THE SEX DIA...

The psychoanalyst stared round-eyed as Nicole raised her skirt to reveal her tiny transparent knickers. A triangle of dark brown curls showed through the clear silk.

'Why are you wearing see-through underwear?' he asked.

'No particular reason.'

'There's always a reason.'

'I didn't come here to be psychoanalysed.'

'Yes, you did. My professional opinion is that you are wearing this blatantly exhibitionistic *cache-sexe* because you feel the need to bare your heart,' the analyst said solemnly. 'I think we can take the knickers to be symbolic.'

'Take them however you like,' said Nicole, turning to show him the thin string of the garment disappearing into the crack between the smooth cheeks of her bottom. 'Personally, I think you should take them off . . .'

Also available from Headline Delta

Naked in Paradise
Passion in Paradise
Exposure in Paradise
Amour Encore
The Blue Lantern
Good Vibrations
Groupies
Groupies II
In the Mood
Sex and Mrs Saxon
Sin and Mrs Saxon
Love Italian Style
Ecstasy Italian Style
Rapture Italian Style
Amorous Liaisons
Lustful Liaisons
Reckless Liaisons
Carnal Days
Carnal Nights
The Delicious Daughter
Hidden Rapture
A Lady of Quality
Hot Type
Playtime
The Sensual Mirror

The Sex Diary of Nicole Dupont

Nicole D

Delta

Copyright © 1997 Nicole Dupont

The right of Nicole Dupont to be identified as the Author of the Work has been asserted by her in accordance with the Copyright, Designs and Patents Act 1988.

First published in 1997
by HEADLINE BOOK PUBLISHING

A HEADLINE DELTA paperback

10 9 8 7 6 5 4 3 2 1

All rights reserved. No part of this publication may be reproduced, stored in a retrieval system, or transmitted, in any form or by any means without the prior written permission of the publisher, nor be otherwise circulated in any form of binding or cover other than that in which it is published and without a similar condition being imposed on the subsequent purchaser.

All characters in this publication are fictitious and any resemblance to real persons, living or dead, is purely coincidental.

ISBN 0 7472 5680 2

Typeset by Palimpsest Book Production Limited,
Polmont, Stirlingshire
Printed and bound in Great Britain by
Mackays of Chatham plc, Chatham, Kent

HEADLINE BOOK PUBLISHING
A division of Hodder Headline PLC
338 Euston Road
London NW1 3BH

The Sex Diary of Nicole Dupont

From Nicole's Diary –
May 3 – Thursday

Before the taxi was more than two metres from the kerb, Remy was leaning over me with his arm round my waist. His mouth was pressed against mine in a long hot kiss.

His hand was inside my short fur jacket to cup a breast, so forcefully that it was almost painful. But it was a delicious ache, a sensation of being used for his pleasure – the concept was exciting. His mouth moved away for half a second while he breathed my name.

'Nicole, Nicole . . . *je t'adore,*' he murmured.

His mouth came back to mine and his tongue touched my lips as he tried to force it between them and slip inside my mouth. His hand moved away from the breast he had handled and pushed my knees apart.

This is one of the most sublime moments at the start of a love affair – when the man first gently prises the woman's legs apart to touch her high up between them. I opened my mouth just a little to let his tongue enter and exchange soft wet touches with my own tongue. And at the same time I let my knees open a little – enough for his hand to go up my skirt.

A long shudder of pleasure ran through my body at the warm touch of his fingers on the smooth flesh of my thighs above my stockings.

'Remy, wait—' I tried to say to him.

Not that I wanted him to stop. Anyway, I couldn't say it – his lips were closed over mine and his tongue was in my mouth. My words of protest were no more than a muffled moan. To judge from the increasing ardour of his kiss, he took my little moan to be a sound of approval of what he was doing to me – and an encouragement to do more yet.

His forearm was up my skirt to the elbow and his fingers reached for the join of my thighs. Then they were inside my knickers and I moaned again when I felt his fingertips brush over the tight little curls of my *joujou*.

I had first met Remy Toussaint – this fascinating man – only a few days before, at a Sunday lunch given by Annette Lecomte and her husband Jacques. There were ten of us, but I was drawn to Remy from the first moment he kissed my hand. He was tall and broad-shouldered and he had dark brown eyes and very dark curly hair.

We were introduced by Annette, one of my dearest friends. Remy and I said a few words to each other, the banalities of social occasions. On the surface, that was all. But in my heart I knew that much, much more would result from this cool encounter.

Almost a week passed – then I saw Remy again by chance. It was four in the afternoon and I had been walking for half an hour in the Luxembourg Gardens to take the air. I was on my way back to my apartment, strolling along the broad and busy Boulevard du Montparnasse, thinking spring had been warm and soft and perhaps summer was arriving early this year.

Then I saw Remy Toussaint. He was sitting alone at a table outside the Dome brasserie, with an empty glass in front of him. He was wearing a stylish grey jacket and a pink shirt without a tie. He looked casual and interesting, sporty and intellectual, all at the same time – if that is possible.

He saw me. He stood up, a charming smile on his face, inviting me to sit down for a moment and join him in a drink. No second invitation was needed – I wanted to know him better. He was drinking white vermouth with a thin slice of fresh lemon in it and I asked for the same.

We chatted, we mentioned Annette and the excellence of the food she served at her lunch party. We stared into each other's eyes and there was another conversation going on in secret – a conversation that had no words but which we both understood.

Remy was saying silently that he wanted to rip my clothes

off and make love to me there and then – bend me backward over the little round café table on the pavement, in full sight of the passers-by. He wanted to stand between my legs and open his trousers to slide his stiff part into me. He would make me scream with delight, so loud that they would hear me at least a kilometre away.

I was wordlessly agreeing to anything he wanted to do. I wanted to sit on his lap there at the table and feel inside his trousers for his strong and beautiful part. I would play with it until he was gasping and shaking on his chair and begging me to let him put it in me – then I would change position to straddle his thighs and slide his hardness into me at the very moment that he spurted his desire.

But this is absurd, I said to myself even then. I was as warm between the legs as a schoolgirl mooning over a pop star – but I was twenty four years old, an alluring young woman, experienced in the ways of love. Yet I was hot for this man I didn't know. I wanted him to put his hand up my skirt and push his fingers into me.

He knew it – he read it in my eyes. As I read in his eyes that he wanted to sweep the glasses off the table and put me face-down over it and flip my dress up over my back and drag my knickers down my thighs – and force his strong male part into me from behind. I would certainly let him. *Yes, yes, yes,* I was saying to him in my mind, *I want to feel your hard flesh penetrate me and stretch me – I want the strong sensation of your shaft bounding inside me.*

All this passed between us without a word being spoken. But we knew, we both knew. He put money on the table for the waiter and we left our drinks unfinished. We were arm-in-arm as we walked very fast to the cab-rank – we almost ran across the pavement in our eagerness.

He gave the driver an address in the Boulevard Raspail – I guessed it was his apartment. He opened the taxi door and before I could climb in he threw his arms around me and hugged me tightly while he kissed me.

It was a cinematic kiss, no other word for it – he bent me backward and held me with one hand under my shoulder-blades and the other on my bottom. I felt his fingers digging into the flesh of my cheek – and the stiffness of his upright part pressing against my belly through his clothes and mine. *Yes Remy, yes, do it to me here in the street*, I was crying out silently in my thoughts.

The address he had given the driver wasn't very far and we could have walked there, especially on so fine a day. But Remy was too impatient for that, he had a monstrous bulge in his trousers and he was desperate to strip my clothes off and kiss my naked body.

We sat close together in the back of an old black Citroen taxi and my skirt was halfway up my thighs. His hand was up between my legs, his eager fingers were inside my knickers, stroking the lips of my *joujou* – and I was moist already. I groped blindly in his lap – through the thin cloth of his trousers I held his stiff shaft and felt it jump and quiver between my fingers.

There was no time to see anything at all of his apartment – he took me straight to the bedroom. I slipped my little fur jacket off and stood by the bed, while he reached down for my hem and stripped my dress over my head and threw it in the approximate direction of a chair.

In seconds he had my bra and knickers off. I stood there with a smile on my face and only a suspender belt and stockings on my body. His hands roamed over my bare flesh, he kissed me again, bending me backward while his hand slid over my breasts. I reached down for his zipper and had his male part out and clasped tight in my hand.

'Oh yes,' he said with a chuckle, 'you want it, *chérie*.'

He was making an effort to maintain his self-possession and his sense of male initiative – in actuality he was so captivated by the beauty of my naked body that his instinct was to go down on his knees in front of me and press respectful kisses on my perfect belly.

Needless to say, I knew very well the effect I always had on men when my clothes came off – I was accustomed to male adoration and devotion and I honoured it and treasured it. I smiled encouragement at Remy amd cupped my naked breasts in my hands as if offering them to him.

'*Dieu—*' he sighed.

He took a step back while he ripped his own clothes off and let them drop to the floor where he stood. His skin was smooth, only his chest was covered by dark curls. His shaft was pointing fiercely up at me – I held it in my hand and thought how beautiful it was, so long and thick and straight – and so strong.

We lay on the bed while his hands moved over my body – as if he was testing everywhere – my breasts and neck, my belly and down between my thighs. He pressed kisses on my nipples and tongued them hotly, he licked my belly and tried to push the tip of his tongue into the deep button. My suspender belt was in his way – he dragged that and my stockings down my legs and off.

Now I was completely naked for him. He kissed my *joujou* and forced his tongue into me. All this time I was lying on my back on his bed, with my legs well apart, on the very edge of orgasm. My hands were on his shoulders, holding tightly on to him while I urged him to slide his body over mine and lie on me . . .

But, but, but . . . if I am to tell the story of my love affair with Remy truthfully and intelligently, it cannot simply be by copying extracts from my intimate journals. These entries were written down in all the exultation of next-day remembrance of hours of passion and delight. They are like photographs stuck in an album – snapshots of happy moments to be remembered for ever after.

To get at the truth about what happened between us it is necessary to step back from the event itself, to put some emotional distance between what I felt and wrote then, and what I know about Remy now. It is necessary to set the narrative free from the restraints of the ego.

The intense desire for Remy I felt in those first days and weeks was so overwhelming that everything was possible – all he had to do was ask. I would gladly have walked the length of the Champs Elysees naked, in high-heeled shoes, if he had asked me to – with every tourist in Paris goggling open-mouthed at my elegant bare body and pointing their cameras at me.

If that had happened in reality, the tourists would have taken home picture souvenirs of the most ardent love affair in all Paris. Not the posed pictures of fake passion they buy in the shady little shops in Montmartre, round the Place Blanche and the Place Pigalle. No, these photographs would have been representations of a true passion.

And at the end of this imaginary naked promenade along the pavement past the cafes and shops and the airline offices, I would have stood without shame with my back to a tree in the Tuileries Garden, while Remy pressed close to my belly with his trousers gaping undone and did it to me in full public view.

That was how I felt about him then. But so much has happened between him and me, in so short a time, that I have become a different person to the woman who took that taxi ride with him from the Boulevard du Montparnasse to his apartment, with his hand between my legs. That being so, I am compelled to regard the Nicole of the intimate journals as another person, not myself.

I must put a breathing space between us, so I can see her – the Nicole of those days – as a character in someone else's drama. Or as a film star in a grand movie – I imagine her on a screen in a cinema on the Boulevard St. Michel, playing a role in a complex plot. She speaks and she kisses and she loves – yes, that way I can understand her.

Therefore – from this moment on there is no more *I* in this narration. Instead, there is an alluring young woman by the name of Nicole Dupont. She is not me, that must be understood, though we live in the same body, she and I. She fell in love with a certain man one day in summer and she did strange and unaccountable things because of him.

The story of her love affair may be said to begin over lunch on a particular Sunday at Annette Lecomte's – or a week later with a drink at a table on the terrace of the Dome – but the real beginning is surely when she lay on her back on a man's bed. She was naked and her legs were wide apart in a gesture of total abandon.

Her hands held his shoulders and tugged at him. He, the man with black curls on his head and on his chest and clustering thickly round the base of his upraised part – this man named Remy – he smiled as he slid his body on top of Nicole and let her feel his weight pinning her to the bed.

'*Chéri, chéri,* I want you so much,' she moaned, her fingers sunk deep into the fleshy cheeks of his bottom.

He smiled down at her again, his charming smile, and pressed the big unhooded head of his shaft to her *joujou* – the lips were open and wet – a long push took him into her. Now his belly was on hers, just as she had wanted and he was sliding his hard part in and out effortlessly. The movement was light and easy, but the sensations that rolled through her body drove her almost frantic.

'Remy . . . oh yes, yes . . .' she was wailing, her long legs wrapped round his waist and gripping him tightly to her belly.

His smile had vanished – on his face now was an intent look as what he was doing to her aroused him more and more. His strokes were longer, he slid all the way into her slippery *joujou* with each strong forward push, the rhythm was faster and more insistent.

'*Je t'adore*, Nicole,' he sighed.

He gasped and a sudden urgency entered his in-out rhythm – it carried Nicole up the long ladder of sexual arousal and flung her headlong off the top into panting and writhing ecstasy. The sheer force of her orgasm swept Remy along with it – he cried out and jerked helplessly on her belly while he spurted his desire into her.

It goes without saying that there are no words adequate to convey the sensations of delight a man and a woman feel in these stunning moments of penetration and of engulfment and of release. Earthquakes and avalanches and other huge convulsions of nature are metaphors used to suggest what is happening in the bodies and souls of a man and a woman locked together in ecstasy. But these metaphors can only hint at the reality.

Lovers after they have pleasured each other lie entwined and touch their lips together in slow little kisses. They sigh and they smile at each other, they stroke each other in a familiar manner – their faces and hair, they trail fingertips down their sides to their hips.

They talk, they say *je t'aime* to each other, whether it is true or not. They ask questions and they tell each other about themselves. Not always entirely honestly, that goes without saying, but lovers are not in a courtroom on oath – at least what they tell each other is always interesting.

Nicole knew – because she had been told by Annette Lecomte – that this handsome and fascinating thirty-year-old Remy was an interior designer by profession. He did not decorate sitting-rooms to impress visitors or bedrooms to ravish lovers. He and a partner named Moreau worked together to design very superior offices for the directors of superior companies.

Nicole would have found that boring, if it had been another man. But because it was Remy, it was of the utmost charm. She had not the least idea of how an office might be furnished and decorated to make it superior, nor the least interest in what superior men actually did in Remy-designed offices.

She knew Remy was married – Annette had also told her that. She asked him about it now they were close. He explained that he and his wife had been separated for two years – which was what Annette had said. And he told Nicole there was a little boy, five years old, who lived with the estranged wife.

The exchange of personal information and emotions leads on to greater confidence and closeness – or it is supposed to. But Remy was a little too casual when he said that he'd phoned Annette the day after meeting Nicole, to ask what this marvellous woman did all day long – and Annette told him that Nicole was a writer.

He made the mistake of shrugging as he said this. Nicole sat up in bed and stared coldly at him.

'What?' she exclaimed. 'Did you expect to hear a tedious domestic tale of a husband and children in my background? You think that I do nothing of importance all day long?'

'No – I didn't mean that. I gathered from Annette that your family is well-to-do and you have no need to earn a living – you can indulge your talents freely.'

'Let me assure you,' she said fiercely. 'To be a writer is

to live intensely. It requires far more courage and endurance than making money.'

Remy saw he had taken a very false step and waited for her indignation to subside.

'I write in order to make sense of my life and my emotions,' she went on. 'I deal in values, in absolutes, and in nuances – I am engaged in a search for perfection.'

'Yes, yes, I understand,' Remy said quickly, his tone very sincere now. 'I realised from the very first moment I saw you that you are an extraordinary and astonishing woman. There is an impassioned air about you – it signifies to me that you are startling in your enthusiasm for life – and you are dangerous to know.'

Nicole liked the sound of that. Some of the inflexibility left the set of her long back and her shoulders and she made a reassuring gesture – she slid her palm over Remy's chest.

'It pleases me you are perceptive enough to realise I can at times be dangerous to know,' she said, almost purring like a cat stroked behind the ears. 'There have been men who never guessed that about me until it was too late for them. They thought that I was a toy for their male vanity, a pretty plaything to spread on her back with her legs apart . . .'

'Ah,' Remy sounded thoughtful.

'Poor fools,' she said sadly. 'They were consumed in the flames of passion they never expected and could not survive.'

Whatever Remy made of that he kept to himself.

'Where are they now, these unfortunates?' he whispered.

'They stumble about Paris,' she said dismissively. 'They are burnt-out hulks of men, derelict ships with no course to steer or port to reach. They paw at women's bodies to try to snatch a miserable little pleasure. In their despair some are married to ordinary women who demand nothing of them beyond clothes to wear and food to eat and an apartment to live in. They make love three times a week like robots without a soul, these men, to women who lie on their backs and think of something else.'

'Well yes . . . but there cannot be many of these walking dead,' Remy suggested. 'You are too young.'

'Two or three perhaps,' she agreed with an enchanting smile.

Her gesture of reconciliation went so far as to stroke the inside of Remy's thigh, a slow massage with her smooth palm, moving up a little with each stroke. Her fingertips touched his dark-haired pompoms and explored their weightiness.

'I hope I shall survive your passion, Nicole,' he said, opening his legs wider to let her fingers probe his groins. His limp part was stirring a little, she smiled to see how it quivered – soon it would be hard and strong again.

Also From The Diary – May 3

Remy lay naked on his bed with his legs apart while Nicole stroked up his thigh and took his dark-haired pompoms in her hand. She tugged gently at them, she stretched them a little, watching his limp part stir as it gradually recovered its strength.

He'd asked her how many men had been devastated by her love – but his question didn't sound wholly sincere. He imagined it was some sort of joke, perhaps. Not that she would tell him, even if he had asked it seriously. Nicole shared her secrets only with her intimate journal. And sometimes with her dear friend Annette.

But Remy's casual question had turned her thoughts toward Gerard Constant, a man she had known and loved the autumn before. He was very different in his appearance and his temperament from Remy, this Gerard. He was slightly built and had light brown hair and eyes. But because of his instinctive grasp of her artistic talent – or so she had falsely believed at the time – he seemed very sympathetic to her and she had fallen in love.

They had been lovers for six weeks when Gerard informed Nicole that he was planning to marry someone he had known for three years. To make matters even worse, he told Nicole in bed. They were both naked and she was in his arms – and he had just half a minute before rolled off her hot and contented body.

She, lying comfortably on her back, in the tingling afterglow of a delicious orgasm, felt a cold finger touch her heart at his words. She controlled her emotions. She was a woman of proud and independent mind and she refused to be hurt by this idiot of a man lying beside her. She shrugged and kept her voice casual while she asked: *what of it?*

Gerard shrugged too, but not so carefree, as he lay facing her, his hand on her curved bare hip. He said in some confusion that he thought she would be furious with him and tell him to leave and never come back. From the oddly strained note in his voice, Nicole realised that he was racked by guilt.

This was something new for her, a man's self-reproach. It had to be investigated and tasted and understood. It was her artistic duty to do so. She was proud to be a writer and an interpreter of the *human comedy* – that greatest of all writers Balzac, had given life as it is lived that name. So she rolled over Gerard and pushed him flat on his back – she rubbed her bare breasts over his limp and sticky part.

Even when it was soft and slack, it was still large. This was a distinction of Gerard's she had discovered when she saw him undressed the first time. The majority of men can offer fifteen centimetres of stiff flesh to the woman they adore and embrace – and in this respect Gerard enjoyed a certain superiority. His was longer and thicker – and because he was slender of body and limb, his exceptional part seemed even bigger than it was.

The name of the intrusive person he intended to marry was Yvette. He didn't name her at first, but Nicole demanded to be told. Though what difference it made to know her name and her appearance was not clear even to Nicole herself. But she demanded to know. Yvette was ash-blonde and pretty, Gerard admitted, but more than that he wouldn't say.

Whatever resistance to Nicole he was planning in his mind, now that he had confessed his secret to her, his body had another reaction. As Nicole rubbed her breasts over his male part she soon felt it standing hard and pressing into her flesh. Just as she had expected. Her fingers played over his flat red-brown nipples, tickling them to arouse him again. He lay passive and sighed with pleasure while she played with him.

By the time he was ready, which did not take long, he'd forgotten all about Yvette and that he was going to marry her – he forgot her so very completely that he begged Nicole to let him put it in her. *Just this once*, he pleaded, *for the sake of what we have been to each other*. She thought that was insulting, but she said nothing and he gripped her by her hips to turn her on to her back.

Nicole shook her head and withstood his urging. She plucked at his nipples and rolled her breasts over his twitching shaft. Eventually he surrendered to her will and lay silent while she continued her little game – a little game that went on and on, becoming ever more insistent – until he gasped and jerked under her and she felt his warm wet spurt on her right breast.

He was greatly surprised when, far from not wanting to see him again, Nicole told him to come back the next day. He shook his head and slid out from beneath her and went into the bathroom to wash himself before he left. She lay on the bed with a smile on her face and watched him put on his trousers and shirt, his oversized part dangling loose between his legs now.

Reluctant he might be, but he came back to her apartment the next day. It was clear to Nicole that he was feeling guiltier than ever. She guessed that in the meantime he had seen Yvette and told her how much he adored her. He'd tried to reconcile his actions and his feelings with his conscience and had not been very successful.

Day after day, always in the afternoons, Nicole made Gerard come to her apartment. She opened the door when he rang and had his trousers undone and her hand inside them almost before he was across the threshold. She never bothered to greet him or kiss him now.

She dragged him willy-nilly to the bedroom, using his fast-hardening and magnificent length as a convenient handle. She pushed him on the bed on his back and was astride him in an instant, laughing at his muttered protestations. He was still fully dressed, of course, his legs hanging over the side of the bed. His jacket was unbuttoned and his trousers were gaping wide open to let his shaft stick out.

There was no point in making him undress, Nicole had decided. Whatever he might in his folly believe, the truth was that he wasn't there in her bedroom to make love. He was there to be humiliated – as a reward for humiliating her by declaring his attachment to another woman.

Nor did Nicole flatter his male vanity or gratify him by taking her own clothes off to let him see her beautiful naked body – that was far too good for him now. By his own crass insensitivity and stupidity he'd forfeited all rights to her love.

For these afternoon occasions she wore a loose skirt and a blouse, nothing else. Without knickers she could sit over him and spike herself on his long thick upright without hindrance.

Perhaps he thought about Yvette and how he loved her while he lay on his back, staring mutely up at Nicole astride him. She unbuttoned her blouse and let it hang loosely open, to give him a tantalising glimpse of her bare round breasts. Not to please him, but to taunt him, though he was too much of an idiot to realise that.

At first Gerard didn't understand what was going on between them. He had the natural vanity of all young men – he believed that Nicole was frantic for him, now that she knew their love affair was at an end. He persuaded himself that he was performing a true act of mercy by letting her sit on his belly with her bare breasts bouncing to the rhythm of her ride.

After a few days of this treatment Gerard had unknowingly learned the lesson of submission. He became dependent on Nicole for his pleasure – the pleasure he must have again and again, like an addict of a habit-forming drug.

When he was away from Nicole's influence over him and with Yvette, his secret almost suffocated him. He undressed Yvette and lay on her narrow belly – but it was only his male pride and his sense of obligation that drove him – the woman whose body he truly desired was Nicole.

Day after day, his feelings of guilt grew stronger. He was betraying Yvette – the woman he was going to marry – he was betraying her trust shamelessly. His remorse and mortification were doubled, because he also felt guilty toward Nicole – he was convinced she was desperately in love with him and couldn't live without his love-making.

In this predicament, unable to tell north from south, as the saying goes, Gerard became withdrawn and morose, *triste* and restless. He was enslaved by a woman – by her mind and her body. He told himself despondently that he wouldn't last even a week without his afternoons on Nicole's bed. Yet he was within weeks of marriage to Yvette.

Gerard couldn't understand how he could love both women at the same time. Not in the same way, of course. Nicole and Yvette were too unlike each other for that. Night and day, sleepless nights and tiring days, he asked himself how this had come about – why had fate conspired against him in this atrocious manner?

The long entries in Nicole's intimate journal for these days were amusing to write at the time and amusing to read again afterward. There was the day when Gerard, with his resolution made stubborn by a would-be tender encounter with Yvette the evening before, tried to make a final break with Nicole.

She had him on his back and ravished him – he pushed her away and struggled off the bed after a first brisk climax. He made a dash for the door, insisting he had no time to stay. He was stuffing his shrinking wet part into his trousers and doing them up as he ran.

Nicole went after him barefoot, across the bedroom and along the passage. She caught him at the apartment door, when his hand was already on the lock. Another two seconds and the door would be open and he would be through it and gone.

She hurled herself at his back and pressed her body hard to him to pin him against the door. Gerard was a slightly-built man and no taller than Nicole. His will had been sapped by days of being ridden on his back. She was able to hold him secure, with his cheek pressed to the painted wooden door, while her hands went round him and dragged his half zipped trousers open again.

'*No more of this*,' he gasped, '*I beg you to stop, Nicole.*' She paid no attention to him. She had his thick fleshy part in one hand and his pompoms cupped in the other. '*Don't be in such a hurry, chéri,*' she said, her mouth touching his ear. Her hand was flicking up and down easily.

Gerard wanted to break free – he told himself that he must break away from her, he must! He struggled to release himself from the arms around him and to escape the pressure of the hot body that trapped him against the apartment door.

But for whatever reason, he didn't struggle nearly hard enough to avoid his fate – his shaft was growing thicker and longer and harder in her busy fingers. He moaned pitifully, his cheek flat to the door, his knees trembling. The length of flesh in Nicole's manipulating hand had grown to an enormous size and was bounding violently.

'*Ha!*' Nicole exclaimed triumphantly as she felt spasms grip his body – he was spurting on to her apartment door. When his legs stopped shaking, she let go of him and took a step back. '*Tomorrow at three,*' she said, '*I shall expect you, Gerard.*'

For Gerard, the days after he told Nicole about Yvette were a time of sleepless nights and heart-searching, of shame at his weakness and remorse for his betrayals – and desperate anxiety that he would be found out by Yvette.

Every day he went to Nicole's apartment and she used him as she wished – yet she hardly spoke to him. As for him, he had nothing much to say to her. He wanted to be free of her – and yet he didn't want to lose her. He was in a state of confusion and all that passed between them was the sighing and moaning of growing excitement and of sexual climax.

As Gerard's feelings of guilt became darker, Nicole enjoyed his discomfiture more and more. He was so feeble – he had submitted totally, and she had come to despise him. And she felt a certain contempt for herself, for ever believing that she loved him.

How could an aware woman like herself have been so mistaken about him? What emotional blindness was this in herself, not to recognise him for what he was – a worm with no appeal at all for an intelligent woman.

The humiliation of Gerard went on for nine days without a break. On the tenth day, Nicole pushed him down on his back on the bed and straddled him on her knees, her skirt raised in her hands. Before she had time to impale her beautiful body on his huge upright, Gerard gasped out in a miserable voice that he couldn't make love to Yvette any more.

He confessed that he'd bared Yvette's breasts the evening before and kissed them. He'd taken down her knickers and stroked her. Yvette lay on her back and spread her legs for him – but his treacherous part refused to stand stiff.

'It's stiff enough now,' Nicole said, sounding very unsympathetic. She was holding his massive length between her fingers, ready to guide it up into herself when she sat down across his belly.

'For you, always, Nicole,' he moaned.

'But of course,' she said, raising her eyebrows.

She rode him forcefully as ever and made him spurt into her. Then she slid off the bed and stood facing him – she held her loose flower-patterned skirt up round her waist, so he could see her neatly trimmed little triangle of brunette curls. And the long moist lips of her *joujou*. They were wet and slippery inside because he had made it so.

'A last long look to remember me by, Gerard,' she said with a smile. 'Do not come back here any more, I do not want to see you ever again.'

Naturally, she wasn't going to tell the marvellous new man she had met, Remy, anything about poor weak Gerard. Gerard was one of those consumed in the flames of passion they had not expected and were too feeble to cope with. Sad perhaps, *mais c'est la vie*.

'I have loved enough men to realise I must be very discriminating in who I let approach me,' she said coolly.

'Then I am greatly honoured to be allowed so intimately close to you,' Remy said. 'I understand that your writing must be formidable and devastating. Shall I be allowed to read something by you?'

'Not yet,' she said with a quick shake of her head that made her bare breasts quiver. Her hand went gliding down to Remy's belly, where his limp part lay. 'Not until I know you better – otherwise it would be revealing a candle-flame to a moth.'

He smiled and said he understood, whether he did or not. And while her palm was sliding over his male part, he understood something – though it was not necessarily her view of her own consequence.

He wriggled up on the bed until he could lean his back on the wooden headboard and sit with his legs stretched straight out before him. Nicole was between his knees, her hand clasped round his male part, stroking it to stiffen it again.

The antagonism he had half-aroused by being casual about her talents had disappeared – she was all charms and smiles and eagerness again. He told himself to be cautious in future if the conversation ever turned to her writing.

She had made his shaft big and hard and she was staring down at it with a rapt expression on her face. It stood up boldly from its nest of dark curls. It was not as long or as thick as Gerard's, but big enough and hard enough to delight her – and most certainly strong enough. Her fingers moved lightly up and down, exploring its tautness and solidity.

'It is superb,' she said. 'So powerful, so dominant.'

'Yes,' he agreed, pleased by her words of praise. And more pleased by her evident admiration.

Her fingers wrapped themselves round the solid length to excite him more and more.

'The first moment I saw you,' she said, 'I knew that when I held this darling in my hand it would be the most beautiful one in the world.'

'Ah, ah, ah,' he murmured, little waves of pleasure flicking through him from her softly moving hand.

She stretched herself out between his legs, lying face down, and took the pink-purple head into her wet mouth.

'Nicole . . . Nicole . . . *je t'adore*,' she heard him moan. As any man should, to be so favoured by her.

His hand stroked her dark-brown hair back from her forehead. An hour ago, when he saw her passing by his table outside the Dome, he wanted to hold her and strip her naked and take her to bed. He guessed then that she would be superb to lie upon and make love to. But never for a moment had he expected her to be so eager for him as this.

Perhaps she could read his thoughts – or guess at what was going through his mind. She turned her head up to look into his eyes and she let his long throbbing part slide away from her wet lips.

'So you truly believe I will let you use my mouth for your

pleasure?' she asked, her dark eyebrows arching in a look of comical surprise. 'You would like that, I'm certain, *chéri*? You would be pleased to loll on a bed like a Pasha in a harem, with your legs apart, while I am the slave to make love to you with your mouth?'

'Ah yes . . .' he sighed.

'But I hardly know you yet,' she said with a quick grin.

'Whether you know me or not, you want me as furiously as I want you,' Remy said, being audacious.

'Are you certain of that?' she said, 'I know you want me desperately – this lovely long hard thing tells me that, by the way it leaps when I touch it with my tongue. But – do I really want you, Remy? Or am I only studying your reactions when I touch you and play with you? You must ask yourself that question.'

'I don't understand – what do you mean, *chérie*?' he sighed while his hands cupped her perfect breasts.

'Try hard now – you must think the unthinkable – perhaps all this is only an experiment, my poor Remy.'

'An experiment in love,' he suggested hopefully.

Nicole stuck her long pink tongue out at him and shook her head. She bowed her head and licked slowly up and down the whole length of his stiff shaft, until she had made it wet and shiny all the way.

'My heart is yours,' Remy sighed, 'I am lost and confounded. If this is an experiment, then I am your tame guinea pig.'

His upright part was shaking to the touch of her tongue. She moved her head back and looked at it with a inquiring grin.

'Nicole,' he gasped, his legs trembling from thighs to ankles. 'Your touch overwhelms me . . . in two more seconds I shall—'

'I know,' she said tenderly, watching the long persistent throbbing of his hard part, 'I understand you far better than you realise.'

She moved quickly to perch over him and straddle his lap, as he leaned back against the headboard. She put a hand between her splayed thighs to open herself and she sank down on him.

He moaned and his body jerked as he felt his shaft slide up into her slippery warmth.

Then she was bouncing up and down briskly, her hands on his shoulders, gripping lightly. Her head was upright and her eyes were open, her long bare back was as straight as if she were riding a cantering horse along a bridle path on a sunny day in the Bois de Boulogne.

She was willing Remy to wail in ecstasy and spurt into her. But in another moment she learned that he was no Gerard, to be subdued easily under a woman's body.

His arms were round her like steel bands, he clamped her to him – her breasts to his dark-haired chest, her smooth belly to his muscular belly – he rolled over sideways, taking her with him, forcing her under him.

She cried out, lost in the surprise of his sudden action. She was across the bed, with her head hanging down over the side and her legs wound about Remy's waist. His hard flesh penetrated deep into her wet *joujou*, stretching her open and filling her with a sense of tremendous longing.

'Remy . . .' she moaned as he stabbed hard and fast into her.

His hands were flat on her shoulders, pressing her down on the bed. His mouth found hers and closed over it in a long hot kiss – and all the while his hard belly was smacking against hers, to the rhythm of his thrusting into her.

'Yes, Remy . . . you must adore me as I adore you . . .' she gasped out.

Her back arched up off the bed as ecstasy overwhelmed her.

More From The Diary – May 4 – Friday

After such pleasure, such intimacy – after my first time with Remy – I was bursting to tell my dearest friend, Annette, about this fantastic new love affair. Annette and I grew up together – there was a distant family connection. My mother's mother and her mother's father were cousins, I think it was.

After Annette married Jacques Lecomte they moved to a house at Passy. A house where there was space to entertain their friends – and space for the three children Annette intended to have. And there was space for Jacques' consulting-room.

Besides that he had an office for a secretary who kept his records and made appointments and kept track of which patients paid their bills and which of them needed a little reminder. Jacques was a psychoanalyst, he devoted himself to well-to-do people who liked to be taken seriously – and could afford to pay good money for the privilege.

In the middle of the afternoon Nicole emerged up the steps from the Passy Metro station and walked in the direction of the Trocadero Gardens, past the Balzac Museum. She was very chic that day in a dark-blue Chanel jacket and skirt – with nothing under the jacket except her bra – so that a long and delicious cleavage was presented.

Whenever she went to visit Annette she felt it important to be dressed formally. She wasn't entirely clear why she felt this way – it certainly wasn't to impress Annette – that would have been absurd after they had known each other so well for so many years. But during the visit she might see Annette's husband Jacques and for a reason she had never satisfactorily explained to herself, Nicole felt it necessary to be formal for Jacques.

Because of his profession, Jacques was an earnest and serious-minded man. He had to be – to listen all day long to people complaining about their lives and their ridiculous little problems – without losing his patience. He had to take them seriously or he'd burst out laughing. And that would be an end of his comfortable living.

Nicole suspected Jacques regarded her as frivolous – not that he'd ever said anything to that effect. But she was doubtful whether he took her writing seriously. Her fear was that a man who had studied and trained for years to understand people and their motives would be reluctant to accept that she – by her innate talent – also had insights into other people's emotions and personalities.

Whatever her unconscious motive might be, she dressed well but quietly whenever she went to visit the Lecomtes. The dark Chanel suit seemed to her very appropriate.

As ever, Annette was delighted to see Nicole. She showed her the baby, now almost a year old. Then they sat in the pretty drawing room, with its view through big windows of the quiet street outside while they drank Brazilian coffee, lightened with rich cream and nibbled finger-shaped sponge biscuits that tasted of almonds and vanilla.

'Tell me all your news,' Annette said. 'You sounded so thrilled on the phone. As I understand it from your babbling, you've managed to get Remy Toussaint into bed. I knew for sure you would, when I saw how you talked to each other not two minutes after you'd been introduced.'

'Dear Annette – you make it sound like a planned campaign to get the man's trousers down.'

'Is he any good at it?'

'He's a master,' Nicole told her, a little breathlessly. 'A lion in the bedroom. My knees shake when I think about him. But I didn't plan it and I didn't stalk him – it was fate. I swear we met by chance.'

'Of course you did, *chérie*. The same way you fell down on your back by accident when you found yourself alone with him.'

'We met on the terrace of the Dome,' Nicole insisted. 'I was out for a walk. He was sitting alone. He bought me a drink and we talked. He looked into my eyes with a glance that probed my very soul – and invited me to his apartment.'

'And, and, and?'

'Darling, it was stupendous. He dragged me straight into the bedroom and ripped my clothes off. He threw me down on the bed and ravaged me mercilessly – I thought my last hour had come.'

Her account of what had taken place in Remy's bedroom was not entirely accurate, but what of it? Annette was smiling – she expected nothing less of her childhood friend.

'I believe you,' she said. 'Remy is tall and strongly built – he's a man with fire in his heart. I have no difficulty in visualising him as a ravenous beast in the bedroom. Has he got a big one?'

'Long and thick and beautiful – and absolutely tireless.'

'Ah good! After all, a woman who accepts an invitation to visit a man's apartment in the middle of the afternoon knows what she's there for – and hopes she's not going to be disappointed when she gets a look at what's on offer.'

'Is that so?' Nicole said with a grin. 'Then what about Carole Roquet? She went off with the man she met in a bookshop on the Avenue de l'Opera – you remember what she told us that afternoon when we were talking in the Café de la Paix? Or was it in the Printemps café?'

'We were in the Café de la Paix,' Annette said.

'Carole said she thought they were going to his apartment to discuss whatever it was they'd chatted about in the shop – something historical or philosophical, I believe,' Nicole said.

Carole was a good friend of both of them – which gave them a perfect right to gossip about her behind her back.

'Philosophy in the bedroom,' Annette said with a lift of her eyebrows, 'I've never for one moment believed Carole is as trusting as that. And the apartment turned out to be a single room in some awful old building in a backstreet, or so she said.'

'At which point,' Nicole took up the tale again. 'Her new friend the philosopher turned the key in the door and chased her round the room with his trousers open and his shaft sticking out like a shotgun.'

'Ha – but we are talking of Carole and so this is no hunting story of a loaded shotgun potting a rabbit,' Annette exclaimed. 'She said that when her philosophical friend undid his trousers what he showed her was as long as a pencil and almost as thin.'

'She also said that he flung her face-down over a scruffy divan,' said Nicole, 'and tore her knickers off – tore them to shreds.'

'You said that's what Remy did to you,' Annette reminded her.

'He did, he did,' Nicole insisted, 'but that's quite different. I never really believed Carole's story – not when she let slip that she stayed with this man with the pencil for two whole days in his room.'

'It must have been good for something, his pencil,' Annette said with a chuckle. 'Evidently he wrote certain words with it that Carole found interesting – or she wouldn't have stayed so long. How long did *you* stay in Remy's apartment?'

'Until we were hungry and went out to eat.'

'That would be about eight o'clock then,' Annette surmised. 'Where did he take you for dinner?'

'We walked back to the Dome – it's not far from where he lives. I was absolutely ravenous – I ate an enormous meal and drank most of a bottle of wine all by myself.'

'A good sign, hunger after love. And you had more love after eating, I suppose, when you went back to Remy's for dessert?'

'Certainly not,' Nicole said, her eyes wide open.

'No dessert? You said *au revoir* and kissed him and went quietly home to bed all alone – is that what you expect me to believe?'

'I took Remy home with me,' Nicole told her with a little shrug. 'You know I like to wake up in my own bed in the mornings.'

'I should have guessed. So . . . there was more merciless ravaging of your body in your own apartment, yes?'

'We lay naked on my bed and adored each other for

hours – we tasted each other's flesh and we tasted each other's soul.'

'An unusual way of putting it,' Annette commented.

'He made me open my legs wide and he put pillows under my bottom,' said Nicole. 'He lay on me with our mouths touching and our breath mingling, his strong hard part was deep inside me – I gave myself to him as never to a man before—'

'Oh yes?' Annette said in mild disbelief.

'Two bodies became one. The sensuality of that hour was as devastating as a drug, the ecstasy of it lasted for an eternity. It went on and on – until we were gorged with love and fell asleep in each other's arms.'

'And woke up together this morning?'

'Need you ask? Of course he was there close beside me when I woke up this morning. It was late when we fell asleep, but Remy woke like a giant refreshed. Stiff as a steel bar – you know how men wake up in the mornings. I came out of a deep sleep to find his hand between my legs.'

'The best way to start the day,' Annette said. 'I envy you.'

'Remy refused to let me get out of bed until he'd rolled me on my back and welcomed the new day – at least, that's what he called it.'

'He does it to wish you goodnight, he does it to wish you good morning – I wonder he didn't drop in about midday to wish you well again,' said Annette with a grin.

The two women talked on until Annette explained that she had to be at the Gare de Lyon at five to meet Jacques' mother, who was coming to stay for a few days. Nicole offered, half-heartedly, to go with her to the station. She didn't much care for Jacques' mother – few did – and Annette understood her feelings and thanked her and said it wasn't necessary.

'I shall go and say hello to Jacques,' Nicole said.

'He has a patient coming at five – that's why he can't go to meet his mother himself. It's typical of her to catch the one train that arrives at an inconvenient time for us. She'll complain all the rest of the day because her son isn't there to look after her.'

After Annette left for the station, Nicole went across to

the other side of the house, where Jacques had his consulting-rooms. There was no one in the outer office, the secretary's desk was vacant and the magazines for patients waiting lay in a tidy line. Nicole tapped on the inner door and walked in.

Jacques Lecomte was sitting at a desk with a sheaf of papers in his hand, his mouth open and his dark-framed spectacles on his nose. His secretary-receptionist sat on the opposite side of the desk to him, her legs were crossed and her knees uncovered. She had an open notepad in her hand and Jacques was dictating a letter.

It was a large and pleasant room. The handsome dark-wood desk was placed over by the wall, to make it look less like an office. There were old and valuable rugs with gracefully faded colours on the polished parquet floor and there were three or four tranquil and unassuming landscape paintings on the walls.

Almost in the centre of the room stood the most important piece of furniture – a large dark-brown leather couch.

This was where Jacques' patients lay, supposedly at ease, to pour out their secrets to him, their anxieties, their dreams and their fantasies. Psychoanalytic theory held that a patient lying down was more likely to talk freely than if sitting on the other side of the doctor's desk, face to face, which suggested confrontation rather than co-operation.

This lying-down position was especially important when it came to the curious dreams and fantasies that made patients blush in shame to speak of openly. These were the only ones that mattered, according to the psychoanalysts themselves. Hot fantasies of naked love-making in public places, of forbidden lusts and masochistic pleasures.

There was an upright wooden armchair by the head of the couch, where Jacques Lecomte would sit – just out of sight of the patient. He'd have a notebook and a pen in his hand, to record the absurd little secrets he was paid to listen to. It would have been impossible for him to write down half the nonsense his patients came out with, but he pretended to record their babbling.

Jacques was in his thirties and of distinguished appearance. His hair was receding a little from the front of his head and the effect was to make him look impressively high-brow. He glanced up quickly and smiled when Nicole came into his room. The secretary at once tugged her skirt down over her knees and smiled politely but impersonally at Nicole. Jacques took his glasses off and dropped them on the desk, stood up and came to greet her.

He took her hand in both of his own and pressed warmly – during his working hours he never kissed women's hands as a greeting because he thought it might be misunderstood by patients – and the majority of his patients were women. An over-imaginative woman – especially a woman in urgent need of sexual comfort – might misinterpret a kiss on her hand and take it for a subtle suggestion that the elegant and intellectual Jacques would like to kiss her elsewhere.

This hypothetical female patient might feel suddenly warm between her thighs inside her expensive knickers – it went without saying that the women who could afford Jacques' psychoanalysis could afford expensive underwear. She might think, this anonymous patient, that a kiss on her hand could lead on to a kiss on her mouth.

Or even a kiss on her naked breasts, if she was badly starved of male attention. And if she was disconsolate and well experienced, she might imagine that a polite kiss on the back of her hand could lead to a kiss on her . . . but who can say what fancies pass through the minds of rich middle-aged women?

Jacques' secretary, Mademoiselle Anvers, stood up and greeted Nicole. She had seen her there before visiting Jacques and she knew the dictation was at an end for the present. On her way out of the room she acted as a good secretary should and reminded Jacques that Madame Fabre was due at five o'clock.

There existed, between Nicole and Jacques, the husband of her best friend, a complicated relationship that went back for two years. It had begun six months after Annette had married him. When she got to know him, Nicole admired Jacques. In fact, she found him attractive – before long she desired him. Therefore she had him. Perhaps it was not so complicated after all.

Alone with him now in his consulting-room, she stood close enough to let him smell the fragrance of the perfume she was wearing – and to let him look down her jacket, to her pointed breasts half-concealed and half-revealed in a small white bra.

What a pity she was wearing a bra, she said to herself. If she'd worn nothing at all under the jacket he'd have seen her naked breasts. Men always became excited when they sneaked a look down the top of a dress or a jacket – even if all they saw was a nicely-filled bra.

Of course, if they could snatch a glance up a skirt, they went stiff in their underwear immediately. This was a simple fact of nature that Nicole found interesting and useful, if not very comprehensible. The view up a skirt was usually of five or six centimetres of stockinged thigh. Perhaps just a flash of bare skin above the stocking-tops.

A woman had to be deliberately careless before an admirer caught a glimpse of her knickers. That was a clear indication to a man that his further attentions would be welcome – and were expected without delay.

Such fleeting glimpses of skin or underwear could turn a sensible and polite man into a deliciously demanding beast. On this afternoon Nicole had something of the sort planned for Jacques – though it would be more sophisticated than a casual glance up her clothes. And it would be far more devastating.

'Nicole,' Jacques said.

His tone was cool and cautious – but he took her in his arms to kiss her properly, now that the secretary wasn't there to watch him.

'Dear Jacques,' she said in reply.

That was what she said out loud – in her mind she said more. She said silently to herself: *Dear Jacques – you want me as much as I want you – I've always known that, whatever excuses you make, either to me or to yourself. So as you want me, you shall have me. And if you still think that you don't want me, too bad – I shall have you, mon cher.*

Their kiss was tender but brief – it was scarcely more than a touch of Jacques' lips on hers before Nicole twisted away from his arms and reached down to raise her dark-blue skirt up from her knees.

Jacques gulped to see her skirt rising higher and higher, just like a theatre curtain rising on the first act of a drama.

You may be a famous psychoanalyst chéri, Nicole was thinking to herself, with a secret mental grin, *you may claim to be a doctor of the soul who can unravel mysteries and cure people's desperately destructive complexes – but you're only a man, Jacques. I'm sure you're as keen when you travel on the Metro to look down women's dresses as any other man is – and when it's crowded, you rub yourself against women's bottoms and make yourself go stiff, like all the other men in the rush hour. There's no need to pretend to me that you're different – I understand you very well – have a good look at my knickers, Jacques – they're very sexy.*

Jacques was staring down round-eyed at her sheer-stockinged thighs as she lifted her skirt to uncover them. His black eyes were luminous with a mixture of complicated emotions – he was breathing through his mouth, almost sighing. When the skirt was almost up to Nicole's hips, she reached out to put her hands on his shoulders. His hand slid between her uncovered thighs, his wrist held her skirt from slipping back down.

She stared deeply into his eyes while slowly she raised one leg and hooked it round his waist. This stork-like stance opened her thighs and pressed her belly and her *joujou* against Jacques. His hands moved round underneath her bottom and there was a look of surprise on his face when his palms cupped taut bare cheeks where he'd expected to touch silk or nylon or satin.

'Nicole – you know very well this is unprofessional,' he said. 'What on earth am I to do with you?'

'How can what we are doing be unprofessional?' she asked, her dark eyebrows rising up her forehead. 'I am your friend, dear Jacques, not your patient – it is not my head I wish you to examine.'

'If only I could be as sure of that as you are,' he said solemnly. 'It is my professional opinion that what is inside your head needs looking at very carefully.'

Whether it was unprofessional or not, whatever that might

mean, his fingers were fumbling at her hip to undo the fastening of her skirt. He wanted to go further with her, his words and actions were not in accord – which is a very frequent state of affairs for men in the company of a beautiful woman.

Nicole smiled and dropped her leg to stand on two feet again – and to let her skirt slide down her legs to the floor. Jacques put his hands on her hips to hold her a little away from him – there was an odd and thoughtful expression on his face while he looked down at her tiny transparent knickers.

In truth, it was an exaggeration to call them knickers. The garment round her slender loins was really no more than a provocative little *caché-sexé* of the sort worn by showgirls at the Moulin Rouge and at other tourist cabarets. It was of silk and it was about the size of a man's hand.

Nicole's neat little triangle of dark brown curls showed through the clear silk – and there being no more than a string at the back, the smooth cheeks of her bottom were bare under Jacques' grasping hands.

'Why are you wearing see-through underwear?' he asked her.

'Why not? There's no particular reason.'

'There is always a reason, whether you know it or not.'

'I didn't come here to be psychoanalysed,' she reminded him.

'But perhaps you did. I think that you came here today wearing this blatantly exhibitionistic *cache-sexé* because, deep down in your inner self, you feel an urgent need to bare your heart to me,' Jacques said solemnly. 'I think we can take the knickers to be symbolic.'

'You can take them as whatever you like,' Nicole said. 'You can take them off, if you want to.'

'You refuse to listen seriously to my interpretation?'

'What can I say, Jacques? If symbolism was in my mind when I dressed, I was not aware of it. I like sexy underwear, what of it? But let us suppose for one moment that what you say is true – what does it mean?'

'I've already told you what it means.'

'You suggested I want to strip naked for you. You meant that symbolically, I know, but for once I think you could actually be right. I'm here to bare my *joujou* for you to play with.'

From Nicole's Diary – May 4

As all the world knows, Sigmund Freud was the doctor who first thought of psychoanalysis. Jacques told me that Freud's name actually means *pleasure* in his own language. It amused me, to think of a *Dr Pleasure*. I could visualise him as a man who sat waiting for people to visit him and tell him all their sexual dreams and imaginings – so that he could explain them.

But, said Jacques, this *Dr Pleasure* didn't confine himself to theories and words – he had love affairs with women – his wife's sister for one. And students who came to him to learn how to be psychoanalysts. Jacques also said that Dr Pleasure made love to some of his women patients. I was not the least surprised to hear of it.

In the calm and well-planned ambience of Jacques' consulting-room, he and Nicole stood face to face and close together – so very close that they were almost toe-to-toe. She wasn't his patient, though he seemed to slip into the odd assumption that everyone who came to see him was a patient seeking his advice and his encouragement.

Nicole's dark-blue jacket was open to show the prominences of her breasts in the half-cups of her little bra. Jacques was looking at them and his palms slid lightly over them, a little gliding caress that brought a smile to Nicole's face but did nothing to change the melancholy look on his.

'But why so *triste*, Jacques?' she asked softly. 'Am I not beautiful enough for you?'

Her skirt lay on the carpet at her feet and she had kicked off her black high-heeled shoes. Her long shapely legs in sheer stockings were on show to him, all the way down from the expanse of smooth bare thigh between her stockings and her knickers, to her slender ankles and feet.

Jacques sighed and put his hand between her thighs, on the bare skin above her stockings. His hand was warm and she could feel how it trembled a little. She smiled and put her tongue out at him.

'Do you think I am beautiful, Jacques?' she pressed him. Instead of giving her an answer, he moved his hand slowly upward between her legs, until he clasped her brown-haired *joujou* through the gossamer-thin silk of her ridiculously small knickers.

'We both know what it means when you come to me wearing see-through underwear,' he said, while he was feeling her *joujou*.

'Do we?'

'If you could only make an effort to face your neurosis, Nicole, face it squarely and courageously – if you could put it into words—'

'I've already put it into words,' she interrupted, 'I told you that I was going to bare my *joujou* for you to play with. And I have – it didn't require much courage.'

'That's an evasion. You should try to bring yourself to the point of confessing to me, so to speak, speak frankly of your deep-seated anxieties. If you did so, then you would be on the way to understanding yourself and your motives. Together we would be able to do something about this neurosis of yours.'

'I am happy to say that I'm free of neuroses,' she told him, and she wriggled her *joujou* slinkily under his hand. 'As for my motives – I understand them already.'

'You deceive yourself,' he said, and she heard a tremor in his voice at the feel of her soft *joujou* rubbing itself like a kitten against the palm of his hand, 'and you are trying to deceive me.'

'No deception is necessary,' she said with a smile. 'I like handsome and clever men to make love to me – often. To me that seems very simple to understand and appreciate – why do you insist on regarding it as some sort of mystery, Jacques?'

'Sit down,' he murmured. 'We must talk seriously.'

Even as he spoke he was easing her back on to the big leather couch behind her, with one hand on the small of her back and the other cupped between her thighs. She had her arms round his neck while he lowered her to sit on the sofa – she held on tight and gave him no choice but to descend with her.

He leaned forward at the waist while she moved downward, she pulled at him until he bent his knees – by the time her bottom was on the couch, he was kneeling on the carpet in front of her.

'What are you doing, Nicole? I cannot talk to you like this.'

'There is no mystery to talk about,' she said. 'I have no secrets from you. If you wish to explore my mind – or my heart – or my soul – or any other part of me that interests you, then you may do so.'

In spite of his high-minded professional concern, Jacques' immediate interest seemed not to be in Nicole's mind. Or so she concluded, when he pulled her tiny knickers underneath her bottom and she felt the touch of smooth leather against her cheeks.

He was staring down between her parted legs at her *joujou* as he slid her knickers down her legs, all the way down to her slender ankles. He slipped the knickers over her stockinged feet – she was free at last of constraint. He pushed her legs further apart so he could kneel between them.

'Who is the therapist here and who is the patient?' he murmured.

It was a meaningless remark and Nicole didn't bother to reply. As a question it required no answer. Or if it did, then he'd answer it himself.

'I've thought for a long time that the underlying problem is that you adore me, Nicole,' he said. 'I deduce that from your obsessive behaviour. You have a compulsion to come here, pretending it is a social visit to Annette, but really in hope of making love with me.'

'Do you think so, Jacques? Why would I do that?'

'You come here with the intent of persuading me to make love to you in circumstances which are risky, to say the least,' he went on, ignoring her question. 'You want me to take your knickers off and make love to you while my secretary is in the next room and my wife is somewhere in the house.'

'That's not true,' Nicole corrected him. 'Annette is in a taxi on her way to the Gare de Lyon.'

She said nothing about Mademoiselle Anvers, sitting at a typewriter in the outer office. It was her private belief that Jacques had his hand in Josette Anvers' knickers whenever he and she were alone together in his consulting-room.

This big brown leather couch dominating the room was very suggestive. No doubt its principal purpose was for patients to lie on and babble out their anxieties to Jacques. But Nicole believed that Josette also lay on her back on it, full length and with her legs apart – the polite smile gone from her face as she gasped in pleasure and Jacques slid his length into her.

To be truthful, she wasn't bad looking, this Josette Anvers, Nicole conceded. She would be about thirty, slender of body and with dark brown hair worn back over her ears. She was small-breasted under the business-like black dress she was wearing today – but when she was walking out of the room and displaying her rear view, it was impossible not to notice her sensually well-developed bottom and thighs.

Any woman with such well-rounded thighs would be pleased to have a vigorous man lie between them – and the full roundness of her bottom would push her loins upward, arching her back for a man to penetrate her and drive her to squirming ecstasy.

Jacques ignored Nicole's reference to Annette being out of the house and heading away in a taxi. He was not going to let himself be diverted from his theorising.

'The first step is to admit that you have an inner need to conquer me, Nicole,' he said.

'Me?'

'You. It is obvious to me that you feel a need to subdue me – isn't that so? – as if you were a man and I were a woman. This is a case of role-reversal, if you know what the phrase means.'

'You're trying to confuse me,' she murmured.

He was still on his knees between her parted legs, but he wasn't doing anything interesting to her at all, even though her brown-haired *joujou* was bare and within his reach. Now he had revealed it by taking off her little knickers, he seemed to have forgotten what it was for.

His hands were lying lightly on her thighs – on her stockings – about halfway between knees and groins. To take his mind off all this tedious psychoanalysing she rubbed her hand lightly over the front of his grey trousers.

'It is you who subdued me, Jacques, long long ago, when we first met.'

'That's nonsense,' he said, and suddenly his fingertips were smoothing over her *joujou*, through the little curls.

'Say what you like,' she went on. 'It is impossible for you to deny it. You set out to bend me to your will – and you have succeeded. I have no will of my own when I am with you.'

The bulge under her hand had grown hard and big. How easy it was to entice men to do what she wanted, she thought for the millionth time. All that was necessary was to take hold of their upright part and they would do anything.

'You are blind to the reality of the position,' Jacques sighed, 'and deliberately so. The truth is that your obsession with me is so strong that it totally overrides your loyalty to Annette – and by transference it affects me so insidiously that I forget my own sense of professional propriety.'

'So many words, so little sense,' she murmured. 'You are the one who is obsessed, Jacques. You are obsessed by me, obsessed to the point of neglecting your own loyalty to Annette.'

'You are mocking me,' he sighed. 'I am ashamed.'

Nicole slid her flat hand up and down the bulge in the front of his trousers and felt the jumping of the stiff part inside.

'You cannot stop yourself,' she said. 'Whatever I say or do to bring you to your senses and prevent you from making love to me, your desire is so powerful that you push me down on your couch and have me.'

'No,' he said, and it sounded like a sigh.

'I know you,' Nicole said. 'You say no when you mean yes, you say you will never touch me again at the very moment of penetration.'

'We make love together, you and I,' he said, 'but it is for the wrong reasons, Nicole.'

She watched with a smile as he unzipped his trousers and felt inside to pull out his long hard part. He didn't try to push it into her, not at once – he bent down to kiss her bare belly, just above her triangle of brown curls.

She was still smiling when she put her hand on the back of his head and stroked his hair – and he kissed and kissed and kissed her belly. One of the reasons she liked Jacques was that she could easily reduce him to abject worship of her beautiful body. This was flattering to her – because Jacques was a man whose training was to be objective and detached, a man who had been taught how to resist the approaches of over-eager women patients.

Naturally, in the general way of things it delighted Nicole to know that men saw her body as a desirable object, to be possessed for their own pleasure. Remy saw her in that light – he'd given ample proof of wanting to roll her under him and lie on top and stab his shaft into her. He thought that by doing so he possessed her – he didn't realise that it was she who possessed him when they made love.

With Jacques the question didn't really arise. Whenever he undressed her – which had never been more than taking her knickers off – it was to worship her body. Two years ago, the first time she let him, he'd kissed her breasts and belly for so long and so hotly that before he thought of going further he spurted his passion over her bare thigh. On reflection she saw his involuntary action as a warm compliment to her sexual power.

But that was not the mood of the moment. There was a patient coming at five – the politely smiling Mademoiselle Anvers would soon be tapping at the door to announce whoever it was who needed a sympathetic ear. And in the meantime, Jacques was on his knees between Nicole's legs, with his stiff part sticking out of his trousers.

'*Chéri*, put it in me,' she murmured in his ear.

He straightened his back and moved close between her thighs. He held his upright part in his hand to guide it while he was pushing forward. Nicole spread her legs wider and at once felt the blunt head touch the soft lips between them. He pushed again, he slid into her.

'Oh Jacques,' she whispered. 'It feels so thick and strong.'

So it did, his stiff length of flesh inside her. And she was trying to compare the sensations with those of Remy inside her, earlier that day – she was trying to decide which of the two felt thicker and stronger. But between the two well-developed men, it was impossible to decide.

She sighed with satisfaction now she had Jacques where she wanted him at last. She bent her legs and pulled them high, until her knees were almost in her armpits – and she had opened herself wide to his inward thrust. He lay forward over her, he slid his stiffness into her warm wetness – he glided in and out, murmuring that he adored her.

Nicole was very content to lie on the smooth brown leather and let him ravish her body. Her day had turned out well – in the morning big strong Remy had mounted her belly, in her own bed. Now it was dear Jacques, pleasuring her on his consulting-room couch.

On the very couch where she was sure he did it to Josette Anvers when there were no patients. But that couldn't begin to compare with what Jacques was having now – when Nicole spread her legs for a man he was privileged to get the deluxe five-star treatment. Little ripples of pleasure ran through Nicole's body, from down between her parted thighs up to the tips of her firm-pointed breasts.

I am an addict of love, she said to herself happily, *why shouldn't I admit it with pride? Love-making nourishes and sustains my talent as a writer. I need to have the men I adore lie on my belly and worship me – they think they are using my beautiful body for their own pleasure, but, no, it is I who am using them without their knowledge. In the act of love I draw their vigour and their vitality into myself – and then later I transform it into works of literature.*

She felt a change in the tempo of Jacques' thrusting – it had become faster and more determined. *Oh yes,* she murmured aloud as his strokes shortened. He was jerking strongly into her and moaning mindlessly.

'Ah, you told me it was nonsense – but it is true that

you must always dominate me and ravage me,' she cried out.

He was still fully dressed, but she put her hands under his jacket and forced them down into the back of his trousers – she gripped the flesh to drive him deeper into herself.

'You want to crush me, Jacques,' she moaned. 'You cannot deceive me. You want to destroy me because you hate me as much as you adore me – you hate me for making you confront your own nature – and so you are determined to annihilate me.'

Jacques shrieked like an orgasmic woman at the moment he reached the peak of sensation. Nicole felt the strong convulsions of his body as he spurted his desire into her, she cried out herself and her back arched in ecstasy.

'Ah yes, destroy me,' she sobbed. 'Destroy me with love, Jacques—'

Whether he heard her words or not, he thrust hard and fast until it was all over for both of them. But then, as soon as he had recovered a little, he pulled away from Nicole. His wet length slipped out of her and he stood up to tuck it away and do up his trousers. He was red in the face, there was a gleam of perspiration on his high forehead, where the hair had receded.

This was not the first time that Nicole had seen his sudden transformation after climax and she knew how to handle it. She put her legs down and sat up on the couch, her thighs modestly together. Her tiny silk knickers lay beside her – she picked them up and twisted them round her fingers.

Jacques didn't sit beside her, he went to the high-backed chair that stood at the head of the couch.

Now there's symbolism for you, if that's what you want, Nicole thought, trying not to smile, *when he sits in that chair and the patient is on the couch, he feels that he's in control of the situation. We'll soon see about that, dear Jacques, believe me.*

She twisted round to face while they talked.

'I adore you, Jacques,' she said lightly. 'You are so good for me – when you make love to me your determination totally destroys my ego. I feel released and renewed – born again. Am I good for you?'

'Do not pretend with me,' he said unhappily. 'You are a very intelligent person – you know the truth about our relationship as well as I do. It is founded in sex, nothing more.'

'Since when did you despise sex?' she asked, raising a dark eyebrow in question.

'You must let me psychoanalyse you,' he said. 'The situation is far more serious than I thought.'

He'd shrugged aside her question as not seriously intended.

'We can discover the causes of your motives and the problems that arise from them,' he told her earnestly. 'We can resolve your inner tensions and set you free from the pattern of the past. Though I warn you it will take a long time.'

'Thank you for the offer,' she said, 'but I find the idea absurd. When you have beautiful exotic flowers growing in your garden, it is madness to pull them up to look at the roots to see what makes them blossom. If I let you probe my soul as ruthlessly as you penetrate my body, all my talent to write and interpret would be obliterated.'

'Not necessarily,' he said, trying to sound reassuring.

'If you want me on your couch,' she said, 'it will not be for talking about imaginary tensions and mythical complexes – it will be to make love.'

Before he had time to consider his reply, she was up off the couch and then down on her knees on the carpet at his feet. She looked up at him with affection in her eyes – while she pushed his knees apart and undid his trousers again. His male part lolled out, soft and limp.

'*Oh la la*,' she said, rolling it between her fingers. 'It seems that this little gentleman has forgotten his manners and doesn't think that he need stand up for a lady.'

'Nicole, no more now,' Jacques said. 'You know I have an appointment in a few minutes. You must leave now.'

She glanced at her tiny gold wrist-watch.

'No need for panic – we have ten minutes,' she informed him with a charming smile. 'That should be long enough for me to instruct your impolite little friend what is expected of him.'

'No, it is impossible,' he sighed.

He wanted Nicole to go and he wanted her to stay – the usual male dilemma after love-making.

Her fingers clasped around his shaft and she flipped it up and down lightly. The treatment was having a beneficial effect – he was starting to grow a little longer and harder.

'Nicole, you must go, you must,' Jacques said, and he was sounding very agitated now.

'Of course I must,' she answered, 'in two more minutes.'

She wrapped her silk *caché-sexé* around his shaft – and this solid fifteen centimetres of his had become exceptionally hard and thick – she had teased it to full stretch and it slanted up from its nest of crisp curls. Together he and she stared down enchanted at his length swathed in thin transparent silk.

'Oh,' said Jacques, round-eyed.

'*Formidable*,' she exclaimed, as her hand slid neatly up and down. 'I do believe that *petit monsieur* intends to devastate my knickers.'

Even while she was saying it, there came a discreet tap at the door – that would be Mademoiselle Anvers.

'Your patient is early,' Nicole murmured, amused by the look of dismay on Jacques' face. 'What a pity.'

Before he could travel the last little stretch to release, she tucked his hard-straining part under his shirt – it was still wrapped up in her knickers – and zipped his trousers closed.

'Poor little gentleman,' she said, patting the bulge it made. 'But at least he has a silk dressing-gown to remember me by when your patient becomes too boring.'

She stood up and kissed Jacques on the cheek, evading the sudden reach of his hands as he tried to take hold of her bare bottom and pull her to him to complete his pleasure.

'I must leave now,' she told him. 'You said so yourself, two minutes ago. *Au revoir, chéri*.'

Her dark-blue skirt lay on the floor when it had fallen – she stepped into it and pulled it up her long legs. She put her high-heeled shoes on, kicking each leg up in turn behind her – and she left Jacques sitting in his upright chair with a look of astonishment and outrage on his face.

Passing through the outer office she smiled and nodded and said *au revoir* to Mademoiselle Anvers. The expected patient was sitting in an armchair with a fashion magazine – she was an elegantly-dressed woman of perhaps fifty, with lips and fingernails painted a bright red.

Nicole nodded politely as she went past and out. There was an amusing little thought in her mind and she was smiling to herself.

Would it amaze you to learn that I've no knickers under this elegant skirt, Madame? The doctor insisted that I took them off – I suppose it was part of his therapy. The unmentionable fact is that my darling joujou is bare and wet.

I'm sure you'd be thrilled to lie on the couch for Monsieur Jacques to take your knickers down, Madame Fabre. Perhaps he will. I've left him in a madly frustrated condition, with his trousers bulging out over his stiff and throbbing part.

You arrived for your appointment a little too early, Madame Fabre – if you'd been only five minutes later, poor Jacques wouldn't be in the desperate state he is. So perhaps today is your lucky day after all. It's certainly been mine.

From The Diary – July 6

My love affair with Remy was burning hot from the very beginning, from that first day when we ran into each other at the Dome and went to his apartment. This love is like no other I have known in its intensity. My heart and my body are on fire – and so are Remy's too.

When we are together I feel myself enclosed and protected – by the strength of his mind and the strength of his body. I lie naked in bed with him, his hands hold me and caress me and fulfil my longing.

We are together almost everyday and almost every night. We walk hand in hand by the Seine, we saunter along the paths of the Luxembourg Gardens, we sit outside little cafés and drink a glass of cognac, we go shopping in the big department stores on the Boulevard Haussman to buy presents for each other – a silk tie for him, a Hermes scarf for me, silk socks for him, black lace knickers for me.

After nine weeks of being loved by Remy and loving him, our affair is hotter than at the beginning, it has become fiery and devastating. Nine weeks with him – and yet the time has passed so fast that it seems hardly more than nine days.

On a warm summer evening when Nicole and Remy had been out to dinner and dancing afterward at a small *boite* on the Left Bank, they lay in bed together in her apartment. She was holding his hard and dominant male part in her hand, while he caressed her breasts.

'*Ma belle Nicole,*' Remy murmured.

The night was warm and they lay uncovered and naked. He kissed her breasts and her belly, again and again – his hand was clasped between her thighs, cupping her neatly-trimmed *joujou*.

This went on for so long that Nicole could almost believe it was not Remy lying beside her but Jacques Lecomte – Jacques worshipping her body.

'Your beautiful, beautiful body,' Remy murmured ardently. 'I adore your breasts, Nicole, those round perfect breasts with the firm pink buds. And your belly – soft and smooth for me to lie on—'

Nicole had no objection to being adored. But at that moment she wanted to be adored with more than words – she could feel the press of his hard fleshy length against her thigh and would like to feel its sturdiness in another place.

'And I adore you, *cher Remy*,' she said, and she gave his proud part a loving squeeze.

She settled on her back and spread her legs luxuriously for him. He kissed her breasts and slid his body over her, his belly was hot on hers, his long strong legs thrust out straight between her thighs.

Nicole sighed pleasurably and waited eagerly for his long thrust into her – the feel of his solid flesh penetrating her and opening her for ecstasy – there was no sensation in the world to match that push.

But there was a pause of some seconds when nothing happened. No strong and delightful slide into her – instead she heard Remy's exclamation of annoyance. She slipped her hand between their thighs – his male part was soft and useless.

'Oh,' she breathed.

Two minutes ago it had been hard and throbbing against her thigh. She had almost thought that in his extensive adoration of her beautiful body Remy might even do as Jacques had once done – spurt his desire on to her leg. Now it seemed that his desire had evaporated before there was any opportunity of it spurting anywhere.

He was muttering an embarrassed apology and he would have moved off her, but she held his narrow hips to keep him where he was.

'Wait a little,' she said, her mouth close to his ear. 'These things sometimes happen.'

'Nicole,' he said, gratitude and dismay in his voice. He rubbed his belly against hers, his hands were over her breasts, clasping them.

'Give me a moment,' he said.

But after a while he slid off her body and lay facing her. She held his childishly limp part in her hand and wondered what the difficulty could be. In the nine weeks of their lovemaking this had never happened before – not even on the nights when they did it four times between midnight and the time he left the next morning, late for his office.

His moment of annoyance was past and he was murmuring charming and loving little nothings to her while his hand stroked her belly and the insides of her thighs. He clasped her *joujou* – the lips were parted and wet. His middle finger lay along them, she felt it press inside and the sensation was so very delightful after her disappointment that she thought she would climax instantly.

His fingertip found her firm little bud and tantalised it. '*Ah yes,*' she sighed faintly, her outstretched legs were shivering with delight. This was not how she had wanted to be loved – by Remy's finger instead of his long hard shaft – but she needed the release of ecstasy and he was attentive and thoughtful and knew what he had to do.

Their hot bodies were close together, Nicole's arms about his neck, her mouth pressed to his in a passionate kiss. The little throbs of pleasure ran through her, they grew stronger and followed each other faster until she was on the very edge of sensual explosion – and all the time his finger in her soft wet *joujou* was moving delicately.

She clutched him close to her naked body and she groaned suddenly as the golden moments arrived – she sucked his tongue into her mouth almost as if her *joujou* was sucking his male part into her belly. He teased her with an expert finger through her ecstatic throes, and held her close when she subsided at last into trembling contentment.

Her beautiful body was calm now, after what Remy had done to her, but her mind was active. Because earlier she had thought for some fleeting moments about Jacques when Remy was kissing the insides of her thighs before he tried and failed to mount her, she now remembered the words Jacques had said to her in his consulting-room at Passy.

There had been a serious look on his face when he'd said – *there is always a reason, whether you know it or not.*

Jacques had been questioning her about why she had come to see him wearing see-through knickers. Not exactly questioning – he was making a point. She had replied that she wasn't there to be psychoanalysed. But Jacques' words now remembered raised a different question and a doubt in Nicole's mind. Was Remy unable to penetrate her because in his heart he didn't want to?

Impossible, she said to herself, *unthinkable*. She was certain that Remy was as madly devoted to her as she was to him. On the nights when he slept alone in his own apartment, he fell asleep thinking of her and wishing she was in his arms. When he slept he dreamed of her – tender dreams of Nicole coming naked to his bed. Dreams of Nicole leaning over him to let her bare breasts brush warmly over his face.

She was sure all this was true because Remy had told her so, not once but many times. He dreamed of having her naked on the grass of the Bois de Boulogne, arms and legs straight out and apart, so that she looked from above like a beautiful starfish. He dreamed of having her at the top of the Eiffel Tower, her back to the lattice ironwork and her skirt up round her waist to bare her belly and her *joujou* for him.

He woke up in the morning after these enchanting dreams with his male part standing firm. He phoned while he was drinking his breakfast cup of *café-au-lait* to say *bonjour ma chérie* and to tell her he adored her.

And yet, and yet . . . suppose for a moment that Jacques was correct in his endless and tedious psychoanalysing . . . could it really be possible that a slackening of Remy's devotion to her might be responsible for the slackening of his male part at so critical a moment? The moment when his belly pressed down hotly on hers and her legs were parted wide to receive him . . .

No, no, no – it is out of the question, Nicole said to herself, *no man has ever tired of me – it is I who bid them adieu when their charms cease to enchant me*.

She rearranged herself on the bed to lean down and take his limp part into her mouth. *Poor sad and bewildered little thing*, she thought with a surge of affection, *it doesn't know which saint to pray to – I will soon teach it*. She licked the soft head with her warm wet tongue and after a time she felt it stir and stiffen a little.

'*Ça va, chéri,*' she said to encourage Remy.

She raised her head to smile at him, and held his shamed part lightly between her fingers. She stroked up and down to comfort it and urge it to grow longer. Her fingertips slid delicately along the warm shaft, she circled it just below the head with her long thin thumb and her long forefinger.

As she felt it stretch and swell under her touch, she played with it a little quicker, wanting it to become strong. She felt it throb, she knew it was almost ready.

He slid his body over her and lay full-length, letting her feel his dominant weight and strength. Now at last she had what she wanted – she felt his hard shaft open her *joujou* and penetrate her... as it slid into her depths she felt it stretching her and filling her, and she sighed in pleasure.

Remy was thrusting in and out – and she was bucking her belly and her loins to meet him. They sighed and gasped and held each other tight and sought their climax together.

And then afterwards, after the spasms of ecstasy had racked them from head to toe and died away, they lay side by side clasped in each other's arms. Their bare hot bellies were still pressed together as they went to sleep, satisfied and content. When Nicole woke in the morning she was alone in the broad bed and her little bedside blue Limoges clock pointed to ten past ten.

She was in the kitchen making coffee when there was a ring at the door and a bouquet of flowers was delivered. Ten red roses – and a note from Remy, a scribble that said simply *Je t'adore, Nicole*.

The unexpected little incident of the night was forgotten as the days of happiness passed – it was not repeated and neither of them mentioned it. Nicole suppressed the thoughts that had passed through her mind when Remy's fine male part had failed in its duty. She told herself that Jacques Lecomte might be a clever psychoanalyst but he didn't know everything and he could be as mistaken as anyone else.

Two weeks later there was a night when Nicole was alone in her apartment and couldn't go to sleep. She turned in her bed, she lay on her left side and then on her right side. There was something keeping her awake, though she didn't know what it could be.

She switched the light on and arranged the big soft pillows

behind her back. It was futile to try to sleep – perhaps if she read for a while that might make her drowsy.

There were eight or nine books on her bedside table, mostly novels of recent publication. She never read other writers' books seriously or continuously – she feared their words might influence her own style or the way she saw things. Instead of reading a book from page one to the end, as ordinary people usually do, she dipped into them, she dabbled and dropped them.

She came back to books that interested her, she turned the pages at random and read for a while, put it down, perhaps for days or sometimes for weeks, and then dipped in for another page or two. And this would continue until she had finally read the book – or most of it – in bits and pieces.

Tonight she was too distracted to make a conscious choice. She reached over to the row of books standing on the bedside table and took a small book without looking at the author or the title. There was no point in remembering how much of it she had read so far – or what it was about. But for once she opened the book at the first page.

Lulu slept naked because she liked to feel the sheets caressing her body and also because laundry was expensive. Henri protested that you shouldn't go to bed naked like that . . .

Nicole sighed in exasperation – she remembered the story now and she looked at the front cover to confirm who the author of it was. This man has ideas of his own about women, she said to herself. As I recall, it turns out that in spite of being naked in bed with Henri every night, poor Lulu doesn't like what men have between their legs.

To Nicole it was almost incomprehensible that when a woman took a man's shaft in her hand and felt it grow hard and stand up straight – that she should be frightened of it. As this Lulu in the story was said to be. The truth, Nicole said with a little shrug, is that Lulu would prefer to be in bed with another woman. As naked as herself – so that she can kiss and caress and not be bothered by a strong thick shaft ready to slip up her.

Nicole couldn't remember what happened in the story. She turned the pages to find out – and shrugged again – Lulu didn't even manage to get her woman friend into bed with her, the poor fool.

With a little sigh Nicole dropped the book on the bed beside her. Reading about one of life's victims wasn't going to calm her mind and help her go to sleep. Her irritation with Lulu would only make her more wide-awake than ever. The little clock said that it was after midnight. She had been in bed for an hour and was no nearer falling asleep than when she first lay down.

Twenty minutes went by very slowly. She decided to phone Remy, to ask him to come to her apartment. It was terribly late, of course, but this was an emergency. She felt sure that, in his arms, after he had loved her, she would be able to sleep.

She had an extension by the bed. She dialled Remy's number – it was a number she knew by heart. She could hear the phone ringing at the other end and waited eagerly for his voice. He would sound sleepy, having just been woken up, perhaps even a little bad-tempered – but when he knew who was calling him, he would be charming.

The phone rang and rang for the longest time and Nicole was thinking what to say to him – *chéri, I can't sleep and I am desolate – will you come over and hold me in your arms* . . .

After five minutes she knew that no one was going to answer. She rang off and redialled, in case she had made a mistake the first time. But the same thing happened, the phone rang and rang and no one picked it up and answered.

Whatever slender chance of sleep had existed before, there was none at all now. Her vague anxieties had found a focus – Remy was not at home and the time was one in the morning. He'd said nothing to her about going away – and he always told her if he had a business meeting out of Paris.

After another half hour of miserable wakefulness and speculation, lying in bed watching the shadows flit across the ceiling, she gave up. She got out of bed, lifted her short white satin nightie over her head and threw it on the rumpled pillow.

Being sleepless and alone was impossible. Not knowing whether Remy was alive or dead was intolerable and so was not knowing if he was with another woman, a niggling little voice said at the back of her mind. She didn't want to listen to that voice, but suddenly she couldn't get out of her head the memory of the night when he tried to love her and couldn't.

For some moments on that night she had wondered if he was

interested in someone else. She'd dismissed the possibility when he responded so gallantly to her encouragement. But now – what was one to think?

To dress was the work of a minute. She didn't bother with underwear, she pulled a shirt and a pair of slacks on to her beautiful naked body and slipped her bare feet into casual flat-heeled shoes. On a summer night nothing else was needed.

Between one and two in the morning the street where Nicole lived was quiet and deserted, there were no lights at apartment windows, cars were parked nose to tail down both sides, crammed in close together. But when she reached the Boulevard du Montparnasse there was life and action. Cars and taxis drove along the uncluttered boulevard faster than they did in the day.

People were walking – in twos, arm in arm – on their way to bed. There were several nightclubs further along, open for another hour yet, till three in the morning for lovers to drink and dance and fondle each other in the semi-dark. For straying husbands to put their hands up their secretarys' clothes.

An occasional woman wearing too much make-up and too-short a skirt paraded along the pavement, in hope of finding a late-night client.

Nicole realised that she herself was unaccompanied and out very late. She wondered how she would respond – what words would spring to her lips if she was mistaken for a *poule* by a man looking for a half-hour of solace. The way she was dressed she could take a man into a dark doorway and in an instant he could have a hand in her shirt and stroking her bare breasts – or down her slacks and fingering her *joujou*.

Mon dieu, what am I thinking of? she said to herself. She hurried on, averting her gaze from passers-by, across the Boulevard Raspail to the street where Remy lived.

From down on the pavement she could see that his windows on the second floor were dark. That told her nothing – he could be out or he could be asleep in his bed. Except that he didn't answer the phone. She rang the bell by the street door and managed to talk her way in. She walked up the stairs to Remy's apartment and paused.

Suppose he was in bed and asleep? Would he be pleased to be woken at three in the morning? Assuredly yes, when she threw her arms about his neck and kissed him warmly. But, said the devilish little voice in her head, suppose he is in bed with another woman? Suppose they are asleep in each other's arms, after he has done all the delicious things to her that he does to you – what then, Nicole?

No, he's not in bed with a woman, he's out, she told herself firmly. Then who is he out with? the little voice riposted. A beautiful young woman, he is in her bed, she is lying naked in his arms. At this very moment, maybe, he is doing all those delicious things he does to me – for the third time tonight perhaps.

'This is ridiculous,' Nicole said aloud.

She rang the bell and waited. She was dizzy from the turmoil of her emotions and her breath was constricted in her throat. What heartbreak was lurking for her behind this door? she wondered.

Nobody came to the door. She rang again, she knocked. No one, no one, not a breath or a whisper from inside the apartment. After ten minutes of knocking and ringing, the door across the passage opened and a man in blue-striped pyjamas put his head out and complained about the noise.

Nicole apologised with a shrug and decided to give up. The neighbour's hair was standing up from his head like short barbed-wire – he was annoyed at being disturbed in the middle of the night, a man of regular habits, and he launched into a bad-tempered harangue. He went on at length about shady night-drifters ruining the sleep of respectable apartment dwellers.

Nicole was more annoyed than the man – and with more reason. So he was awake for a minute or two in the night, the hateful grudging slug – what of it, when whole nights and days of anguish lay ahead of her from the ruin of her happiness. She gave him an icy glare.

'*Monsieur*,' she interrupted his flow of words. 'I see you are one of those despicable persons whose custom is to expose their miserable sexual parts to women in public places. You are a nasty little pervert and I shall go down and find a policeman to have you arrested.'

The man's jaw fell and he clapped his hands over the front of his pyjama trousers without taking time to look if anything was exposed or not. He dived back into his apartment and shut the door – Nicole grinned sourly and exclaimed *dirty toad* as she left the building.

She was seething with annoyance now. Remy was not at home, that much she had certainly established – where the devil was he? He might be back with his wife, the ugly little voice in her head suggested. That is out of the question, Nicole responded, they parted years ago. They were lovers once, the voice insisted, why shouldn't they be so again?

The turmoil in her head was such that Nicole hardly noticed the walk home in the night. Suddenly she was at her own apartment door, she went in and through to the bedroom. She didn't bother to put the light on – she kicked off her shoes and threw herself on the bed, still in her clothes.

She had convinced herself that Remy was with a woman somewhere. There was a vivid scene in her mind – a room with a broad low bed, and Remy on it. Remy naked, his back propped up on pillows. His legs were splayed out straight in front of him – a woman crouched between them. She was naked too – Nicole could see her back and round-cheeked bottom. The woman's head was down between Remy's thighs.

'No, this is insane,' Nicole said out loud, appalled by her own jealous imagining.

But while the intolerable fantasy held her attention, she had undone the fastening of her slacks – her hand was inside and lying on her belly.

She hadn't put knickers on when she dressed to go looking for the traitor Remy – her body was naked inside her shirt and her slacks. 'I hate him,' she said aloud in the dark, 'I hate him and I shall make him suffer.' Her palm slid down over soft warm flesh until her fingers touched crisp little curls – and she gave a long heart-broken sigh.

More From The Secret Diary – Saturday 7 July

After I returned from my visit by night to Remy's apartment, my mind was in a turmoil. I lay in the dark and suffered all the agonies of unrequited passion. Ah, such suffering as no one else can understand. Toward dawn, emotional exhaustion put me to sleep for a few hours – but it was a fitful and broken sleep, troubled by nightmares . . .

Not once, but again and again, in this haunted sleep, I stood at the door of a room strange to me. Remy was sitting naked on the bed with his back propped on pillows. A woman crouched between his legs, and she too was naked. All I could see of her was her back and the round cheeks of her bottom – she had her head down between Remy's thighs. I didn't have to see her face to know what she was doing to him.

No, no, no – this must stop at once, I kept crying out, but neither of them could hear me. *Stop it, I screamed, I won't let you do this!* But all that happened was that Remy moaned and jerked – he had spurted his passion into the woman's mouth.

The windows were bright when I woke up and the day outside was bright, but to me it seemed grey and desolate. I got off the bed, still dressed in the shirt and slacks of my futile journey last night, and made coffee in the kitchen. I sat alone at the table with my hands wrapped round a cup of *café-au-lait* and fought off the dejection that was threatening to overwhelm me.

There can be no doubt now, I said to myself, Remy has done our special things with another woman. He has gone to find his pleasure elsewhere. Naked all night with a naked stranger. Well then, action is called for, not tears and melancholy.

I reminded myself I was no young girl discovering for the first time that men are untrustworthy. I learned that before I was eighteen.

But this Remy – what has he deserved? I offered him my love and my trust, I gave him my brilliant mind and my beautiful body. And by his faithless response in another woman's bed he had shown how little he valued my gift to him.

He had to be taught the value of what he had so recklessly thrown away. I was not a pair of laddered stockings to be discarded without a thought. One man who learned that lesson was Gerard Constant – he eventually came to understand what a fool he was to break faith with me.

My attachment to Remy had been more important to me than any passing affair with Gerard – with Remy it was a kind of love – and for that reason Remy's lesson was going to cost him dear.

Remy's office was in the Boulevard des Italiens, not far to walk from the Opera Metro station and on the same side as the Credit Lyonnais building. The day was Saturday, but Nicole knew that the office would be open until midday. She stared at her face in the mirror and saw the signs of grief and disturbed sleep – the dark shadows under the eyes and the pallor of the cheeks.

She made up her face carefully and looked through her wardrobe before she decided on a stylish little summer costume – it was a buttercup-yellow jacket and skirt from a good house. A simple necklace, a strand of green jade beads, to draw the eye to the *décolleté* and the elegant cleavage of her breasts.

When she arrived at the office, Remy wasn't there – but she hadn't expected him to be. He was having breakfast with the woman he had spent the night with. Perhaps they were in her kitchen, she sitting on his lap and slipping morsels of sweet croissant dipped in milky coffee into his mouth – while he had his hand inside her dressing gown to feel her.

Remy's partner was in the office – Lucien Moreau – and he was the one Nicole had come to see. She had met him before, of course, on her visits to meet Remy when they were going somewhere together. Lucien was twenty-nine and as fair-haired as Remy was dark. His colouring and sturdiness of build made him more the type one would expect to meet in Normandy rather than Paris.

The secretary in the outer office announced Nicole and stood aside to let her pass. Lucien sat on a high-stool at a drawing board. He was in shirt sleeves and a dark-red bowtie, his jacket hung on the back of a chair by a cluttered desk. He slid to his feet and came forward to meet Nicole, his hand held out and a pleasant smile on his face.

He settled her in a chair which had chrome tube legs and a scarlet seat and perched on the edge of the double-size desk he and Remy shared – he used one side and Remy the other. They talked – or at least, Lucien talked. Nicole said little, she was arranging her thoughts and deciding on her plan.

She was ready – she crossed her legs elegantly and held up her hand to stop Lucien's friendly chatter.

'I am not here to meet Remy,' she told him. 'I am here to talk to you, Lucien. Please be truthful with me.'

'But of course,' he said, and his sandy eyebrows were rising in surprise. 'What do you want me to be truthful about?'

'Remy was not with me last night,' she said, keeping her tone neutral. 'He was not in his apartment all night. He is not there now. Do you know where he is?'

'As it is Saturday he is with his little boy, I imagine. He has rights of visitation on Saturdays.'

'Where was he all last night? That is what I am asking.'

'But how should I know, Nicole?'

'Because you are his friend and men tell each other things.'

Lucien shrugged and looked at her with an expression of innocence in his pale blue eyes.

'His friend, yes, but not his brother,' he said mildly.

'Remy was with a woman last night,' Nicole said. 'Do not try to deceive me, Lucien.'

'It is impossible to believe he would be with anyone else when he could be with you,' he said gallantly. 'I know I wouldn't.'

'I believe you,' she said. 'But the fact is that he was in

someone else's bed last night. Whose, Lucien? It is pointless to pretend you do not know his interests.'

'We don't tell each other everything,' Lucien said.

His cheeks were pink – he was embarrassed by the thought of betraying the confidence of a friend.

'Men always tell each other about their women,' Nicole said with a dismissive flick of her hand. 'There is no need to play the schoolboy to protect a friend. Has Remy gone back to his wife?'

'Back to Dominique? Why no, she has found another man in her life and lives with him.'

Nicole didn't know whether to be glad or sad that Remy was not with his estranged wife. Last night she was racked by the thought that he might be. They were lovers once, she told herself in anguish, they could be lovers again, even after two years apart. How easy for him to go calling, to see his little son – and stay to comfort Dominique.

But that was not it, according to Lucien. And Nicole's opinion of Lucien was that he was a naturally candid person, not given to telling untruths.

'Very well,' she said. 'He was not with Dominique. Then who was he with – tell me?'

She was projecting all her charm and grace at Lucien. Her dark-brown eyes were wide open and luminous, she was leaning forward a little on her chair so that, perched higher on the desk, he could see down the top of her buttercup-yellow jacket to her superb breasts.

'Tell me, Lucien,' she murmured softly as she held out one hand toward him.

'It's wrong to give a friend's secrets away,' he said, his voice husky with emotion. 'But he has behaved so impossibly badly toward you that I feel free of any obligation. You are so beautiful and fascinating that he must be out of his mind to do what he's doing . . . I mean, if I were in his position – if I ever for a moment had the unbelievable good fortune to attract your interest and love, I swear to heaven I'd chop my own fingers off with a kitchen knife before I touched another woman—'

'Yes, yes,' she interrupted, 'I have always known you were

a man of honour. But as for Remy, that's a different story, it seems. How long has he been meeting someone else?'

Lucien had taken the slim hand she held out toward him. He held it as reverently as if it were sacred. He sighed and for a moment she thought he was going to kiss it. She held his eyes, willing him to speak, to tell her all she needed to know – and feared to know.

Lucien couldn't meet her gaze for long, he bowed his head and stared down at his shoes and shuffled them uneasily on the floor.

'About three weeks now,' he said in an undertone.

Nicole looked at him thoughtfully – in her mind she was working out the dates. Three weeks – how did that relate to the night when Remy was in her bed and tried to make love to her but couldn't because he had gone limp? She had asked herself at the time if a slackening of his devotion to her was the reason for a slackening of his male part.

She had told herself that it was impossible, out of the question. She had changed her mind since then – now she had the proof.

'Who is she, Lucien?' she asked.

'Her name is Chantal Lamartine.'

'Tell me about her.'

'She's an important executive of an office furniture company we deal with. We've both known her for a long time. Then about three weeks ago, when Remy and I were sitting in a bar having a drink together after work, he told me, out of the blue, he had spent the night before with her.'

'Is she pretty? Is she dark or fair? How old is she?'

'She is brunette,' Lucien said. 'She's in her twenties, I would say. And some would call her quite attractive, though I personally have never been greatly struck.'

From his awkward and shame-faced words Nicole deduced that this Chantal was wildly attractive to men. The situation was worse than she'd feared. She intended to have Remy back – and at her feet – and to make certain he'd never underrate her again.

'Lucien, we've much to talk about now you've told me this,'

she said. 'And as it is very confidential, send your secretary home.'

He nodded and went to the door. He put his head round it and told the secretary in the outer office that she could go. When he came back Nicole was standing at the window, looking down into the small courtyard below.

'She's gone,' he said, sounding a little agitated, as if he was about to join a desperate conspiracy.

In a sense he was. Nicole had decided the first step in her plan to beat Remy to his knees and bring him crawling to her feet. She intended to give herself to Lucien. If she had read the candour of his character right, he'd be incapable of keeping it a secret. He would be compelled by his own sense of decency to confess to Remy that he'd had Nicole. That would bring Remy up short and make him ponder. So far Remy had been running carefree and jaunty – now suddenly and unexpectedly he was going to run into a plate-glass door.

'Sit down, Lucien,' she said, her hand on the back of the chair where his jacket was hanging.

'You take that chair, I'll take the other one,' he said innocently, meaning they would be facing each other across two metres of polished desktop. She shook her head.

'Sit down, Lucien,' she repeated, her smile charming as she reached out to take his hand.

He pulled the chair away from the desk and sat. An instant later Nicole was on his lap. His knees were spread just a little, to provide a comfortable base for her – it dawned on him that her weight on his thighs was sexy and exciting. She could tell from the curious expression on his face that the astonishing thought had crept into his mind that perhaps there was a hope of making love to her.

But they were some way off from that, there were the usual rituals and stratagems to be gone through first – the little manoeuvres required by decency and the charming subterfuges of self-esteem.

First she must be kissed, of course – her face came round toward him and she had an arm lying lightly around his shoulders. He put an arm about her waist and hugged her affectionately – while he pressed his lips to hers in a kiss meant to be eager and yet respectful.

'Nicole, I never imagined . . .' he murmured. 'I still can't take it in,' he kissed her again, as eagerly if a little less respectfully.

'*Chéri*,' she murmured, when the kiss ended.

His arm about her waist held her close while with his other hand he undid the top button of her jacket and slipped inside to cup her breasts. She was wearing a gossamer-thin bra – he touched her superbly-shaped breasts gently, no sudden grab or squeeze to startle her and break the magic spell.

An enchantment it surely must be, he was telling himself, his mind in a whirl of delight. She was his friend's girl. But what of it? There were no rules in love.

He undid another button of her jacket – there were only three. Why not go all the way? he said to himself. He undid the last button and the jacket fell open to reveal that her little bra was transparent. His fingertips slid softly over the pink buds that showed through the silk or whatever it was – she sighed and her arm round his neck pulled his head closer to hers. This time, she kissed him.

'You have a guilty look about you,' she said with a smile.

'That's not surprising. I can't think of anything I'd rather have happen to me than this – and I can't think of anything less likely to happen. If I seem confused, Nicole, it is because I am.'

'You cannot understand why I am here with you now when I love Remy – is that what is puzzling you?'

'To be truthful, yes.'

'It is not important – put it right out of your mind. There is only one thing we ever learn from love – which is that we learn nothing from it at all.'

Her hand lay on his chest, her palm was gliding in slow circles over his flat nipples. This was more encouraging than ever – he was sure now that she was going to let him make love to her. Here and now. His stiff part inside her, her hands holding him close to his body while he slid in and out of her . . .

As for his partner Remy, perhaps conscience ought to make an intervention before it was too late. Even a token gesture.

But it was already too late. It had been too late from the moment Nicole sat on his lap. There was nothing to be done but shrug and say in his mind *too bad*.

The thought that loyalty to a business partner, even one who was also a good friend, had any significance when so beautiful a woman as Nicole kissed him and sat on his lap and let him fondle her breasts – the idea was insane. It was a concept with no meaning. But the stratagems of *amour-propre* must still be observed, however stiff a man's part may be standing in his trousers.

'I have adored you since the first time you came here to meet Remy,' Lucien said. 'When I saw you I was completely knocked out.'

'I know,' she murmured. 'That's why I'm here.'

Her words were very far from truthful, but he didn't care about that, only about the amazing good fortune that had turned her against Remy and brought her to him, ready to be loved.

'I haven't been able to get you out of my mind for an hour since that morning you first came here,' he said.

'Maybe,' she said, smiling and shrugging. 'But you have a girlfriend, I suppose – I can't believe you think of me when you are with her.'

'But I do,' he said warmly, 'I assure you I do, Nicole. I think of you and wish you were in my arms instead of whoever it may be.'

She laughed at that and hugged him. The perfume she was wearing between her breasts was so sensual and provocative it made him a little dizzy. He bowed his head to nuzzle at the exposed upper slopes of her breasts and touch his tongue to her satin-smooth skin.

'I suppose you dream about me at night too?' she asked, trying not to laugh aloud at him.

'Always,' he told her – he didn't yet realise that she was joking with him, 'I dream of carrying you in my arms to my bed, of putting you down naked and kissing your breasts.'

'Only that?' she asked. 'Kissing my breasts is all that your dream aspires to?'

'Oh by no means,' he said, beginning to see at last that she was not being very serious. 'I kiss your bare belly, I kiss you between the legs.'

'Of course,' she said. 'And in the morning?'

'In the morning I wake from my enchanting dream of you with my shaft standing upright in my pyjamas.'

She chuckled – his words were not very different from Remy's and the intention was exactly the same. Her bottom was soft and warm on his lap – she could feel the thick hard part pressing against her thigh through their clothes. Her knees were apart, he slipped his hand between them, feeling the sleek touch of her stockings. Her large brown eyes stared at him, as if not quite understanding this new move.

He slid his hand up her skirt, up between her thighs, till he felt smooth warm flesh above her stockings.

'Do you love Remy?' he asked. 'I must know the truth.'

'I adore him,' she said lightly, moving her thighs on his lap to press against his covered bulge.

Her arms were about Lucien's neck, her cheek was pressed to his cheek, her face was flushed a pretty pink. She felt his fingers fumbling with her knickers and lifted her bottom from his lap – so he could pull the little garment halfway down her thighs. Then his hand was between them to touch the soft lips of her *joujou*.

She pushed the tip of her tongue into his ear and he pressed two fingers inside her and found her wet and slippery. She made a gasping little noise in her throat and slipped her hand between their bodies to tug at his zip and open his trousers. She had his stiff male part in her hand and was fondling it.

'Oh,' he said, almost speechless with happiness.

They sat like that for some time, lost in their daydream of delight, appreciative fingers playing softly with each other. Fingers moving gently in her wet *joujou*, teasing her little bud, while the ball of his thumb slid over the neatly-trimmed curls down on her belly – and her fingers curling close around his twitching shaft, hardly moving at all – just enough to make him sigh.

Lucien was the man of the two, but it was Nicole who initiated the next stage of their love-making. She stood up from his lap and slipped her knickers right off. She sat on the edge of his desk, facing him, with her knees well apart. Her hands were under her thighs, raising them in invitation.

'Lucien?' she said, her head cocked on one side.

He was on his feet at once, sighing out nonsense, his stiff part was sticking out of his trousers like a direction-sign. He held it in his hand and steered it to the open lips between her legs. He was well endowed, she noted with satisfaction as she let herself fall back on the desk, her knees coming up to grip his hips as he sank his stiff part into her.

'Oh Lucien,' she sighed. 'Oh yes, *chéri*.'

Lucien was beyond himself, still unable to believe this was truly happening. He thrust into her with fast little jabs – it was going to be over far too soon, Nicole realised. But the most important thing was for him to have her and tell Remy about it later. And there was the rest of the day for him to make good on too hurried a debut performance.

She was on her back on the double-desk, her yellow skirt up round her waist, her bare bottom lying on Lucien's blotter and her head on Remy's side.

If you could see me now, dear Remy, she said to herself, *now while your friend Lucien is having me on your desk – I'm quite sure he'll tell you about it when you come to work on Monday morning. You can sit in your chair and look down where I lay on my back with my legs apart and felt Lucien penetrate me – he's brutally exciting – I'm loving every moment of it, Remy.*

And it was true. The strength of Lucien's assault was making her moan and squirm in near-ecstasy on the polished desktop. She felt him grip her shoulders very tightly as he commenced the short strokes – in one more second she shrieked out in her climax before he spurted.

From The Diary – 14 July

Bastille Day – all Paris on holiday. Remy and I had arranged to spend the day together. I was tempted to tell him I loved him still, in spite of his insult to me. The ultimate affront to any woman. He had undressed Chantal and done things to her that he ought to have done only to me. My beautiful breasts were there for him to kiss – he had no need of hers. I would lie on my back with my legs spread apart for him whenever he wished – there was no reason for him to lie on her belly.

But I didn't breathe a word about any of this, not even a hint. Because he would take my confession to be a weakness of character – a failure of integrity and self-esteem – and he would make use of it.

There was another reason, more devastating yet. If I said anything to him at all, I might go too far and tell him that I love him more now than before I found out he had been to bed with Chantal.

Been to bed – what a very inadequate phrase. It diminishes the event, as if it were a single slip by Remy – a drink too many and his hand up a skirt without a thought for the consequences. No, the truth is that he was taking her clothes off two or three times a week – I knew because he couldn't resist telling Lucien – and Lucien told me all.

The growth of my feeling for Remy after his betrayal does not spring from emotional masochism on my part – quite the reverse. This sensual itch he has for Chantal's naked body, when I have bestowed on him the freedom of mine, is a clear sign of a weakness in *his* character – and I intend to exploit this weakness mercilessly.

* * *

Nicole and Remy were among the thousands of Parisians who lined the Champs Elysees to watch the parade. The military bands marched past, drums and trumpets playing at full stretch – the armoured cars drove past in formation, they were flying little tricolours on their radio aerials. The Foreign Legion marched by in their white kepis, with their rifles on their shoulders.

The President of the Republic drove by to great cheers from the crowds and the waving of hand-held little flags. He stood proud and upright in his open car, his head back and his great beak of a nose cleaving the air like the prow of a ship.

Quatorze Juillet – a national day of celebration and people were packed close together along the broad pavements from the Place de la Concorde up to the Arc de Triomphe, to see the parade. There was no possibility of avoiding the constant touch of hands and bodies, hips and thighs, in the crowd. Nor was there much point in trying, Nicole concluded, after her bottom was pinched for the fifteenth or twentieth time that day.

It is of interest, she reflected, to note that only older men pinch women's bottoms in public – fifty-year-old men and upward. They make a sly nip with the fingertips, then a quick retreat, a look of grinning nonchalance on their faces. They are inviting the complicity of the targets of their elderly desires.

Against that, younger men who take women unaware in public places do not bother themselves with a quick pinch of the bottom – they try for a feel, Nicole said to herself.

She had known it on the Metro, times without number, ever since her breasts began to grow at the age of twelve. Not a pinch, not when the groper was a young man, but the sly touch on the thigh. And as she became a grown woman, the palm on the cheek.

All women know the touch in the crowd – it is part of French history and culture. The touch on the thigh or on the bottom – for as long as the groper dares – or for as long as the woman allows, before she reacts sharply against the act of impoliteness. In a swaying crowd, the press of a man's body on the cheeks of her bottom, as she stands trapped and unable to edge away.

Perhaps the man's hand hangs casually down by his side – and seems by accident to touch where the woman's thighs join. The toucher hopes to rub his hand lightly over her *joujou*, through her clothes. Then there's the man coming from the side, with his part stiff and erect in his trousers, pressing himself against a woman's hip. If the woman tries to protect herself, then he presses himself against the back of her hand – his aim to make her aware of his aroused condition.

Nicole told herself that as a serious writer and an interpreter of life and of the human condition in all its fullness, these casual sexual acts were of significance. She had experienced them in crowded Metro trains and in the lifts of department stores. She knew what it felt like to be touched by passing strangers. Old men pinching her bottom, young men's fingers skimming over her thighs.

At that moment she was keeping close to Remy, her side pressed to his side and her arm round his waist to hold on to him – as a clear hands-off warning to the men standing around her in the crowd on the Champs Elysees that Fourteenth of July. It was a warning that was not always heeded by Parisian males.

This advance from pinching a bottom to feeling it indicates a change in the aspirations of succeeding generations of men, Nicole told herself. The older men are survivors from a generation of *boulevardiers* of the typical Maurice Chevalier type. They had about them a certain air of strolling along the Boulevard des Capucins on a long summer evening and winking an eye at passing girls.

Somehow it now seemed *tres Music-Hall*, very old fashioned – and in a curious way, very innocent. It was impossibly far from modern – it was of a by-gone era of gaslight and plump-bodied women in corsets and horse-drawn buses. And for all the good it did the cheeky *boulevardiers* in their search for love and pleasure, they usually ended their evening in a small hotel with a streetgirl, paid with a handful of francs to take her clothes off and lie on her back on a sagging bed.

The younger men have no time for this false *bonhomie*,

Nicole told herself as a warm hand stroked her bottom. She glanced quickly over her shoulder and saw to her relief that it was Remy's hand. She nestled close to him and kissed his cheek.

In the rush-hour young men put their hands on women in full carriages down in the Metro – her train of thought continued – but not to pinch and retreat, as their grandpapas did in their day – and still do now, when the opportunity serves – not just to pinch, but to feel and to assess.

She recalled how in an overfull lift between floors in the Galeries Lafayette department store, a man in a stylish pale blue suit had stood pressed against her back. She was hemmed in and helpless, with packages in both hands. She was wearing a turquoise silk summer dress that day, with a matching jacket open over it.

He was rubbing himself very slowly against the cheeks of her bottom through the thin silk – she could feel the upright shaft between her cheeks. She tried to move forward, to move sideways, to move in any direction to escape his attentions – but the lift was packed tight and she could do nothing but stand and feel the slow rub of his stiff flesh against her.

Between floors is only a matter of half a minute at most. But the man in the expensive suit wanted more from her. He slid his arms round her waist and held her still while he put a hand over the join of her legs and felt her through the silk. *Ah no, that's intolerable*, she exclaimed, butting her bottom backward, hoping to disable him.

She heard him sigh and press his shaft even harder into the divide of her cheeks – while his fingertips were exploring her groins and the lips of her *joujou* through her dress and her flimsy knickers. Then the lift doors slid apart and people swarmed out and the man's hands were gone from her body.

This was not the floor she wanted, but she lurched forward on high heels to escape the intrusive stranger. As the warning sounded and the lift doors closed again, she glared over her shoulder – more people had rushed into the lift and he had been pushed backward as far as he could go and was himself pinned against the back.

But he was watching her and he smiled at her over the heads of those between. His lips moved, but it was impossible to hear his words over the chatter of the crowd. Perhaps he was saying *Au revoir*, perhaps he was saying *Merci, madame*.

This is something that ought to be written about and made plain for everyone to understand, Nicole decided, while she watched the President's escort of cavalry with sabres and silver breast-plates and helmets with plumes clattering past on tall black horses. *There has been a shift in the French soul*, she thought, *to pinch a woman's bottom in the street no longer satisfies the arrogant demands of the male ego – he must feel her now and in this way express his desire more openly*.

If that is so, then what next? she wondered. Perhaps it will be the turn of women to signify their desires to men, instead of waiting to be asked. Or waiting to be groped in public. Since she had grown up Nicole had never failed to indicate to attractive men what she wanted from them. Perhaps it would become universal – perhaps all women would do the same as she did.

And with that thought in mind, under cover of the men and the women crowding around them and waving and cheering the soldiers, she put her hand on Remy's thigh, her palm warm on the fine wool of his trousers. She stroked very deliberately up toward the join of his legs.

'*Oh la la*,' she heard him say softly.

Well why not? she said to herself with a smile, *what is good for the buck is good for the doe*.

Her fingertips touched the heaviness where his thighs joined – even above the cheerful noise of crowd she heard him draw in a quick breath. What lay cupped in her hand was soft and small, but she felt it growing harder and thicker each passing second. When it stood upright inside his underwear, close to his belly, she stroked the long shaft, just below the head, with one fingertip.

She was thinking then about the man in the lift at Galeries Lafayette, and what he had done to her between floors. It had been no more than thirty seconds – but time had no meaning for her in the packed confines of the slowly descending lift, while the young man in the blue suit behind her pressed his hard-standing shaft into the divide of her cheeks.

Only seconds, while the lift sank from the fourth floor to the third floor – only seconds for his fingers to search her groins and glide over the soft lips of her *joujou*, through her silk dress and her flimsy knickers. But these few seconds lay outside ordinary clock time, they had the essence of eternity in them – to judge by the strong impression the incident made on Nicole.

She was being touched in a crowd, as she had been touched thousands of times in her life – yet this touching in the store lift was more than that – it was a ravishing. She felt as if the stranger was rubbing not his fingers but his stiff male part over her *joujou*.

That thought made her gasp at the time and her eyes rolled up in her head. She expected to feel his hand under her skirt and then down inside her knickers, his fingers opening her, caressing her little bud.

To all intents she felt she was being outraged in a public place – she was being emotionally ravished by a stranger while she was surrounded by people unaware of the brutality of the violation being performed on her beautiful body.

Her legs were trembling and her belly was quaking. She was moist and hot between her legs – with bated breath she awaited the thrust of the stranger's hand down inside her knickers and the touch of his fingers on her bare *joujou*. She feared she would go into orgasm the moment she felt him open her lips and caress her bud.

She despised and hated this blue-suited man for molesting her, for the indignity of submission he was forcing on her. If she had a pistol in her Gucci shoulderbag she'd have snatched it out and turned it on him and pulled the trigger. She'd have shot a stream of bullets into his body, to punish him and kill him for ravishing her.

Heaven only knows what might have happened if the lift had travelled all the way without a stop from the highest floor down to the basement. Nicole might have dropped her packages and turned around to rake the ravisher's face and scratch his eyes with her fingernails – or she might have fallen in love with him and invited him to her apartment.

Or again, she might have collapsed against him for support while she slid into a gasping sexual climax where she stood. Before any of this took place, the lift shuddered to a stop and the doors opened – and she pushed forward through the crowd to make her escape.

But she hadn't forgotten the complex and confusing emotions of those dreadful moments in the lift – the scene was vivid in her mind now as she stood on the Champs Elysees and secretly stroked Remy.

He was hard and strong and she could detect the throbbing under her finger. He held her to him, his arm about her waist and his hand on her bottom, his fingers clenched into her warm flesh.

'Nicole – stop, I beg you,' he gasped.

'Ah, you men – strong and conceited and arrogant,' she said. 'You know nothing of what it is like to suffer violation.'

She was not really speaking to Remy – she was addressing a remembered man in a blue suit and a striped tie in a department store lift. Remy's face was flushed and his eyes were bulging – he didn't understand what her words meant. But she took her hand away and smiled at him.

'Conceit can be humbled,' she said pleasantly, 'and perhaps you can be taught. We shall see.'

After the parade ended they made their way slowly, arm in arm, down the Champs Elysees, going at the easy pace of the crowd, to the Place de la Concorde. They had no particular destination in mind, the day was hot and sunny and they were in love. Though perhaps not exactly in the way couples were conventionally in love with each other.

Every café and brasserie they came to was packed, every table outside and inside was packed, the waiters with their tray loads of glasses and coffee cups were coping as best they could.

But at last, after walking and resting and walking on again, Remy and Nicole found themselves in Montmartre, in the Place du Tertre, drinking glasses of *pastis* at a table outside and under the canopy of a little cafe. The square was packed with people in festive mood and there was music to dance to – two accordionists playing a cheerful tune together.

They were both women, the musicians. One was dark-haired and twenty-something, the other looked to be ten years older and she was thick-bodied. The younger one wore a flowered summer dress, the other was in a black skirt and a white blouse – and she had a black beret on her head.

'Husband and wife,' Remy said with a grin.

Nicole shrugged – the two women were not looking at each other as they played, the one in the dress had a look of concentration on her face and the other was almost frowning as she fingered the white and black keys. But it was evident that they belonged together. Which of them lay naked on her back at night with her legs open, and which of them lay naked between them, was of no consequence.

The two women played their accordions and the people were dancing on the cobbles to *Auprès de ma blonde*. Men in suits and open-necked shirts were jigging with their girls, sailors in square collars and round caps with pompoms were clutching girls they had picked up casually, tourists out to see the sights were dancing with their wives.

Nicole hugged to herself in secret the knowledge that Remy knew she had let Lucien enjoy her beautiful body. So far he had said nothing to her about it, not a word of reproach. But several times she had caught him looking at her sideways and biting his tongue.

He is confused, he hates me and he adores me, she said to herself in quiet glee, *before I have finished with him he will respect me*.

Remy emptied his glass and signalled to the busy waiter to bring two more of the same. He held Nicole's hand on the table.

'Those were very strange words you spoke when we were watching the parade,' he said. 'Do you think that I have violated you?'

'Not my body,' she said, digging her thumb-nail into his palm. 'Everything you've done with me has been with my full acceptance. But you have violated my soul, Remy, you have betrayed my confidence.'

'Me?' he exclaimed, 'but you went to my office when I was not there and—'

'Not another word,' she interrupted him, her nails scoring his palm deeply. 'Or I shall feel it necessary to ask about Mademoiselle Chantal Lamartine. Is that what you want, Remy, to answer questions about her?'

'Ah,' Remy said thoughtfully. 'So that's how it is.'

'It is as you have arranged it,' she said with a shrug.

'Then we are finished, you and I – is that what you mean?'

'Certainly not,' she told him. 'You adore me, Remy, and I adore you.'

'Then what?'

She slipped her hand out of his and with a quick smile put it on his thigh under the table.

'You were strong and hard when I touched you before,' she said with a little chuckle. '*C'est formidable*. But now, *chéri*, are you still strong? Or have you gone small and slack?'

The accordionists were playing *La vie en rose* now and the dancers in the street held each other close, cheek to cheek and belly to belly.

'That is a question of great interest,' Remy said. 'The way to answer it is to walk round the corner to the first small hotel we come to and take a room for an hour.'

Nicole nodded and squeezed his thigh.

'*Je t'aime, chéri*,' she said tenderly. 'I shall not let you forget that.'

As is well known, small hotels that let their rooms for an hour and do not ask for registers to be signed or for visitors to have luggage, are abundant in Paris and very abundant in Montmartre. Only a few steps round the corner from the Place du Tertre was the ever-open door of a suitable establishment.

The concierge was a plump middle-aged woman in a black dress. She said nothing at all when they stood before her, arm in arm. She nodded and took Remy's money and handed him a key from the board on the wall behind her.

The round wooden tag attached to the long old-fashioned key had the number eleven stamped into it. Remy led Nicole up the stairs and in a narrow passage that ran the length of the old building they found the right door. The room was small and the window was covered by a net curtain to prevent inquisitive eyes in nearby buildings from seeing what amusing things the occupants of number eleven did to each other.

Most of the room was taken up by a double bed with a green but threadbare coverlet. But there was a handbasin on the wall and a thin but clean towel hanging beside it – and the inevitable bidet. Remy ushered Nicole into the doubtful little room with a gesture as magnificent as if they had a suite at the Hotel Ritz.

They stood by the bed and he kissed her lightly – after what had been said at the cafe about violation and betrayal he was unsure of himself and unsure of her. It was impossible after that to lose himself in the sweet sensations of making love – he was uneasy and unsure of himself.

But however bad a man's conscience is, to be in a bedroom with a beautiful young woman brings about certain effects. His hands found her breasts, he was touching and caressing through the lavender silk of her blouse. He wanted to feel them bare – he started to undress her, not meeting her eyes.

He unbuttoned the blouse and undid the fastening of her skirt – Nicole's clothes fell about her on the floor. She was returning his kiss – only their mouths touched, and she was undressing him, unbuckling his belt and flipping his trousers wide open.

When they were both naked, standing facing each other, hands on each other's hips, Remy said – for the millionth time since they fell in love: *'You are so very beautiful, Nicole'*.

'Am I?' she said softly, 'I'm pleased you recognise that. Men have bad memories sometimes and cannot see past the nose on their own face.'

'Do not reproach me, *chérie*,' he said, 'I know I've been stupid. But I love you to distraction.'

His dark brown eyes were round and wide with admiration as he looked at her body. He bent his back and kissed the pointed buds of her breasts as lightly as a butterfly wing fluttering over them.

'Adore me, Remy,' she murmured.

He picked her up in his arms and held her easily. She put an arm about his neck and her soft cheek close to his, so that he could smell the exquisite Chanel perfume she splashed freely over her body that morning – under her chin and between her breasts and in her smooth bare armpits.

She lay naked in his arms, open to his adoration. He half turned to carry her two steps to the waiting bed and she slid her hand down her smooth belly to touch her neatly-trimmed patch of brown curls.

'*Je t'adore*, Nicole,' he whispered.

Out of sight below her, his upstanding part swayed stiffly to the movement of his two steps to the bed.

He held her with one arm while he flicked the green coverlet away and set her down on the sheet. She closed her eyes and smiled to feel him biting her thighs and licking at her breasts. His fingers were inside her, she was hot and slippery – she was moaning softly for him to press his belly down on hers and penetrate her.

More From Nicole's Diary – 14 July

Each time I lie on my back with my legs apart – and Remy lies on me – his body feels so big and powerful that I slide almost at once into an orgasm. He responds to my passion – I respond to his. He thrusts and ravages me, he dominates me, destroys me – we convulse with pleasure together.

He tells me that he adores me, he begs me to pardon him for breaking faith with me. I push my belly up to meet him – he is still inside me, though I feel him becoming soft and small. I tell him that I adore him too and he kisses me. In my heart I vow never to forgive him, even after he has atoned for his betrayal.

The afternoon was sunny and hot and to stop the hotel room becoming stuffy the long windows stood open. A breeze was stirring the floor-length curtains, billowing them out into the room, so that they almost touched the foot of the bed.

Remy and Nicole lay naked on that bed – she was on her back and his hands were under her bottom, holding the warm cheeks. Her eyes were half-closed and there was a beatific smile on her face. His big white teeth nipped at the smooth flesh of her thighs.

'Ah Remy,' she murmured as she stroked his dark curly hair.

He slithered higher up the sheet and licked at the pink buds of her breasts – they were firm under his tongue. Her long shapely legs were open to let his palm glide over the neat little brown fleece between them. He pressed two fingers into her – he felt how slippery and warm she was. A tremor ran through her entire body when his fingertips touched her small secret bud.

She sighed and tugged at his shoulders to pull him on top of her. She was impatient to feel him lie on her belly and push his stiff male part into her. And he responded eagerly – his uneasiness had evaporated and he was hard and impetuous. He was ready to master her, to dominate her completely and ravish her to ecstasy.

In his pride he was certain she had completely forgiven him because she was too deeply in love with him to do otherwise. He didn't know it, but he was demonstrating the simple truth of the accusation she'd made when they were watching the military parade on the Champs Elysees – he was showing his natural male conceit and arrogance.

'Nicole, *je t'aime*,' he murmured.

He did this to consolidate his moral ascendency, at the same time he displayed his physical ascendency by moving on to her, with his legs between her spread legs.

She reached down to grasp his shaft and it throbbed in her hand. She guided it to where she wanted it – the bared head paused there for just a moment, nuzzling the soft lips between her thighs – then with a long sigh Remy slid into her.

She gasped and squirmed under him when she felt his solid thickness penetrate her – his hard flesh was stretching her open – it was filling her full, it sent tremors of joy racing through her belly and up to the very tips of her breasts.

'Remy . . .' she gasped – her back arched off the bed and she shook in sudden climactic ecstasy.

'Oh Nicole,' and he launched into forceful rhythmic thrusts, spurred on by her fingernails sinking into the flesh of his bottom.

Her smooth belly jerked up to meet his thrusts, her legs left the bed and wound themselves round his waist and pulled him closer to her. The waves of her ecstasy were decreasing in intensity, but they didn't stop. She lay shaking under his thrusts and sighing to the pleasurable spasms of her body – then as he moved faster and harder her excitement flared up again.

Remy moaned her name. He was excited by the grip of her thighs about his body and the smooth rub of her belly on his. He could feel the soft hold of her slippery *joujou* on his plunging shaft – he could feel how it swallowed his stiff length at each thrust, sucking him into her.

He cried out and jerked furiously as he spurted his desire into her – by then she was writhing under him in her second or third orgasm and she was gasping his name brokenly.

After a while they fell asleep, the breeze from the window playing over their hot bodies, cooling them and drying the perspiration of their loving. Remy reached down to the floor beside the bed to find the green coverlet and pull it over them both, but only below the waist, so that their bellies and loins were shielded from the breeze.

The day had been busy – they had watched the Fourteenth of July parade and they had walked through the streets afterwards, pausing at cafés now and then, as far as Montmartre and the Place du Tertre. The wildness of their love-making had tired them for the moment and they fell into a light sleep together.

Nicole lay on her side with a hand under her head. Her perfectly shaped breasts were uncovered – Remy sighed in admiration and looked at them without touching until his eyes closed and he dozed off. He was at peace with the world now – though he had been in a damnably awkward situation after Nicole found out about Chantal.

He'd expected a painful scene of screams and tears, terminating in a hissed order to leave her and never come back again. And that would have been a pity, to say the least of it, as he adored Nicole. And as for his idiot of a partner, Lucien, Remy hadn't known whether to laugh or punch him in the face when he confessed that he'd made love to Nicole – and in their office, on their shared desk.

If it had been anyone else Remy would have broken up the partnership at once. But Lucien Moreau was remarkably good at designing superior offices and persuading important people to pay for them – at an impressive profit to the partnership. And apart from that, Remy was genuinely fond of him.

There had been a day or two of not speaking to each other, a cold and pointed silence between them – but relations had somehow drifted back to their normal easy-going acceptance.

All in all, the inconveniences had righted themselves. Nicole's eagerness to be loved not ten minutes ago was proof she had swallowed her feelings and adored Remy as much as ever. He was very pleased with himself – *I'm a lucky devil*, he thought with a feeling of warm self-satisfaction, *and why not – who deserves it more?* There was a faint grin on his face as he nodded off.

He slept lightly for about an hour. When he woke he reached out for Nicole, to take her naked body in his arms, but she wasn't beside him. She was sitting cross-legged on the bed by his feet and watching him. The light from the window was behind her, her beautiful face and her breasts were in shadow. The neatly-clipped fleece between her legs was a dark patch, as if hidden from him, though her thighs were spread by the way she sat upright with her ankles crossed.

'While you were sleeping,' she said in a thoughtful tone of voice, 'I kept watch over you and pondered the urgent rhythms of love.'

'Mm,' said Remy, wondering what she meant.

'For me there is the exultation of seeing a lover dashing toward me while I dash toward him with equal enthusiasm – I am speaking of the emotions, you understand, not of physical *rapprochement* – although in a sense I am speaking of both. Consider the imperative drive toward each other across the emptiness of ordinary human indifference, then the demanding meeting at mid-point, the kisses and embraces.'

'Ah yes,' Remy said, recognising her writer's mood – he was very concerned not to say the wrong thing and be thought an idiot.

'There is no place for regret or treachery or deception in these life-enhancing unions,' she said. 'We who love must be free and open, or we are nothing.'

Remy nodded and kept quiet – he realised that she was going to talk about his nights with Chantal and he was in for a difficult quarter of an hour.

'Explain to me,' she said.

She took a deep breath that made her bare breasts sway in the shadow of evening. Remy knew what she wanted explaining, without being told in detail. If she really wanted explanations – which he doubted. After all, what was there to be said, except that he'd had a chance to get another woman's clothes off and kiss her breasts – and he'd taken it?

Nicole knew that already – it would serve no good purpose to say it to her. An apology was surely what she was waiting for, not a tale of what he'd done. She wanted him to abase himself.

He sat up and moved closer to her. He folded his legs under him and put a hand lightly on her knee. He wanted some form of contact between them, not the separation of distance and antipathy. She glanced for an instant at his hand, but left it where it was.

'We men,' he said with a big shrug. 'What can one say?'

She looked at him, waiting.

'We are too coarse to sustain the great and noble emotions you expect of us,' he said, shaking his head regretfully.

'No mystery there,' she said. 'But it is too easy an escape.'

Remy saw that he must lie extravagantly to satisfy her.

'We claim to be creatures of logic,' he said, 'we believe that we are guided by reason – but events prove that this is not often so. The truth is that we do things which are clearly against our own best interests. I adore you more than you know, I would be lost and devastated without you – and yet I have offended you by an act of folly.'

'Folly?' she repeated, seeming to weigh the word.

He nodded and shrugged again.

'The fact is, Nicole, I am not worth the love you give. No man ever could be. I know that – and you know it too. But what can we do, if we love each other?'

He thought his words sounded very persuasive.

'Yes,' she agreed softly. 'That is to your advantage – at least you understand that the love I give you is above your deserts. But I cannot help myself.'

With that she uncrossed her legs and turned to lie across his lap, her arms up and round his neck to pull his face down to hers. They kissed, and Remy silently congratulated himself on finding a way out of an awkward corner. But in this he was over-optimistic.

When they were hungry at last it was only a few steps to

go to find a restaurant for dinner. They walked hand in hand back up the steep and narrow cobbled street to the Place du Tertre, and to *La Mere Catherine*. Nicole declared herself famished after the exertions of the day – the patriotic fervour of the parade and the walking through crowds of Parisians on holiday and the loving and the high-pitched emotions. Remy was pleased to see how well she ate and drank – it indicated a mood of content.

After the meal there were more exertions to come. They found a small nightclub not frequented by tourists because the cabaret was in French and not the tourist English of the big attractions. They sat at a small table in semi-darkness and sipped glasses of wine while entertainers sang. In between the music and the singing they danced cheek to cheek on the tiny floor, their thighs brushing together in unhurried amity.

The star of the show was a wasp-waisted girl in a short silver evening dress that displayed slim legs and high-heeled diamanté shoes. Gigi, she called herself – she had long black eyelashes and a red-painted mouth. Her dress was cut straight across below armpit level and gave a glimpse of small young breasts.

She sang in a little voice, swaying her slender hips, *Autumn Leaves*, a song once made famous by Yves Montand.

'She is too young,' said Remy, who was more than a little drunk by now. 'She's hardly more than a child.'

'Too young for what?' Nicole asked. 'Your *she* is a *he*.'

'What? Of course, I see it now. *Quelle horreur* – but I am amazed.'

'You would be more amazed still if you had put your hand up Gigi's skirt and discovered her little secret in that way.'

'Amazed and confounded,' Remy agreed with a laugh.

'But only suppose,' said Nicole, her mind fixed on the thought, 'a nightclub is one thing, things are not what they seem – but if you had met Gigi at a party and you were deceived by appearances – as you were a moment ago. It is possible, you agree? Suppose that you were attracted and took her somewhere – to your apartment, perhaps – and you kissed her and fondled her little breasts—'

'No, no, no,' Remy said firmly, 'I wouldn't be at any party where that could happen.'

'And suppose she kissed you,' Nicole continued, 'and then she touched you – I'm sure you would be aroused – there would be something long and stiff in your trousers. Suppose she unzipped you and took it in her hand—'

'All this supposing is absurd,' said Remy. 'She is a he, nothing of the sort could possibly take place – I should know the truth as soon as we introduced and shook hands.'

At three-thirty in the morning they were strolling arm in arm down the Montmartre hill by way of the rue des Martyrs, heading for the Boulevard Clichy, to find a taxi to take them home at last. Nicole said she was hungry. Remy agreed he could also eat a bite or two – it had been a long time since dinner and they had danced many times in the club.

The Boulevard Clichy was by no means deserted, even at three-thirty in the morning. On the Place Pigalle stood a little group of street-girls in bright tight clothes and crippling high heels. They were smoking cigarettes and gossiping while they waited hopefully for a last client of the night.

Nicole wished them goodnight as she and Remy walked past. She found it hard not to stare at a plump woman in white kneeboots and a scarlet dress with a zip up the side, from the hem to her armpit.

'They are too old,' Nicole said to Remy when white-boots and the others were out of earshot. 'There isn't one of them under forty.'

'The young and pretty ones have finished work for the night and are tucked up asleep in their beds,' said Remy, as if he knew all about such arrangements. 'These poor dears are past their prime, but they have no other way of life – they wait for the drunks weaving along the boulevard on their way home.'

'That's very sad,' Nicole decided.

'Perhaps – but we all have to live. And if a man is drunk enough he doesn't care what his companion for half an hour looks like, so long as she has what he needs between her legs.'

'It is as you said in the hotel,' Nicole told him. 'Men

are too coarse to sustain the noble emotions we expect of them.'

'But you women love us anyway, with all our shortcomings,' said Remy.

As soon as he spoke the words he wished he hadn't – Nicole might take it into her head that perhaps too many women loved him. Or one too many, at least. But she said nothing and a cruising policecar passed them, windows down and a flic with his head out, keeping a watchful eye on anyone out and about at this time of night.

They were heading toward the Place Blanche, where the Moulin Rouge had stood since the days when Henri de Toulouse-Lautrec went there every evening to sketch the Can-Can dancers and the customers. Nowadays it had become the haunt of American and German tourists.

Before Remy and Nicole reached the Place Blanche they came to an all-night steak restaurant. Even in the small hours of the night it was half-full. They took a table and ordered, holding hands like young lovers from the country. There was no menu, the proprietor offered only one dish, all day and all night, morning, afternoon, evening and after midnight – rump steak and *pommes frites*. With a carafe of Beaujolais.

Nicole had never been there before and she was fascinated. She looked round curiously, wanting to understand everything. At a table near the entrance sat two sailors, drunk and staring in front of them without speaking. A street-girl with the top three buttons of her thin blouse undone was trying to get their attention and failing.

There were several men in sharp suits, talking business very quietly over their empty plates, half-empty glasses and full ashtrays. Heaven alone knew what business was discussed at four in the morning – nothing that honest people wanted to know about.

Nicole saw several obvious foreign tourists – they'd probably started their evening at the Moulin Rouge down the road and then later discovered the less respectable attractions of Montmartre. They were yawning and wishing they were in bed in their hotels and they seemed to be gathering their strength for a final effort to get there.

'You never really answered my question – what can it be like, making love to a man who thinks he is a girl?' she asked Remy, as she sliced her sizzling steak neatly.

'For me it would be mortification,' said he. 'To start to make love to a pretty girl and then find in the last moments that between her legs she lacked what was necessary and possessed what was superfluous—'

'Perhaps for me the shock would be the same – but in reverse,' Nicole said. 'If I was with a man who was really a woman disguised in men's clothes – evidently when I undid his trousers I'd find that what I required was missing – and what I had no need of was present.'

'You are making my head reel,' Remy said, though in fact he was more sober now he'd eaten the steak and chips. 'Let us limit our interest to the customary uncomplicated man-and-woman alliance.'

'Uncomplicated?' Nicole said, raising an eyebrow, 'is that what you believe, *chéri*?'

By the time they arrived at her apartment it was broad daylight. They went into the bedroom and sat on the side of the broad bed while they helped each other to undress. Remy had his hand between Nicole's thighs to clasp her neatly-clipped *joujou* and stroke it. He pressed his middle finger between the lips and found that she was slippery inside.

He wanted her to lie on her back and let him lie on her belly, but she had other thoughts in her mind. She mounted the bed and posed there on her hands and knees.

'This way,' she said, looking over her shoulder at him.

'The thirty-six positions of love,' he said with a broad grin. 'Number twelve.'

He knelt behind her round bottom to put his hands on it and feel the cheeks and squeeze them. She sighed and giggled – and then when her expectation was at its highest, he held a cheek firmly in each hand and prised them apart. She felt him run the tip of a finger along the lips of her *joujou* and slowly increase the pressure until his fingertip sank in and he was caressing her bud.

He used both thumbs to open her wide and hold the lips apart while he moved in closer, aiming his waving shaft. She gave a little shriek when the smooth end touched between the parted lips and then pressed inside. He pushed in slowly, quivering with the pleasure of her slippery flesh clasping his shaft.

His hands were on her hips, holding her fast while he slid in deeper – until his bare belly was pressed against the cheeks of her bottom and he was all the way into her.

'*Chérie, chérie,*' he was sighing.

'I am yours, Remy,' she moaned, leading him on. 'Use me, destroy me.'

He lay forward over her back, letting her feel the weight of his body on her. Her soft bottom was jerking against him with nervous little movements – he groped underneath her to take hold of her hanging breasts and squeeze them in his palms.

All was set – the position was perfect, their parts were joined, his shaft was impaling her and her *joujou* was clasping his stiffness softly. He started a firm rhythmic thrust, sliding forcefully into and out of her warm wetness.

'I'm being ravaged,' Nicole sighed pleasurably. 'Is this how you would do it with Gigi – down on his hands and knees?'

He understood then that she was playing a game with him – she hadn't given up on getting an answer to the questions she asked in the nightclub and in the steak restaurant. She'd set him up to make him consider his reaction to sexual ambiguity.

'No, no,' he gasped. 'This is atrocious . . .'

But complaint was useless – the sensations that were running through him from the sliding of his hard part inside her were compelling and irresistible – his body was shaking on her broad back and in another two seconds he spurted his hot desire into her.

'Yes, absolutely atrocious, *chéri*,' she agreed in a trembling voice. Her hands were flat on the carpet, she braced her arms to support his convulsing weight and wailed in delight as ecstasy took her.

23 July – Monday

It was unexpected, this meeting in the afternoon – it took us both by surprise. Give me another chance, he pleaded, I need you, Nicole. I reminded him that turning the hands of the clock back cannot change the past. He said he couldn't break free from me – he was haunted by the image of me naked in the arms of another man – he'd never known such distress. I felt a sort of pity for him then, I let him take my arm and lead me to a café where we could sit and talk for half an hour. Later I let him kiss me. Was it a mistake?

It was a fine afternoon – Nicole was strolling along the Quai Conti. The stone parapet of the embankment and the Seine were on her left. Across the sunlit water, opposite her on the island, stood the imposing bulk of the Palais de Justice. Further along on the island she could see the square twin towers of Notre Dame, and between them the magnificent rose window behind the statue of St. Marie.

All along the Quai, at her elbow, were the little stalls of the secondhand booksellers. She wasn't interested in secondhand books, but many of the stalls also had interesting old prints for sale. Sometimes she bought unusual prints and had them framed.

She was looking at a mezzotint of the Place Vendome, as it was in the nineteenth century – when the old column stood in the middle, before it was torn down by rioters in 1871 and then rebuilt.

The painter Gustave Courbet led the rioters to attack the column. His landscapes were good enough, Nicole thought, but his best pictures were of half-dressed girls exposing bare bottoms. His most famous painting was a close-up view of a girlfriend's *joujou*. She was on her back on a bed, her legs wide apart – the artist must have been kneeling between them to get the angle of his picture.

He would have been better advised to stay in his studio and play with pretty young women – when the riots were finally put down he was sent to prison for six months and made to pay for the restoration of the column – which left him hard-up and bitter. Now, long, long after his death, his paintings hung in the Louvre and were seen by schoolchildren.

Was the mezzotint worth buying? Nicole was asking herself. And if so, how much to offer for it – not the price the stallholder was asking. She heard her name spoken by a man behind her – she turned and there stood Gerard Constant in a white summer suit.

She hadn't thought about him for a long time. Hardly at all, in fact, since the day she straddled him on the bed for the last time – and rode him until she made him spurt into her and cry out. That was a day to remember – before he had his breath back she was off him and off the bed altogether – she stood beside it with her legs apart to show him her little triangle of brown curls.

While he stared open-mouthed, his exploited part starting to droop, she'd parted the curls to reveal the long moist lips of her *joujou* – it was wet and slippery after what she'd done to him. In fact she'd been giving Gerard a *Courbet* view of her belly and thighs – and the delight that lay between them. And she told Gerard *take a last look to remember me by*. She'd said it smiling, *I do not want to see you ever again*.

Now here he was, and he looked prosperous and well-turned-out – not the speechless and trembling wreck she'd turned him into, before she kicked him out. He'd infuriated her by telling her he was engaged to be married to Yvette Somebody-or-Other and she made him suffer for that.

He wore a wedding ring, she noted, a wide gold ring on his hand. So he had married Yvette, as he said he would. Yvette evidently had restored his self-confidence and transformed him back from the gibbering ruin Nicole made of him into a contented and well-fed husband.

He was slightly built, Gerard, but his face was a little

plumper now than last year. His jacket was open, his black leather belt was pulled tight round his waist – it seemed to Nicole that his belly had the beginning of a little pot.

To her the meeting by the riverside bookstalls was casual – a word or two, a touch of hands, a parting and an instant forgetting. Gerard endowed the encounter with more significance – he held on to Nicole's hand, he gazed earnestly at her, he smiled continuously as if to ingratiate himself with her.

He wanted to talk, that was obvious. He was talkative – there was a smell of good cognac about him. He begged for a few minutes of her time – what harm could it do? She let him persuade her to walk with him up and away from the river, towards the Boulevard St. Germain – and a café where they could sit outside with a cool drink and talk to each other for a little while.

Gerard worked in the textile business – in a family concern he might one day control. They bought from the makers of the most luxurious fabrics and sold them at a high price to *haut couture* houses and others. Gerard's long familiarity with the extravagance of silks and satins endowed him with an artistic understanding of Nicole's talent, or so she had believed at the time – she had fallen half in love with him.

She had been mistaken about him – she had found that he was only a man, like other men. He had been a lover, he became an enemy to be hurt – now he was only an acquaintance. Of all this he was unaware. With a boyish grin he explained his presence on the Quai Conti in the middle of the afternoon by saying he'd been lunching with a client and he was walking off the effects before going back to the office. Nicole realised that he was a little drunk.

They sat on the café terrace chatting for half an hour. Gerard had charm – great charm – otherwise he would never have been accepted as a lover in the first place. He set out to please her and to amuse her – to flatter her. He told her how beautiful she was and how chic – as indeed she was. She was dressed casually for a summer stroll – a white linen jacket over a sleeveless pink silk shirt, white trousers cut so well that her shapely bottom and thighs were ideally shown off.

She smiled graciously and listened, remembering the days

when Gerard had seemed perfect to her – or as near it as a man can be. He surprised her by asking her to give him another chance – there was a half-smile on his face when he said it, making it hard to know if he was serious.

'Why?' she asked. 'Give me a good reason.'

'You will laugh at me,' he said. 'I sound like a boy in love for the first time but after all these months I still can't free myself of the image of you naked in the arms of another man. There – I've said it and you can laugh in my face.'

Why Nicole let him walk her back to her apartment wasn't very clear to her – she wasn't sorry that it distressed him to think of her naked in another man's arms – and she was sure she didn't want to be naked in his arms again. But whatever we may decide, events have their own momentum, especially on a long lazy hot July afternoon.

She wasn't going to let him anywhere near the bedroom – that was out of the question. She opened a bottle of chilled white Macon and they sat on the sofa, talking like old friends. Gerard's arm was about her waist in an amiable sort of way. She had taken her white jacket off – it was hot in her apartment, even with the long windows of the sitting-room standing open.

Before very long her pink silk blouse was out of the waistband of her slacks and Gerard's hand was inside it to cup her breasts and stroke them slowly through her little bra.

'Don't let your hopes carry you away,' she said. 'We are friends and nothing more than that – I am not going to let you make love to me. You must go home to Yvette if you are in a bedroom mood.'

'You shouldn't wear trousers,' he said, as if he hadn't heard what she said. 'Your legs are so perfect that it is a great pity to hide them.'

That was true, she agreed silently, her legs were long and very well-shaped. She was sorry for women who had short legs or thick legs – they had been cheated by Providence of a major female attraction. While she was congratulating herself on her good fortune in being born beautiful in body and face, Gerard was slyly undoing her slacks.

'Oh!' she said in sudden surprise when his hand slid down inside her knickers and closed over the neat little triangle of dark brown curls between her thighs.

'*Je t'aime*, Nicole. I was an imbecile to do what I did – and I am still paying for my stupidity.'

'Really?' she said, sounding casual, parting her legs a little on the sofa to let his hand rest easily between them. 'Then you must continue to pay for what you did – I can do nothing for you.'

'Oh but you can,' he breathed, his fingertips caressing the long soft lips of her *joujou*. 'You can end my misery now, very simply.'

While he said it he advanced as far as pressing the tip of his middle finger between the warm lips and then eased it up to part them.

'No,' she said. 'That won't do you any good at all, my mind is made up.'

He murmured that he understood why she felt like that about him – he spoke in a soothing tone, accusing himself of being a fool and having a broken heart and he kept his fingertip just touching her little bud.

'Time does not run backward, Gerard,' she said. 'You can turn the hands of a clock back, but it doesn't change anything. We were lovers until you wanted Yvette, not me. Now you want me and not her – we are not a pair of dolls to change as you wish for your little games.'

'You're not taking me seriously,' he said sadly. 'Look down for a moment.'

Nicole glanced down and saw that he had unzipped himself and his male part was standing up hard and strong out of his open trousers. She didn't try to touch it, remarkable though it was. It stood up like a fleshy column between his thighs – a triumphant column like that in the Place Vendome which the deranged artist had destroyed.

She smiled a little – she remembered that column of Gerard's well and it lived up to her memories of it. *Gerard-le-Grand* she used to call it, when they were lovers. Meanwhile, his fingertip was gliding over her bud and giving her little thrills. She pretended to be indifferent for as long as she could, but after a while her thighs were trembling and she was breathing fast.

'*Je t'adore*,' he said – her knees were apart and her bud was wet and slippery to his touch.

Her eyes were closed and there was a little smile on her face now. She was thinking about the days when she was busily destroying him – after he'd told her about Yvette Whatever – and the occasion when he'd made a dash for the door to escape. Nicole had gone after him from the bedroom and caught him at the apartment door.

It was comical at the time and it was even more comical now in memory. She'd pinned him to the door, his face pressed to the panel, forcing him against it while she reached round him and dragged his thick fleshy part out of his trousers.

He had begged her to stop – she laughed at him while her hand flicked up and down rapidly. He stopped begging and began to moan softly. She felt his knees tremble under him and the hot shaft in her hand seemed to have grown to an impossible size.

That was then – in those days when she controlled him and manipulated his emotions in her thirst for revenge. But now – she could see the comedy of it. Then it occurred to her – the situation was reversed – Gerard was manipulating her emotions and she was letting him.

'This is intolerable—' she started to say, but it was too late for protests now – her head jerked back and she moaned as climactic spasms shook her belly.

Gerard was watching her face intently as his finger drove her through the long orgasmic thrills. When she had calmed down again he asked what she had been trying to say.

'Nothing really,' she said, staring at him curiously. 'The gasps of pleasure.'

Her mind was in a whirl – Gerard was exploiting her – he was trying to control her body and her mind. He'd learned nothing, it seemed, and he had to be taught all over again.

'I'm very hot,' she said with a smile. 'It's all your fault. I must take my clothes off and cool down.'

He followed her into the bedroom without being invited, his long hard part sticking out of his trousers and nodding up and down as he walked. She could see how sure he was that she had succumbed to his charm and was waiting for him to lie on top of her. He slipped his white jacket off – and his tie – and dropped them on a chair.

'Stop,' she said instantly. 'I said nothing about you taking your clothes off. Do not tempt fortune, Gerard – just sit here on the side of the bed and talk to me.'

He did as she asked, confident that it was only a matter of minutes before his massive part was inside her. She undressed and lay on the bed in a small black satin bra and knickers – all the rest of her beautiful body was naked for him to look at. He sat staring down with burning eyes at her long smooth thighs emerging from her tiny black knickers – and at her perfect belly with its round dimple of a button.

The bra was small – it concealed the pink buds of her breasts and not much more. Nicole lay at ease, her legs stretched out and her ankles crossed, her hands under her head on the square pillow. She could feel Gerard's admiration as a tangible thing – his eyes stared so hard that it was as his hands were running over her breasts and her bare belly.

'You are too beautiful,' he murmured, his eyes ravishing her from her calm face down past her superb breasts to her long smooth belly and the mound concealed by the thin satin of her knickers.

'Yes,' she agreed, smiling to see how his upright part was throbbing.

'Ah, I hear a little touch of vanity, *chérie* – though it is absolutely justified,' he said.

'I adore being adored,' she said, 'I know that I am very desirable and it pleases me beyond words to be kissed and touched and played with.'

He thought it was an invitation and reached out to stroke her belly.

'I truly adore you, Nicole, I worship your beautiful body.'

She smacked his hand away quickly.

'If you cannot control yourself you must leave now,' she said.

'Do not be cruel,' he said ruefully. 'You are too exciting – how can I control my feelings?'

'You must. I am in love with someone – I won't let you touch me. You ought not to be in my bedroom at all, but we are old friends.'

'If only I knew how to persuade you,' he breathed.

He leaned down and, for a moment, put his cheek lightly against her belly. His eyes closed in delight at the fragrance of expensive Chanel perfume she splashed over her body. He was desperate to kiss her, but he kept himself in check, hoping to persuade her by being patient.

'You cannot entice me to make love to you,' she said. 'You must put it out of your mind, Gerard.'

'I love you,' he said, sitting upright. 'You are the most exciting woman I've ever met – I'm dying to do delicious things to you.'

'You had that chance once,' she said. 'It is too late now.'

He gave a great sigh – and summoned up all his courage to do what he was on fire to do – whether she would let him or not. He lay face down on the white coverlet with his face between her legs and kissed her through her thin knickers.

Nicole gave a little cry of surprise to feel the hot tip of his tongue lick up and down the lips of her *joujou*. Her loins jerked up off the bed for an instant. Then she settled herself comfortably and let him continue.

'My poor Gerard,' she said. 'You are letting yourself become over-excited. You imagine I shall take pity on you and let you make love to me. You are wrong – however hot you may be – and however desperate – the answer is *no no no*.'

Words are one thing, actions another. He pulled her little knickers down to her thighs without being checked. He pushed his tongue between the soft lips and found her bud with the tip of it.

'You always were good at that,' she said, with a smile he couldn't see. 'I haven't forgotten, *chéri*. But it is futile to try it now – you will gain nothing.'

His hands were on her smooth tbare highs, gently pushing them open – as far as her underwear allowed. He made no comment on her words of discouragement because his tongue was otherwise occupied. He had opened her and he was lapping delicately at her little bud. *Oh*, she gasped, and he took heart from that and drew her bud between his lips. He sucked gently and felt how her loins were lifting off the soft coverlet.

He thought she was lost in sensation and beyond saying no to anything he did to her. He was mistaken – her mind was still working in spite of the little tremors of pleasure running through her. *The situation is too risky with Gerard in this condition*, she thought. *He must be disarmed – a very simple affair as I recall – two second's rubbing and he's gone.*

She reached down to take him by the ears and tug him up from between her legs – he thought she wanted him to lie on her and he slid his body upwards till his mouth was on her breasts. He flicked his tongue over those pink buds before sliding up higher still to mount her.

'You are beautiful, beautiful,' he murmured. 'Let me love you, Nicole, or I shall die.'

His hands were all over her, touching her bare breasts and her belly – his lips followed his fingers, kissing her firm pink buds and the smooth expanse of her belly down to her little triangle of curls. She felt his hands shake as he put them on her long slender thighs to push them apart and kiss her *joujou* again.

He kissed those long pink lips between her legs fervently – his mouth was hot and eager.

'*Je t'aime, je t'aime, Nicole,*' he moaned, in between forcing his wet tongue into her now equally wet *joujou*.

'Do you, *chéri*? Do you love me – or do you only want to make love to me? Be truthful now.'

'I shall die without you,' he sighed.

Poor Gerard – she was well in control and never intended to let him have what he wanted from her. While he sighed over her breasts her hand was down between their bodies to take hold of the massive throbbing part standing out of his open trousers. She clasped it tight in her palm – she felt the hard length and thickness of it, the hot life of the flesh.

'So huge and strong,' she murmured, her fingers flicking up and down rapidly to relieve him of his aching desire.

'*Chérie*, no, no,' he gasped out in dismay as the inevitable happened – he spurted wildly over her smooth bare belly.

'Ah yes . . . come to me,' she whispered.

Gerard was done for, as she intended. His shaft no longer throbbed or jerked – it was wet and sticky and in her hand. Nicole pretended not to know, she forced her legs as far apart as the knickers round her thighs allowed her and put the head of his cheated part to the soft lips between.

'Slowly, slowly,' she murmured, her hands on his bottom to force him into her.

His massive length slid in, centimetre by centimetre. These moments were overwhelming for Nicole, her plan was a success, the sensations were tremendous – she gave a cry and dissolved into ecstasy. Her back arched off the bed.

Gerard was only at half penetration, but he was still firm enough to slide the rest of the way into her. She writhed and moaned under him in her sudden ecstasy, but his pleasure was past and in his heart was disappointment and chagrin.

'Love me, Gerard,' Nicole moaned. 'Destroy me, *chéri*.'

From The Diary – 27 July

I lie in bed till ten in the morning asking myself if I dare make an appointment to see Jacques Lecomte. Not as a friend, an intimate friend – no appointment is needed for that. But to see him as a patient. I have no need of psychoanalysis, but he might be able to advise me how to deal with my confusion.

After all, that's his job, that's what people pay him for. Though I do not expect to pay him money. Annette must not know about the appointment with him – it would make me feel a fool to tell her that I was in a muddle over a man.

Like everyone else Annette and Jacques are going away for the month of August – Paris is inhabited solely by foreign tourists and café owners for the high summer weeks. They do not go to the coast – Annette thinks the heat is unhealthy for the baby. They go to the Dordorgne, where they have a cottage, not too far from Bordeaux.

Satin sheets are sumptuous – ivory satin, of course. I lie naked in bed with my legs apart and feel the soft slinkiness of the sheet on my breasts and on my belly. I close my eyes and imagine having Jacques in bed with me for an hour – two hours – of being loved luxuriously by him, not the hasty pleasures in his consulting room, on the chair or on the desk, with Mademoiselle Anvers probably listening behind the door.

He is strong when he makes love to me, dear Jacques, he is masterful and demanding, even if he pretends that I am trying to subdue him – as if I would ever be satisfied by a willing victim. He has a theory about me – he calls it role-reversal. The idea is absurd.

If I ever get him into my bed, I shall prove to him for once and for all that I seek no reversal of male and female roles – I shall be at my most feminine for him, I shall be as submissive as he wishes, I shall lie here on my cool satin sheets and let him ravage me to the limit of his strength.

Annette left Paris yesterday, taking the baby and the housemaid, to get the cottage ready for Jacques when he arrives next week. It seems he has his life well arranged. As I wore the Chanel suit the last time I saw him, I decide to wear the yellow silk this time. It is not formal, but it is very chic – formality does not suit my present mood. If Jacques thinks me frivolous, what does he know?

Nicole was a little early for her four-thirty appointment. She looked sexy, expensive and stunning, when she presented herself to the receptionist. There was a surprise waiting for her – Josette Anvers wasn't wearing the business-like black dress of secretaries and office employees. She sat behind her desk wearing a stylish ivory blouse with a big bow at the neck. Her hair was not pulled back plainly over her ears today – it was fluffed up into soft waves.

She stood up to greet Nicole and she could be seen to be wearing a close-fitting black linen skirt that revealed the shape of her thighs and the round cheeks of her well-developed bottom.

Oh la la, Nicole said to herself, *this one has dressed herself up for Jacques while Annette is out of the way. I knew it – he has her in his consulting-room. She sits on his lap and he has his hand in her blouse to feel those skinny little breasts of hers while he dictates reports on his patients. She adores him – that's obvious – and he takes every advantage of her, beast that he is – though a madly sexy beast.*

'Monsieur Lecomte is expecting me,' Nicole said pleasantly. 'Is he free – or shall I take a seat?'

'There is no one with him at this moment,' Josette conceded. 'But he is making an important telephone call. Please have a seat – I'm sure he won't be more than a few minutes. He knows you are due.'

'Your hair is very elegant today,' Nicole said. She was trying to start a conversation that might reveal more of the secret dealings between Jacques and his receptionist.

'Thank you,' Josette answered. She had no difficulty in

guessing the reason behind the compliment and her cheeks were slightly pink.

Perhaps he makes her sit on the side of the desk facing him, Nicole thought, *he did that to me once. He slides his hands up her skirt to stroke her thighs and feel her – exactly as he did to me. He had his hand in my knickers and played with me until I was gasping for breath and I begged him to finish me off.*

I bet he does that to Mademoiselle Anvers twice a day. To judge by the way she's dressed, she's asking for it today. – But what am I saying? – It's half-past four, he's done it to her at least once already today.

'There was a patient waiting to see Monsieur Lecomte the last time I was here,' Nicole said. 'An elegantly dressed woman in black and grey – she had a big diamond brooch on her lapel. I think her name is Madame Fabre.'

Josette looked at her without expression.

'I'm sure I know her from somewhere, but for the life of me I can't recall where or when,' Nicole added.

'Yes, her name is Madame Fabre,' Josette confirmed.

The look on her face was not encouraging. Nicole saw that for some reason the receptionist was jealous of Madame Fabre – her money and her clothes perhaps? Did she suspect that Jacques' hand was up Madame's clothes when the door closed behind her? Even though Madame was of a certain age?

There are depths in dear Jacques I have only suspected, Nicole said to herself, *there is so much I want to ask him when I get him to myself and have his important part in my hand.*

'I know I've met her somewhere,' she said. 'Socially, I mean. At the house of a friend in politics.'

'It is possible,' Josette said, tight-lipped with disapproval. 'But she didn't recognise you, did she?'

The conversation was going nowhere and Nicole dropped it.

I wonder how often Jacques makes little Josette lie on the couch and take her knickers down, she was thinking, *surely he cannot expend too much of his energy on her, not with Annette expecting his attentions in bed at night? Though they say that a change of woman acts on a man as an aphrodisiac and he is able to perform above his usual achievement. That is also something I shall ask him about when I have him naked in my bed.*

Another thought occurred to her. She knew psychoanalysts wrote detailed reports on what their patients told them and what they made of it. She was about to see Jacques officially, not as a friend – would he dictate a report on her to Mademoiselle Anvers for the files? Because if he did, then this plump-bottomed woman was going to know far more about Nicole than Nicole wanted her to know.

On the other hand, did it matter what she knew?

Jacques was pleased to see Nicole. He came round from behind his desk to take her hand. He was wearing an elegant dark-grey suit and had his spectacles in his hand. He smiled and said he hadn't expected to see her as a patient, even though he'd told her more than once that he felt she would benefit from a course of psychoanalysis.

She shrugged and let him think what he pleased. They sat facing each other on leather armchairs. She had no intention of lying on the couch – not yet. Jacques might mistake her for Josette Anvers and put his hand up her skirt. Before things went that far Nicole wanted to have his advice.

'How can I help you, Nicole?' he asked, his voice resonant with professional sincerity and sympathy.

'I am not here to be psychoanalysed,' she said, crossing her knees carefully under her yellow skirt. 'I know more about myself than you'd find out in ten years listening to me. What I am sure of is that I am an addict of love.'

'Are you accusing yourself of nymphomania?' Jacques asked, raising an eyebrow up his domed intellectual forehead.

'You misunderstand me already,' she said, shaking her head sadly. 'As I understand it, nymphomania is a disorder of middle-aged women who run after young men and drag them into bed. What I am speaking about is entirely different – I am trying to explain to you the well-spring of my creative abilities.'

Jacques nodded wisely – whether he believed her was another matter.

'Love-making sustains my talent as a writer,' Nicole told

him. 'I need to be adored, I need to be worshipped – I need men to lie on my belly and thrill me.'

Jacques' dark brown eyes never left her face for a moment, his gentle stare was full of understanding – or so he thought.

'In their simplicity the men I choose to adore me believe that they are using my body for their pleasure,' she went on, 'as they are – but that is completely incidental. The truth is I am using them – without their knowledge. I draw their vigour and their vitality into myself – and this I transform into literature. Can you understand that?'

Jacques nodded, not committing himself to anything. Nicole told him about Gerard – all about him, from the chance meeting on the Quai Conti to the final downfall of his male pride in her bed.

'Tell me what was happening in your mind,' Jacques said. 'What were you thinking when you met him and later when you undressed and made him sit on the bedside.'

'I don't know what was in my mind,' she said. 'I suppose there must have been a stirring of the old emotions from the time we were lovers last year. Yet I do not respect Gerard – in fact I despise him.'

'Then what was the purpose of letting him see you naked? To bare your body in front of a man is to offer him your trust. You knew exactly what it meant when you came here last time wearing see-through underwear.'

'That was different,' she said. 'I wanted you to feel my *joujou*. And you did – you knew what it meant too.'

'In what way was it different when you lay on the bed for Gerard to see your body? Surely the purpose was the same.'

'Why should there be any purpose,' she said, crossing her elegantly stockinged legs the other way. 'Perhaps I felt a flicker of sensuality – Gerard is exceptionally well endowed.'

'You are evading the question, Nicole – there is always a purpose, even if it is hidden in your unconscious mind. Try to recover it – think.'

Jacques was staring at her knees now – her skirt seemed to have ridden up to uncover them. She glanced at his lap, trying to discern any hint of a bulge there.

'The whole experience was strange,' she said. 'I find it

difficult to think about it rationally. When Gerard undressed me and kissed my body from mouth to toes I felt no pleasure – I was entirely passive.'

That was very far from the truth, but who revealed the whole truth to a psychoanalyst?

'Hm,' said Jacques doubtfully – psychoanalysts are used to being lied to and learn to recognise it. 'A moment ago you said you took your own clothes off while he watched – now you say he undressed you. There is an important shift of emphasis here.'

Nicole ignored all that as too tedious to bother with.

'I think I believed it was important to conquer Gerard,' she said. 'If only to remind myself of the importance of not letting him conquer me.'

'*Conquer* is not a word associated with love – or even with liking.'

'But that's how it was,' she said with a little shrug.

'Why do you want to tell me about this episode with a former lover?' Jacques asked. 'Does it disturb you, that you have let him back into your life?'

'In a way,' she said. 'But I thought after he had gone that I may have let him make love to me to score over Remy.'

'With whom you have been having an affair for months now, yes?'

'I met him in your house, you remember. I love him and I need him to adore me. To a point he does, but he has another woman, and that tells me that he is not totally committed to me.'

Nicole was fairly sure now that she could make out a bulge in Jacques' dark grey trousers. He noticed she was looking at his lap and crossed his legs as casually as he could. his cheeks faintly pink.

'But from what you have told me, you didn't really give yourself to Gerard,' he said. 'How could you be said to score over Remy? Tell me once more what happened between you in the bedroom.'

Nicole smiled at him sweetly. His question sounded innocent enough – a scientific desire to understand the situation in detail. But if Jacques was becoming excited – as she guessed he was – then what he wanted was an erotic description to add to his pleasure.

Very well then, she said to herself, *Jacques shall have what he wants – and I see no need to confine myself to the strict truth*.

'We were in my bedroom,' she said. 'It is a very pretty room – what a pity you never call on me – I could show you how pretty it is. Gerard went down on his knees and undressed me. I stood there proudly in bra and knickers – a set of lingerie made of delicate black lace.'

Jacques almost sighed, but contained it in time.

'It was impossible to hide any part of myself from his desire,' she said. 'I let him take off my underwear and kiss my belly and between my legs – he was trembling like a leaf.'

'Yes,' Jacques said, trying to be non-committal and failing.

'He picked me up and laid me on the bed. His hands were all over me, touching and stroking – everywhere, my breasts and my belly – he kissed my little triangle of curls. He pushed my thighs apart and slipped his tongue into me – his mouth was hot and eager.'

'You said before that he was still dressed,' Jacques said. 'Was that true – you were naked and he had his clothes on?'

'He took his jacket off,' she said. 'I opened his trousers to feel his massive part – it throbbed in my hand – huge and strong.'

'Ah,' Jacques sighed, unable to stop himself this time. 'You find it of great importance, the size of a man's member?'

'I couldn't control myself,' Nicole told him. 'I slid my hand up and down that magnificent shaft – in two seconds he gasped and spurted over my belly.'

'Yet you forced him to continue,' Jacques said, his voice shaky. 'Or so you said before – why did you do that, Nicole?'

'Why? Because I wanted to feel that superb shaft inside me,' she said with a smile. 'No, it was more than wanting – it was an irresistible urge. Gerard lay over me and slid it in a centimetre at a time – I felt it stretch me open and fill me.'

Jacques' eyes were bulging from his head.

'I reached my climax before he was more than halfway in,'

she added, then fell silent, letting Jacques imagine the scene in his mind's-eye.

His face was flushed red and he was visibly much affected by what she had told him. He crossed his legs the other way and tried to recover his calm so he could approach Nicole with professional detachment. But this was impossible, he knew her too well, they had made love in the past.

'By your unconsidered actions you have made yourself the important woman in this man's life,' Jacques said. 'You raised his hopes when you let him make love to you, however bizarre the events in the bedroom. Now you will destroy his confidence again.'

When she shrugged and said nothing in reply he looked at her curiously.

'It was just once, wasn't it?' he asked. 'I mean, you don't intend to continue with this ill-fated affair?'

'I really can't say,' she told him, her forehead wrinkled for a moment with doubt. 'It would be cruel to say no to him so very soon. Besides – Remy is unfaithful to me with another woman – why shouldn't I amuse myself with another man?'

'I understood you were doing that with his partner Lucien.'

'Yes I am, but that doesn't seem to be having much effect. I thought Remy would be jealous of Lucien and give up his other woman and beg me to forgive him.'

'A dangerous assumption,' Jacques said at once. 'It seems that the only one who has asked you to forgive him is this Gerard.'

'It is infuriating!' Nicole declared. She stamped her foot in annoyance and her skirt slid higher up her thigh – Jacques couldn't take his eyes off that long expanse of leg – perhaps he was imagining how it would be to put his hand on it and slide it up under her skirt to where her legs joined.

'You have given yourself complications,' he said softly, and his glance never wavered from her thighs.

'I have thirty-six types of complication,' she said. 'Gerard comes to me and Remy goes to Chantal. Against all reason and good sense, he and Lucien are friends again. He expects me to say nothing and be there for him whenever he chooses.'

'Have you considered giving Remy up?'

'No,' she said at once, 'I adore him and I mean to have him and keep him.'

'Do you mean that you want to marry him?'

'Of course not,' she said crossly. 'I have no wish to play a wife's role for him, any more than with you, Jacques. It would not suit me at all. I want him to be my lover, to be there when I need his attentions, to amuse me and take me to dine or dance. And I want him to go away to his own place when I have to be alone to write.'

'If that's your ideal arrangement,' Jacques said. 'It seems to me that you have it already.'

'No, I haven't,' she said. 'When Remy is not with me he's in bed with another woman. I do not wish to share him.'

Jacques sat thinking for a few moments.

'Why have you come to see me?' he asked finally.

'For your expert advice,' she said. 'You have years of experience with women who find themselves in awkward affairs.'

'I do not dispense advice to the love-lorn,' said Jacques. 'I am not a writer in a magazine, I do not tell horoscopes.'

'But you are my good friend,' she reminded him.

'No, you have chosen to be a patient,' he reminded her.

'I resign as a patient and reclaim your friendship,' she said at once. 'Come and sit with me on the confession couch, Jacques. There are things I must ask you as a good friend.'

When he hesitated, she stood up and lifted her skirt to show him the rest of her long thighs.

'Calm yourself, Jacques,' she said, 'I am not wearing see-through knickers today.'

It was true, they were virgin-white, very small, and cut to show her thighs right up to her hips.

In another moment Jacques and Nicole were sitting on the brown leather couch together. He had an arm about her waist to hold her close while his other hand undid the top button of her jacket and slipped inside. She was wearing a gossamer-thin white bra – and that was see-through. He sighed when he saw the pink tip of her other breast.

'The last time you were here you left me in an impossible situation,' he said. 'You rushed away leaving me with your ridiculously small underwear stuffed down my trousers. And Mademoiselle Anvers was about to usher a patient in – I didn't know what to do.'

Nicole giggled and put her hand between his thighs. He was hard as iron, she stroked over his trousers, teasing him.

'I thought about you all the way home,' she said.

'It will not happen today,' he said, his hand up her skirt to feel her *joujou*. 'My schedule is free for the rest of the day – no patient to be shown in at the wrong moment.'

'In that case there is only Mademoiselle Anvers to interrupt you,' Nicole said, unzipping his trousers. 'Would she dare?'

'No, she has strict instructions.'

Nicole put her legs up on the long leather couch and pulled Jacques' throbbing length out of his trousers. It was hard and strong in her hand.

'I want you to take me to dinner this evening,' she said while he was sliding her virginal little white knickers down her legs. 'And then I shall take you to my apartment. I want you to see my pretty bedroom.'

Jacques agreed eagerly – her hand was stroking his stiff part and he was in a state where he'd agree to anything she suggested.

'I lay in bed this morning and thought about you,' she said, her head back to let him kiss her throat while his fingers between her legs were teasing her wet little bud.

'I wanted you there with me,' she said, 'I was naked and I wanted you naked there beside me. I closed my eyes and stroked my belly and made believe it was your hand touching me.'

Jacques sighed and his long shaft jumped in her hand.

'I opened my legs and touched myself,' she said. 'I pretended your fingers were in me – it was so very thrilling . . .'

'Nicole,' he sighed, 'you know I adore you . . .'

'Tonight,' she said as he slid on top of her, 'I shall lie on my bed and let you psychoanalyse me.'

'What do you mean?' he gasped.

'You will probe all my secrets with this long hard shaft,' she said. 'You will explore my obsessions—'

'Yes,' Jacques moaned, 'yes, Nicole.'

Nicole's Diary – Aug 7 – Tuesday

We have been here by the sea for three days now and I still cannot make myself believe I'll be here with Remy for the whole month. But it's true – and Remy has promised never to see Chantal again. We are at St. Raphael on the Mediterranean coast. We lie in bed at night with the long windows open to let the sound of the sea lull us to sleep.

Last night I woke at two in the morning. The day had been perfect, filled with love and laughter, the night was calm and bright with moonlight. Remy lay asleep by my side, we were naked, with only a thin sheet over us. The bed was rumpled from our love-making. He lay on his back with his head turned to the side, even in the half light I could see his clear profile and his dark curly hair.

Every part of my body remembered that love-making. My eyelids still felt the touch of his kisses, my breasts the caress of his hand – and the hot touch of his tongue. Between my legs I still felt his fingers, dabbling in my wetness and in the palm of my hand I retained the impression of his male part.

I wanted him to wake up and hold me in his arms again. I was hungry for the smack of his belly on mine as he drove into me . . . I felt under the sheet to hold his sleeping part – it was small and soft and not yet completely dry. As I held it tenderly I felt it growing thicker in my palm. I played with it very gently so as not to wake him – even though I wanted him to lie on my belly again.

Then he was hard and powerful. He stirred and murmured my name in a whisper of adoration, his hand crept between my thighs . . . but I am again slipping into the error of copying extracts from my journal. This gives only the half-truths of love. To understand myself it is necessary to step away from my own personality – I must see Nicole as a different person, not as myself.

It was after two in the morning Remy and Nicole left their hotel and ran hand in hand across the deserted beach. She was naked underneath a white sundress she had slipped over her head. Remy had paused only to pull on a loose shirt and a pair of trousers – there was a long hard bulge in the front of his trousers – Nicole caused that by waking him from sleep by stroking him – she was proud of what she'd achieved and meant to achieve more yet before she let Remy sleep again.

The moonlight was so bright that the sand shone white. The ocean was making a dull hissing sound as the little waves rolled in and broke on the sand. Nicole stripped off her dress and dropped it behind her on the sand as she walked naked toward the sea, her body luminous.

Remy stared after her, watching how the bare cheeks of her bottom slid and rolled to the rhythm of her walking. And all the time he was hopping from one foot to the other to get his trousers off. He ran naked after her – by the time he reached the white-edged sea she was some way out, wading slowly through the deepening water.

The swell was lapping over her bottom when he splashed after her. He called to her to wait for him – she was in a moonstruck mood and gave no sign that she heard him. She waded out until the water was halfway up her back, then dived forward and kicked up her legs behind her. Remy saw a gleam of white cheeks, a glimpse of dark curls, and then white foam as her feet thrashed – she was swimming slowly and gracefully, heading away from the shore.

The water was warm as a bath – he went after her, a fast crawl stroke to catch up. He pulled level, she smiled sideways at him, the rhythm of her movements unbroken. He smiled back and made a shallow dive under her and came up the other side. He felt her belly rub slowly along his back as he passed beneath. She laughed, he turned with vigorous strokes and dived under her again, back the other way.

He trod water and put his arms round her, pressed her to him, her wet belly to his and her breasts squashed against his chest. His proud part stood out stiffly from his body – Nicole took hold of it and they swam back toward the beach together. They faced each other in a lazy side-stroke, her hand clasping him to keep him close to her.

At the sea's edge, where the waves lapped to their ankles, Remy knelt and licked her belly, tasting the salt tang on her skin. His hands were on her bottom, holding her fast – his lips moved down her belly to her little triangle of curls – the dark hair was plastered wetly against her smooth skin. He kissed her *joujou*, his fingers crept between her thighs to touch the soft lips.

She let him adore her for a while, feeling his warm tongue along the soft lips between her spread legs. Charming little sensations flicked through her – she wanted him to keep on doing it, to open her and press his tongue into her and lick her bud until she dissolved in ecstasy. Then he'd pull her down into the sea – she knew he would – he'd slide on top of her, his wet body on hers.

She would feel his weight pressing her into the soft and shifting sand under her back, while little waves broke over her shoulder and her hip – his hard shaft would push right into her *joujou* and penetrate her, she would feel it slide all the way in, filling her full.

That would be if she submitted to Remy. As she had submitted to him many times before, and always with delight. But . . . he was a man – like all men he wanted to climb on as many women's bellies as he could, he wanted to assert his male pride and his desire. Nicole understood that perfectly well – she had no quarrel with that, she adored being rolled on her back and dominated.

But, but, but . . . there must be a new beginning between them, not a continuation of the old ways. Not after his betrayal – that had ended the old trust and love. A new trust had to grow between them – and while it did, she wanted Remy to know that she was his equal in love and she expected his respect and his honesty.

She twined her fingers in the thick curly hair above his ears to haul him to his feet. She kissed his mouth briefly and knelt before him in the swirling sea. She held his trembling part in both hands, her fingers slid along the long sea-wet shaft. It was big and strong and she felt it throb eagerly. In his natural arrogance he saw her kneeling and thought she was abasing herself before him – he believed she was acknowledging him to be her master.

She took his pulsing shaft into her mouth, her tongue rolled over the bare head. Remy's hands were on her shoulders, his loins jerked and he thrust slowly in and out of her mouth, sighing and gasping. Nicole was his to do whatever he wanted, she had forgiven him his little slip with Chantal and was offering her mouth and her body for his delight.

In three more seconds he was going to push her down on her back on the sand. He was going to ravage her in the breaking and ebbing waves. She was his love, his delight, his plaything. He moaned softly to feel the clasp of her hand under his tight and hairy pompoms – the fingers of her other hand were gliding up and down his quivering shaft. And all the while her mouth sucked at him rhythmically and her tongue lapped at his pride.

His eyes were closed in pleasure, his fingers were clenched tight on Nicole's sea-wet shoulders. Oh *yes, yes,* he said to himself, *push her down on her back, make her open her legs wide for the waves to surge up between, warm salt waves breaking over her brown-haired joujou – I'll lie between her thighs and push it into her . . . do it to her hard and fast . . . she will love me all the more for it . . .*

'Nicole,' he groaned, 'I adore you . . .'

He'd got it wrong, of course, he was mistaken about what was happening between them on the seashore. She was asserting her right to use him as she pleased, and not the other way round. The suck of her mouth became stronger, her hand slid further between his legs until he could feel a fingertip pressed against the tight little knot of muscle between the cheeks of his bottom.

'Oh,' he gasped, 'oh Nicole,' – then her finger probed into him and her mouth ravished him and he spurted wildly.

Afterwards, when his tremendous spasms had abated and his breathing was slowing back to near-normal, he looked down at the naked woman on her knees below him. She cupped sea water in her hand to rinse her mouth – with a smile she let it spill back into the waves – Remy saw the white foam of his desire carried away by the ebbing sea.

'*Je t'adore, Remy,*' Nicole said, looking up at him with a fond smile on her face in the bright moonlight.

They had been at St. Raphael for about ten days when she offered to let him read part of her intimate journal. That surprised him and it pleased him because it was a mark of her confidence. He'd seen her scribbling in the journal most days they'd been on holiday – it was a large blank page book bound in red leather.

By the time they went on vacation together Remy had read the published work Nicole was so proud of – or at least, he'd read one of her three novels – or most of it. He'd chosen the one called *The Anxious Heart* for no better reason than that it was the shortest of the three.

When Nicole asked him afterwards what he thought of it, Remy said it showed tremendous sensitivity and integrity. From that she concluded that he didn't really like it.

He was expecting her diary to be much like her novel and did not expect to like it much. Fortunately for him he didn't know she had another seven other large diaries in her apartment in Paris, their pages filled with a record of her thoughts and adventures for past years. Since she was eighteen, in fact, and fell in love for the first time.

The page she let Remy read was dated MAY 3 THURSDAY – and it recorded their chance meeting at the Dome and her emotions on seeing him. Remy read with growing amazement – it was nothing like *The Anxious Heart*. He was astonished by the frankness and sincerity with which she confessed her deep and most secret emotions. And he was equally astonished by the fierceness of these emotions.

He read of how she had looked at him across the table on the terrace of the Dome and guessed that he was burning to rip her clothes off and make love to her – to bend her backward over the little table in full sight of passers-by.

'It is true,' he said, looking up to smile at her. 'You must have read my mind that day. I wanted to throw you down and stand between your legs and make you scream with delight.'

'I wanted you to,' she said. 'You've read what I wrote – I was dying to sit on your lap and play with you till you were panting and trembling – and then I'd straddle your thighs and slide you up into me.'

'We'll do it now,' he said with a hot grin.

They were sitting at an outside table under a café awning, with a cold drink, watching the world go by. The sea was an intense blue – and so was the sky.

'Finish reading the page,' Nicole told him.

'*Ah mon Dieu,*' he sighed. 'What is this about walking naked down the Champs Elysees, if I asked you to? Would you truly have done that to impress me, Nicole?'

'Without hesitation,' she said.

'And this,' he said, his long forefinger tapping the page. 'Would you really stand naked against a tree in the Tuileries Garden while I made love to you – in full public view?'

'Day after day,' she said.

Remy was greatly moved by what he had read – but before he turned the page and found details of other events which would not please him, she took the journal from him and closed it. She did not intend to let him read about her visit to Annette the next day to tell her about getting into Remy's bed with him. And she certainly did not mean to let him read about her private discussion with Jacques Lecomte – such matters were not for Remy's eyes.

Especially not the fact that she was wearing tiny see-through knickers that day and Jacques put his hand between her thighs and felt her. As a beginning, of course. Then he'd mounted her on his brown leather couch. Jacques was an old and trusted friend, but to let Remy read that page would only disturb him.

As matters stood, after reading the page about himself, Remy's heart was overflowing with tender love for Nicole. He threw money on the table for the waiter and led her by the hand back to their hotel. It was eleven in the morning and the hotel employee at the reception desk gave them an impassive smile as they made for the stairs. When couples came in holding hands in the middle of the morning and went up to their room there was no mystery about what they were going to do to each other.

But first Nicole put her journal safely away in her suitcase and locked it. She trusted Remy, of course, but there was no point in taking unnecessary chances – now he knew what a work of art her journal was he might become inquisitive and read something not intended for his eyes.

Such as the lines she had written weeks ago about the size of Gerard Constant's male part. There was no exaggeration – it truly was huge and dominating – and there was certainly no slight intended to anyone else. But she knew that normally endowed men were apt to become jealous and very angry about that sort of incident, because they made a comparison with themselves.

For Remy to read her memories of how she lay on her back with her legs apart while Gerard's massive length slid into her – and gave her such powerful sensations that she melted into ecstasy before it was all the way in – no, no, no – it would surely destroy all Remy's love and trust if he read that.

She left her locked suitcase and stood close to Remy, beside the bed. He kissed her again and again and again until she was breathless – and he slid his hands up and down the beautiful curves of her body. She was wearing a short white skirt and a pink silk shirt – he had both off her in a second and pressed her down to sit on the bed while he knelt to remove her sandals. Her legs were long and bare and sungold – he took each foot in his hand in turn and kissed the sole and instep and each pink-nailed toe.

He kissed up the length of her leg, up her thigh, he eased her tiny see-through knickers off, so he could kiss her brown-haired *joujou*. She couldn't be certain, but they were probably the same ones Jacques had taken down that day in Passy – she had five similar pairs. To have a man take off her knickers had always been a moment of great significance in Nicole's life – the action symbolised so very much.

She lay naked on her back on the well-used hotel bed. Remy was on his knees between her parted legs, his head down to kiss her belly and lick it – and open her with loving fingers, to kiss her little bud. He was naked and his long hard part was throbbing – Nicole was sighing – he could see her belly tremble as he touched the head of his stiff shaft to the lips of her *joujou* and pushed in.

He rode her with long rhythmic thrusts, murmuring her name, telling her that he adored her, over and over again. Nicole said nothing rational – she moaned and sighed and gave little jerky sobs as she clung to him with all her strength. Her deepest emotions had been stirred by Remy's adoration of her – the adoration that sprang from all he had read about himself in her journal.

In fact, her emotions were so strongly affected that she had slipped into orgasm the moment he penetrated her. She squirmed and jerked under him while her ecstasy went on and on, shaking her belly and ravaging her mind with sensation. Remy took his time, sliding and murmuring, till he spurted his desire into her. By then Nicole felt she had been more superbly destroyed than ever before in her life.

'Remy, *je t'adore*,' she murmured faintly. She tried to hold on to him, but her hands were suddenly weak. She was only half-conscious, in the long contented after-tremors of her stupendous passion.

The perfect summer days passed, in eating and drinking and swimming and sitting in the sun and making love – always that, always the love-making. After so much happiness, Nicole was determined never to mention the name of the other woman. But as everyone knows, even the best of intentions are never enough – female curiosity is stronger than that of the cat in the proverb. After ten days, she couldn't resist asking him about Chantal Lamartine.

'Is she very beautiful?' Nicole asked, pushing her sunglasses up her forehead to stare at Remy with big eyes.

They were lying on the hot sand on a coloured straw mat. Nicole wore a white swimsuit with a Greek key pattern in black – the material clung closely to her body and accentuated her curves. Every man on the beach looked at her slyly when he thought he was unobserved, to see the shape of her breasts under her swimsuit.

Remy was in small tight black trunks – until this moment a distinct bulge had been visible in the front as the result of Nicole's nearness and the midday sun beating down on it.

He didn't want to talk about Chantal – discussion could only lead to grief and misunderstandings, he feared. But he had no choice, Nicole wouldn't let it drop now she'd broached the dangerous topic. Remy went warily, trying not to offend her. He was so cautious he almost gave the impression he'd made love to Chantal as a matter of promoting good business relations.

He didn't actually say so, but he made it sound as if he'd made love to her against his better judgement. And very much against his feelings. If Nicole had believed him she might have seen him as a martyr to his profession, so to speak, a toy in the hands of a hot-blooded and unscrupulous woman, who made use of his body for her own pleasure.

But Nicole eyed him sceptically. He saw this and tried again, a different approach – a more intricate excuse, but it was still only an excuse for his faithlessness.

'It may seem strange to you,' he said, 'but Chantal doesn't really like making love. She is not a sensual person. She saw something in me that was missing in her life – a strength, perhaps, a completeness – she clung to me for the sake of that. Perhaps it would be truer to say she clung to whatever it was she saw in me – I was never a lover, not in any real sense, I was only the bearer of a message, so to speak.'

'That's all very well – but you haven't told me if she's beautiful,' said Nicole.

'Yes, I suppose you could call her attractive,' Remy said, doing his best to sound casual. 'She's a thinnish brunette.'

'How did it begin?' Nicole asked.

'By chance,' Remy told her, not sounding at all convincing. 'We were discussing a contract for an office suite I am designing and furnishing for Laburette Freres and I took her to lunch to persuade her to drop the price of the furniture. We talked and ate, we drank a bottle of wine, and a couple of cognacs – she said she had a new design to show me.'

'Ah,' said Nicole. 'Let me guess – it wasn't at her office, you had to go to her apartment.'

'Why yes,' Remy tried to sound surprised and failed. 'Well, when we got there she poured more cognac while I flipped through a new catalogue of designs she had – *et voilà*.'

'What do you mean, *that's it*?' Nicole demanded. 'That's what? Did this woman throw you down on your back and sit astride you while she raped you – against your will? Is that what you want me to believe?'

'She went out of the room while I was looking at the new designs,' he said. 'When she came back she was naked. I was a little drunk by then, you understand, I lost all control of myself – I am ashamed to speak of these things to you, Nicole.'

'Then we'll forget all about the unfortunate episode,' she said with a fond smile. Though she knew there had been more than one occasion when he had *forgotten where his only real love lay*, as he put it to her.

There had been other times when he'd taken her to dinner and gone back to her apartment with her. And to bed with her – Nicole would never forget the night she'd been unable to sleep and had gone to his apartment at two in the morning – to find him missing. But though these injuries could never be forgotten, they had to be forgiven, or else her love affair with him was finished. She wasn't ready for that.

After lunch that day they went up to their room in the hotel – for a siesta, Remy said, which naturally meant to make love before they had a little nap. Nicole undressed and put on a short and flimsy white dressing-gown while she sat at the mirror to comb her hair and cleanse her face of the sun lotion she'd put on that morning on the beach.

Remy was standing at the long open window, waiting patiently for her. There was a cry outside – a curse – a shout.

'Come and look at this,' Remy said with a chuckle.

Nicole went to stand beside him, an arm round his waist. Down below, between the hotel and the beach, two men in shirts and shorts were shouting and threatening each other, their arms waving and their fists clenched. A young girl in a tight blue swimsuit was cowering away from the fraças.

'But what can it be about?' Nicole asked. 'Is it a furious father saving his daughter from an older admirer – or are two admirers falling out over the same girl?'

'She can't be more than sixteen, by the look of her,' Remy said, 'but she's pretty enough.'

He slid round behind Nicole and stood close to her back with his hands on her hips, looking over her shoulder at the angry scene below. He put his hand up her short dressing gown to stroke her bottom. No knickers, just the feel of warm smooth flesh under his hand.

'Ah,' Nicole sighed, wriggling luxuriously under his stroking hand.

'Her young breasts are like two little oranges in her swimsuit,' he said appreciatively. 'If she were mine I would suck the sweetness from them. Put your arms on the rail, *chérie*, no one can see what we're doing up here.'

Her face was pink as she did as he said – she leaned her folded arms along the balcony railing. Remy lifted her dressing-gown at the back to bare her cheeks – he put his hand between her thighs to feel her *joujou*.

'This is too bizarre,' she said. 'Let's lie on the bed.'

'In a moment, *chérie*,' he agreed.

'You are absurd, *chéri*,' she said affectionately.

He pressed himself to her bottom while he put an arm around and under her to stroke her from below. The lips between her legs were soon loose and open – he slid two fingers inside and found her wet and slippy. She made little gasping sounds in her throat, her bottom pressed against his belly and the stiff length in his trousers.

She felt him fumble between their bodies – then his trousers were open and his hard length was steered between her thighs and into the open wet lips.

'Oh Remy, what a way to do it,' she gasped – with a long push he was up inside her, his hands on her hips to hold her close and tight.

In the street below the two men were still in dispute over the young girl in the blue swimsuit – each had her by a wrist and they seemed ready to pull her in half if need be. She too was shouting now – at both of the men indiscriminately.

Nicole sighed and shook as Remy slid rapidly in and out. He was holding her very tight – in three more seconds he spurted fiercely and clung to her back. Nicole cried out open-mouthed as she was pushed to a climax of delight.

She stared sightlessly down at the street, where a little crowd had gathered laughing around the quarrelling and noisy trio. On the edge of the crowd a man in a pink shirt looked up and saw Nicole at the window – his interest was captured by the expression on her beautiful face while she was shaking and moaning in orgasm and he kissed his hand to her.

August 25 – Wednesday

More and more I feel the truth of what I tried to explain to Jacques – I am an addict of love – it sustains my talents as a writer. To the men I most admire I give the pleasures of my beautiful body – in these acts of love I take their strength into myself to make into literature.

They do not know this. Their pride would never permit them to accept a woman who has made use of them for an intellectual purpose. I thought that Jacques would understand, as he is trained to unravel the motives and mysteries of the soul.

Even Jacques failed to grasp the truth about me – because he too had surrendered to pleasure and was lying on top of me on his brown leather couch. So the secret of my being is still my secret, unshared by anyone. I write because I love. If ever I needed a reminder of it, my meeting today with Alexis Roche impressed the actuality on me again.

Remy was playing at *boules* on the beach with a group of men he'd got into conversation with. Nicole left them to their game and strolled a little in the sun and then sat at a table under a café awning with a tall glass of iced coffee. A voice murmured *May I?* – a man was standing at her table.

'There is something of very great importance that I have to tell you,' he went on.

Nicole pushed her dark glasses up her forehead to see him more clearly. He was young – surely only twenty or twenty-one. His casual shirt had an expensive look about it, and so did his white trousers.

'What can you possibly tell me that I want to hear?' she said with a smile. 'Nothing, I'm sure.'

'If I tell you that you saved my sanity – and perhaps my life, surely that would be of some interest to you, no?' he asked, smiling back.

His smile was charming, she thought. He slid into the chair next to her without any further invitation.

'And just when did I render you this important service?' she asked. 'I have no recollection of it.'

He told her his name was Alexis and he was here on honeymoon with his wife. They were deeply in love and their first two weeks by the sea was a time of great happiness for them both. Then one evening after dinner they quarrelled, as lovers do, over nothing much. Neither would give way, the quarrel turned to icy silence and unspoken condemnation.

'Lovers' tears and quarrels are easily put right in bed,' Nicole told Alexis.

'We'd never quarrelled before – we didn't know how to make up. Perhaps we weren't willing to make the effort to forgive. We went to bed late and not speaking to each other – she lay as far from me as the bed allowed, with her back to me.'

'Why are you telling me this?' Nicole asked.

'In a moment you will understand,' he said.

'What is your wife's name – without a name I cannot imagine her as a living breathing loving person – and if she does not exist in my mind, I cannot picture the scene you describe.'

'Her name is Nicole too and she is twenty years old and very pretty, and I love her to distraction.'

'That's better – please go on.'

Alexis explained how he had tried to sleep and forget his feelings of desolation – but naturally, sleep was impossible. After a long time, he got out of bed in despair and pulled on his clothes. He left the hotel, meaning to walk until he felt tired – after an hour or two he was tired but he knew he still wouldn't be able to sleep.

'It was after two in the morning,' he said, 'I stood alone on the beach in the moonlight. I looked at the sea and I was so miserable that I even considered walking out into it and letting myself drown.'

'*Bon Dieu, non,*' Nicole exclaimed.

'I sat down on the sand to think this over before deciding,' Alexis said. 'And two naked people came out of the ocean – a man and a woman. They were laughing and happy together – they didn't see me, they had eyes for no one but each other.'

'Ah,' Nicole said thoughtfully.

'The woman knelt in the swirling sea at the man's feet,' Alexis went on. 'His shaft was standing hard away from his body – she took it into her mouth. I could hardly draw breath, I was so enchanted by the love and desire between these two. The man was tall and sturdy, the woman was slender and very beautiful – he put his hands on her shoulders and his body was jerking . . . there is no need for me to describe this tender scene further.'

'No, there isn't,' she agreed.

'The bitter unhappiness that had gripped me and tormented me released its hold as I watched those moments of love,' Alexis said. 'The man cried out the woman's name in his ecstasy.'

'They often do,' Nicole said.

'When he cried "Nicole" – my wife's name – my anger and despair vanished,' he said as he smiled at her in a friendly way. 'The thought of drowning myself in the sea seemed totally absurd. I hurried back to the hotel room – even in the dark I could tell my Nicole was lying awake and unhappy – whereas I was full of the will to live and to love—'

'And no doubt stiff inside your underwear from what you'd witnessed on the sand,' said Nicole with a grin.

'I flung back the sheet, ripped open my trousers and hurled myself onto my darling,' Alexis said, his eyes shining. 'She cried out and resisted me at first – she beat at me with her little fists and heaved underneath me to escape. But after all I had seen I was unstoppable, I was overflowing with love for her and desire for her.'

Nicole raised her eyebrows, in doubt what to think about his confession.

'After a few moments my emotions transferred themselves

to her,' he went on, his eyes closed in happy memory. 'She pulled her nightie up to her waist and spread her legs wide.'

'A charming little story,' said Nicole. 'I'm pleased I could be of assistance to you, even if I never knew.'

'We reached a climax of ecstasy together, Nicole and I,' he said, as if she hadn't spoken. 'Then we wept and laughed and kissed a thousand times and fell asleep in each other's arms. Sometime before dawn we woke at the same moment and we made love again – it was as sudden and furious as the first time – cries and moans and her legs so tight round my waist that I was her prisoner even while I dominated her.'

Nicole listened with her head on one side, smiling a little at his seriousness.

'Again we slept,' said Alexis, 'Nicole's hand lay between my legs and my arms were about her. It was halfway through the morning before we woke again, still embraced in each other's arms. This time we made love slowly and tenderly, sobbing out our adoration to each other all the time.'

'*Oh la la*,' said Nicole with a charming smile. 'That was a night to remember.'

'Yes,' he agreed solemnly. 'Nicole and I are more in love than before. She knows nothing of her debt to you because I haven't told her of the adventure on the beach.'

'That was sensible of you. Otherwise she might wonder who you were thinking of while you were making love to her.'

'To be truthful,' he said, 'I wondered the same myself. But at least *I* know how much I owe you – and I've been looking for you ever since to tell you so, Nicole.'

'Well, you know my name,' she said smiling, 'and you've told me where you heard it. But all that was a week or more ago – why are you telling me this today?'

'All I knew was Nicole – I didn't know your last name or where you were staying. I couldn't visit every hotel and describe you to the porter, could I?'

'And today you found me by chance sitting here alone and you decided to thank me for saving your life?'

'To tell the truth,' he said, grinning broadly, 'I found you yesterday – by chance. There was a little disagreement taking place in the street, two men and a young girl. I stopped to watch for a moment, then I looked up for no reason at all and saw you at an open window. The same man was with you – the man from the beach – he is your lover, of course.'

'You see things not intended for your eyes,' Nicole told him severely. 'First on the beach by night and then at a window by day.'

'He was making love to you,' Alexis said with a comical look on his face. 'You were leaning with your arms on the balcony rail. I'm sure his zipper was wide open and something of his was up between your beautiful thighs, Nicole.'

'My thighs are beautiful,' she agreed, glancing down at her lap. She was wearing white shorts and a blue shirt – the shirt was tied underneath her breasts to leave her golden-tanned belly bare.

'I saw them on the beach by night,' he said, 'I saw all of you that night – you are very beautiful.'

'That's true,' she said, pleased by his words of praise.

'At the hotel window,' he said, 'there was a moment of intensity – a look of pure delight came to your face. I knew why – you'd reached the moment of ecstasy. I hurried back to my hotel and threw darling Nicole on the bed . . .'

'Of course,' Nicole said softly.

She looked into his eyes, brown and bright. He looked into her eyes. Nothing was said, nothing need be said at such an exquisite moment, but both knew what the other was thinking. They got up from the little table together and he led her, his hand under her arm, to his hotel.

The room had no sea view, it was on the side of the building, with no balcony outside the window. The shutters stood open and the view was of another building across the way.

'We do not have very much time,' he said huskily, while he pulled her to him until their bellies were together, 'Nicole is at the hairdressers.'

'We do not need much time,' Nicole said.

She felt a strength and a determination in Alexis that would inspire her writing for a long time to come. His mouth was on hers in a furious kiss – his hand was down inside her shorts and he was clasping her between the legs.

She wanted to lie on the bed – there on the bed where

he had made love to Nicole. She wanted to feel his weight pressing down on her. But he had other ideas.

'If only there was a long window and a balcony rail,' he sighed, his middle finger was pressing in between the lips of her *joujou*.

'You are not him,' she said. 'Be yourself, Alexis.'

She was wet and slippery inside – she had been so since he related his strange story at the café table. There was a fixed idea in his mind that he could not shake free from – he wanted to be Remy and to have Nicole by moonlight at the edge of the sea – or failing that, he wanted to have her standing at an open window, as Remy had.

It was a moment for compromise – he pushed her down to kneel by the bedside – she was leaning forward over it, on her arms. He knelt behind her and slid her shorts and her tiny knickers down her legs – his hands were on her bare bottom feeling the smooth cheeks and squeezing them.

Nicole gasped when he ran a trembling finger down the warm lips of her *joujou*. The finger sank into her slowly until he was touching her secret bud and sending little spasms of pleasure through her belly.

'I must tell you this, Nicole,' he sighed. 'If I were not tremendously and eternally in love with Nicole, I would fall in love with you.'

'Do you mean that?' she murmured. 'But perhaps I wouldn't let you fall in love with me, Alexis.'

His thumbs opened her neatly – he shuffled closer on his knees until the smooth head of his stiff male part touched her and pressed between the parted lips. He pushed in strongly, murmuring at the pleasure of her soft *joujou* clasping him. She felt him slide in deeper – deeper – his belly was hot against the bare cheeks of her bottom.

She let her head sag forward and leaned on her arms – he untied her shirt and put his hands inside to hold her breasts. She was wearing no bra, he stroked the soft bare flesh and he touched the firm little buds to make them firmer – and all the time he was jabbing rapidly into her. She responded with sighs and little jerks of her bottom to meet his thrusts.

He's doing exactly the same as Remy did yesterday, Nicole

thought, *he thinks he has to prove he's as good a lover as Remy . . .*

'*Je t'adore, Nicole*,' Alexis gasped.

A strange thought came into her mind — although Alexis was a stranger to her the simple truth was that the pleasure he was giving her was the same as when Remy did it to her.

'*Ah mon Dieu non*,' she sighed aloud, 'ah Alexis—'

Her train of thought in these moments of delight led her to a curious speculation. If it was true that a man whose shaft was standing up hard was so undiscriminating that any woman who would lie down and spread her legs was acceptable, then perhaps it was equally true that when his hard part was inside an excited woman it didn't matter to her which man was on the other end of it.

Surely that can't be so, she said to herself, *I refuse to believe it — the idea is absurd . . .*

'Nicole,' Alexis was moaning.

'*Chéri*,' she moaned back, smacking her bottom against his belly to his every thrust.

There was the rattle of a key in the door.

'Oh my God,' he gasped, 'Nicole is back already—'

His hard and fast pumping into her came to a sudden stop. He seemed paralysed with shock. He held her tightly, his hands over her breasts inside her shirt, as the lock turned and the door opened. But his stiff male length refused to be brought to so sudden and cruel a standstill — it ignored the command of his mind and continued to jerk rhythmically inside Nicole.

She too was beyond exercising rational control. Her body shook and she sobbed under her breath as her wet *joujou* clenched and unclenched on the throbbing shaft inside her.

They both stared wide-eyed at the door as it swung open — in came a chambermaid with bath towels over her arm. She stared in amazement at the couple on their knees by the bed. They were sideways on to her, with their heads turned to face her as she came through the door. Alexis' trousers were round his ankles and his belly was against Nicole's bare bottom.

The chambermaid saw Nicole's blue shirt was open all the way and her beautiful breasts were under Alexis' grasping hands. He had frozen on the in stroke, she could see nothing of their wet and joined sexual parts unless he pulled back. Her face turned bright red, she stammered an apology while she was backing away.

Alexis was completely incapable of speech – he was poised on the edge of orgasm and was trying to stop it happening without pulling out of Nicole and exposing himself further. And Nicole's face was pink, her mouth open and her eyelids hooded. She tried to smile reassuringly at the retreating maid and couldn't.

The maid turned and almost ran out of the room, pulling the door to behind her. As if a bad spell had been lifted, sudden waves of ecstasy flooded through Nicole. The squeeze and tug of her wet *joujou* on Alexis' throbbing part took him the rest of the way – he hadn't far to go – he cried out in relief and surprise as he spurted hard.

Twenty-five minutes later Nicole was back in her own hotel room. There were important events to be recorded in her journal, but that could be done later. She was in the shower when Remy returned from his boules match on the beach.

She put her head round the shower curtain to ask if he'd won. He shook his head and said it had been a close thing.

'Were you playing for money?' she asked.

'So I lost a few francs,' he said.

He peeled his clothes off while they talked. He was hot and sweaty from his hour in the sun – in two more seconds he was under the spray with her. The water was at body temperature, not hot and not cold – it was refreshing and pleasing.

'But you are sweating, my poor Remy,' Nicole said. She made him lean back against the tiled wall while she soaped his body from neck to knees, her hands gliding sensually over his chest and belly and between his sturdy thighs.

She had washed all trace of Alexis from herself – all that was left of him was in her mind, and would before the end of the day be in her journal. Her body had the delicate perfume of expensive toilet soap.

'Ah,' Remy sighed.

He leaned back against the cool tiles while Nicole was washing him down with loving hands. At her word he raised his arms over his head for her to soap his dark-haired armpits. She hadn't touched his male part but it raised its head and was standing up stiffly.

'He is reliable, your little friend,' she said, touching a wet fingertip to the nodding head. 'Always ready.'

'Little friend?' Remy said in mock outrage. 'Little?'

Nicole shrugged casually and let the water wash away the creamy lather from his chest and down his belly into the thatch of dark curls around the root of his upstanding part. She soaped it and clasped it in her hand and slid the thick lather up and down.

Remy pulled her to him with an arm about her waist. Their mouths met and he kissed her lovingly while the water sluiced down between their bodies, over her breasts and between their pressed together bellies.

'Put my dear and not-so-little friend in,' he suggested in a murmur close to her ear, 'I'm sure he'll be welcome.'

He dipped a little at the knees and when she had positioned his quivering part between her thighs he pushed slowly upward into her. He gripped the cheeks of her bottom and supported her, while he rocked backward and forward in an easy motion that made her breasts roll up and down to his rhythm.

With Remy love is so natural, Nicole said to herself, her arms about his neck and her cheek against his cheek, *this is why I love him – he does it to me whenever the mood takes him, no matter where we are – this is part of why I love him – his calm assurance*.

'Ah Nicole,' he gasped as he thrust into her with short fast strokes that made her moan with pleasure.

Her breasts were bouncing up and down to his vigorous movements – she panted and jerked against his wet body in sudden climactic spasms. His own crisis arrived two seconds later and sent his hot desire spurting into her.

'Yes, yes, yes,' she moaned, '*je t'adore*, Remy.'

This pleasure under the shower was material for her journal when she had time to bring it up to date – the excitement of being loved by Remy and by Alexis, within half an hour of each other. How alike they were, these two men, clever and strong, with stiff lengths of flesh they wanted to slide up inside her belly and snatch their satisfaction.

Yet different they were, Remy and Alexis – one was assured and calm, the other was filled with uncertainty and anxiety he masked under a bold face. She adored them both.

From The Diary – Sept 11 – Tuesday

A night of madness. I have survived the madness – but I am amazed by what I have done – I am amazed that the thought of doing such things could enter my mind and overwhelm my heart. I am amazed by my own passionate nature – and by the generosity with which I can give myself to another, even when my heart is broken.

Less than two weeks after Nicole and Remy returned to Paris from the Mediterranean coast, Lucien phoned her at home and asked her to meet him after he finished work. He rang off abruptly – before she could ask him any questions.

Nicole liked Remy's fair-haired business partner – though not in a serious way, of course. She considered him a friend – he was a friend she sometimes let make love to her. At the beginning she'd intended it to be only that once, on the desk in the office he and Remy shared. She wanted to humble Remy after she'd learned of his betrayal – she wanted to shame him and humiliate him.

For that reason she took her knickers off and sat on the edge of the double desk facing Lucien, with her knees apart. She put her hands under her thighs and raised them in invitation, she was offering Lucien her beautiful *joujou*.

He hadn't hesitated, partner or not – he sank his stiff part into her. She let herself fall back on the desk and brought her knees up to grip him. Until that moment it was no more than a cold-blooded exercise – she was letting her body be used in order to hurt Remy for hurting her.

Events sometimes outrun intentions. Lucien's muscular rhythm made her gasp and writhe on the polished desktop – she cried out in orgasm even before he spurted.

After that day there were other occasions during July – once more in the office, but later in the evening, when the building was empty. She insisted on lying across Remy's side of the double desk – to spite him – while Lucien mounted her and made her cry out with pleasure. She wished there could be some mark left on the polished desk top as an indication to Remy of where her bare bottom had rested while his partner had her.

And once that month they met at Lucien's apartment near the Gare St. Lazare. The simple truth was that Nicole delighted in Lucien's robust love-making and she didn't want to give it up. Not yet.

Lucien was intelligent and educated, he was a designer of distinction, but he was easily led – Nicole thought of him as a countryman – as her little peasant, so to speak.

Love-making with him was uncomplicated and robust – almost brutal in its simplicity. He'd put it in – and he was satisfactorily endowed – he thrust and drove, he was tireless and he was as regular as a machine. Nicole arrived at her terminus before him every time – sometimes twice. And after only fifteen or twenty minutes repose he was ready again.

His seemingly inexhaustible male energy impressed her and intrigued her. The last time they met before she went away on holiday with Remy was at Lucien's apartment. She thought it would be fascinating to find out how long he could go on before he was completely exhausted. After a good but light dinner they were in his apartment by nine o'clock – by midnight he'd had her on her back three times and she was very content.

She got off the bed to fetch herself a glass of cold water – she felt hot and flushed. Lucien was lying with his legs apart, eyes closed and a pleased smile on his face. After a minute or two he followed her into the tiny kitchen of his apartment – she was standing by the refrigerator with a glass of Vichy water in her hand, the glass misted from the ice-cubes she'd dropped into it.

He put his strong arms round her from behind – they were both naked and barefoot. Nicole sighed pleasurably. She put the glass down – his hands covered her breasts and caressed them. *Chérie*, he whispered, with his mouth against her ear. She stroked her belly with quick little movements. Her hand glided down the smooth flesh, till her fingertips touched the neat little tuft of dark-brown curls.

'Lucien, this is crazy,' she said with a chuckle. 'I don't love you, but I want you. And you want me – but I don't think I can any more, not just now, because you've worn me out.'

'I love you, Nicole,' he said solemnly.

'Of course you do, *chéri*,' she said, reaching up over her shoulder to stroke his face. 'I believe you.'

Under his big hands her breasts felt hot and full. Lucien picked her up and carried her back to the bedroom. She hung limply in his arms, her eyes closed – her mouth was open a little but she was hardly breathing. Lucien put her down on the bed on her back and lay beside her. She was like a rag doll, unmoved, while his mouth fastened on her breast and his hand stroked between her thigh. His stiff-again part prodded at her hip.

Her beautiful body was slack and pliant when he slid his belly on to hers and forced his long hard part into the wet warmth between her legs. It brought her back to life, that thick sturdy shaft of his, it filled her flesh with its solidity and filled her soul with the desire to live and love and respond to him.

She woke up the next morning about nine – she'd been in Lucien's bed for twelve hours. He was gone, he'd got up without disturbing her and gone to work. The white sheets were crumpled under her naked back, she lay with her long legs apart and thought of the events of the night and Lucien's tireless thrust into her belly.

The twelve hours in bed with him had been memorable – she liked him a lot. But she didn't love him and it would have been better if it had been Remy in bed with her for those twelve hours. She closed her eyes and stroked her bare belly softly. And then her tousled little triangle of curls – and then the well-ravished lips between her legs – and soon she was hot and slippery.

After her month away with Remy she almost decided not to see Lucien again – which is to say, she felt it sensible not to let him make love to her again. Which was a great pity, because he was so exciting in bed, and so obliging. But having Lucien had never been more than a ploy to bring Remy back to her – and that was now accomplished. During their weeks at the seaside he'd sworn his everlasting devotion to her at least a thousand times.

Naturally, Lucien wanted to see her again, and expected to. After that long night in July at his apartment he certainly anticipated having her in his bed again. To be fair to him, he knew no other women as desirable as Nicole – how could he, when there were only a few in the whole of Paris as desirable as she was?

And that, she said to herself, is why he phoned her. She'd been away for a month and he'd missed her. No doubt he'd taken other women to bed in her absence, but that could only have been a disappointment for him. Clearly he planned to take her to his apartment this evening and make up for lost time. But it's all over, she said to herself, Lucien has served his purpose nobly, but now it is time to extricate myself as gracefully as possible from his expectations.

They met at the Café Flore – Nicole easily guessed why he'd chosen to meet there, on the Boulevard St. Germain. On the Left Bank he had put the Seine between himself and the office and Remy.

He was there at a table on the café terrace when she arrived – he rose to take her hand and kiss her cheek. He looked serious. He was drinking cognac, and he had a glass ready for her. Without any delay he blurted out his appalling news – Remy was seeing Chantal again.

'What?' Nicole demanded, her voice almost shrill. 'What are you telling me – ten days back in Paris and he's seeing that woman again? I refuse to believe it – you are making it up because you are jealous.'

Lucien assured her that it was the truth, that his heart was torn with grief for Nicole, that he despised Remy for his actions – and much more of the same.

'When?' Nicole asked, her heart heavy.

'You know when,' Lucien told her. 'It was at the end of last week when he went to Lyon to see a good client of ours.

He took Chantal with him to advise on furniture, he said. But they shared the same hotel room.'

'*Ah Dieu*,' Nicole said brokenly.

'My heart goes out to you,' Lucien said. 'I cannot understand how he can even look at another woman when he has your love. If he hadn't told me about sharing a room with Chantal I wouldn't have believed it.'

'I know why he told you,' Nicole said, summoning all her resolution. 'He told you so that you would tell me.'

'Surely not – what possible reason could he have?'

She didn't answer, she was deep in her own thoughts. She finished her glass of cognac and Lucien told the waiter to bring more. After a while she was able to speak again – they sat at the café table and talked and drank while the evening light slowly faded.

'Are you hungry?' Lucien asked. 'Could you eat?'

She was too agitated to eat. She was certainly too agitated to go with him to his apartment, he saw that for himself and didn't suggest it. She didn't want to be alone in her own apartment – she was too restless.

'Walk with me, Lucien,' she said, getting up from her chair.

She was too shaken to wait for him. She walked off – by the time he'd paid the waiter for the drinks she was lost to sight. He hurried after her swearing under his breath – if she'd turned off the Boulevard he'd never find her in the gathering dusk. He spotted her ahead, among the sauntering evening crowd – she was wearing a yellow-checked jacket over a white silk rolltop sweater – he almost ran to catch up with her and take her arm.

'Nicole, what can I say to ease your suffering?'

'You are a good friend, Lucien,' she told him. 'The tragedy of love is that men are by nature too coarse to sustain the noble emotions women expect of them.'

'It's true,' he said mournfully. 'We are not worthy of your love – and yet you love us.'

They walked on in silence, not caring where they were going. Traffic roared along the boulevard, people passed them on the pavement without noticing them. They crossed the Boulevard St. Michel and wandered into a side street. Before long Lucien had no idea where they were – it was a narrow and gloomy street of shuttered houses and widely spaced streetlights.

'Nicole, we do not want to be here,' Lucien said.

'You are a good friend,' she said again, squeezing his arm.

They were abreast of a dark doorway – she pulled him into it with her and held him close. It seemed sensible to kiss her in the dark and so he did. Her hands were on his waist, holding him close to her, he responded by putting his hands on her breasts inside her jacket.

'I am only a friend, but you love Remy,' he said.

'For the man I love I would walk naked down Champs Elysées at midday,' she said, recalling the words she had written in her journal only a few weeks ago. 'To show him I loved him I'd stand naked with my back to a tree in the Tuileries Garden, for him to have me in public view. That is how I loved Remy – I do not love him now.'

Lucien's fantasies were stirred hotly by the mental picture of her strolling naked in the street in her high-heeled shoes, while tourists pointed cameras at her beautiful body and gaped open-mouthed.

'Do you understand?' she asked.

'No one has ever loved me like that,' he said sadly – and he slid his hand under Nicole's skirt. His fingers were between her thighs and his hot palm pressed against the thin nylon of her knickers to touch her *joujou*, his thumb in her groin. He was making her aware of his longing – she had provoked this confession of utter devotion.

'I almost wish I loved you, Lucien,' she said.

It was enough for him, her admission. He pulled her knickers down her legs and off – he put them in his jacket pocket. Nicole sighed and shivered pleasurably to feel his hands on the bare cheeks of her bottom.

'Kiss me,' she said urgently – his lips touched hers and she turned her face away.

'Not on the mouth,' she said. 'Below – kiss me.'

There in the street, half-hidden in the shadows of a doorway, he sank to his knees on the pavement and pressed his lips to her *joujou*. Her smooth bare thigh touched his ear.

'Nicole,' he sighed, looking up at her, his face pale.

'Do you truly adore me, Lucien?'

'Truly, truly,' he sighed.

'Kiss me again.'

His hot tongue licked along the lips between her thighs. She was wet and slippery with a strange feverish desire, her belly was shaking. She wanted to feel his strength inside her, she wanted the reassurance of his strong male certainty. He stood up – she ripped his zipper open and took his long hard part in her eager hand.

'*Je t'aime, Nicole, je t'aime*,' he murmured.

She moved her feet apart on the stone step and guided him up into her. *Ah ah* she sighed when she felt that stiff length sliding in. His body was close to hers, he kissed her and his tongue slipped into her mouth, he thrust into her *joujou* with fast little jabs. She closed her eyes and hung on to him, waiting for the orgasm she felt hurtling toward her.

'I will make you love me,' Lucien sighed.

She moaned and shook fiercely, his hands were clenched hard on the bare cheeks of her bottom while he spurted his desire. She thrust and rubbed herself against him while his throes lasted, willing him to wipe out her unhappy memories with urgent sensation.

Making that furtive love in the street liberated Nicole and calmed her. She held Lucien a little way away from her and stared at him with a serious expression on her face. A taxi drove past in the narrow street, two dark figures in the back, their heads close together. She kissed Lucien on the cheek and told him she was hungry and could eat a hearty meal.

Lucien laughed and put his arm round her waist while they walked and found their way back to the Boulevard St. Michel. They went into the first restaurant they came to and Nicole ate greedily and drank half a bottle of good wine.

At nine-thirty they were still sitting at the table, talking over a glass of cognac. Lucien was pleased to see the improvement in Nicole's mood – he put his hand on hers on the table and suggested they went to his apartment.

'Not yet,' she said, her face darkening. 'There is something I want to do first – something important.'

Lucien shrugged, suddenly aware that she was not yet back to normal good spirits. They found a taxi further down the boulevard and Nicole told the driver to take them to the Boulevard Clichy.

'Why are we going there?' Lucien asked.

'I cannot explain it to you,' she said. 'Will you trust me, *chéri*?'

In the dark of the taxi she put her hand between his legs and cupped his long limp part to persuade him.

'I trust you,' he said. 'I adore you.'

It was in his mind to put his hand up her skirt and between her legs – she had not asked for her knickers back and they were in his jacket pocket. Her beautiful *joujou* was uncovered and bare – if he slipped his hand up her skirt he could touch it and stroke it with his fingertips.

But when he tried, she pressed her thighs together and whispered *not now, chéri, you must trust me a little longer*. Her palm was warm over the bulge in his trousers as it grew thicker – he was content to lean back in his seat and let her stroke him through his trousers to keep him calm for the rest of the journey.

They left the taxi at the crowded Place Pigalle – brightly lit by the garish neon signs of the stripshows that jostled side by side round the square. There were tourists and streetgirls everywhere – the girls were chatting to each other while they waited for their next client. Nicole linked her arm in Lucien's and dragged him through the restless crowds on a tour of inspection.

'What are we doing here?' he asked.

'You will see in a moment,' she said.

She stopped by a girl in a shiny black plastic raincoat and wished her *Bon soir*. It was a warm dry evening but the raincoat was belted tightly round the waist and buttoned up to the throat. The wearer was a light brunette – her hair was stacked on top of her head to make her taller.

Lucien couldn't understand what was going on. Nicole was talking to the girl in an undertone. The girl winked at Lucien and undid her belt – she flicked her raincoat open for half a second to let him see all she had on under it were black lace knickers and high-heeled shoes.

Then the show was over – as if the curtain had fallen at the theatre – the plastic coat was closed and belted again. Lucien was left with an impression of big soft low-slung breasts and a broad belly with a deep button in it.

'Bernadette has promised to take us to a hotel not far from here,' Nicole said solemnly. 'You have enough money with you, I hope?'

Lucien's confusion was complete. He couldn't imagine what she wanted with a Place Pigalle street-girl – but he didn't know Nicole had been here before with Remy, on Bastille Day. Even so, a dim idea was starting to form in his mind that she was trying to get back at Remy for his misdeeds but it was impossible to see how. One thing was certain – whatever predicament she might get herself into, Lucien was going to be there to look after her.

Bernadette led them round the corner and into a small hotel. The man in charge was half-bald and wore a brown suit without a tie – he nodded to Bernadette as to an old acquaintance. He stared at Nicole and Lucien with an unpleasantly knowing look in his cloudy eyes. He handed a key to Lucien and doubled the usual price of the room, just as Bernadette had doubled her usual charge when Lucien negotiated with her out in the noisy Place Pigalle.

The room looked clean, the bed was low and large and ample for its one purpose. Bernadette took her shiny black raincoat off and hung it up. She kicked her high-heeled shoes off and took her knickers down – and stood waiting to see what they wanted to do.

Nicole looked with a curious interest at Bernadette's big bare breasts and broad hips – and the soft cheeks of her bottom and the dark-brown curls between her sturdy thighs. *Ah bon*, she said, and stripped naked herself – and threw her arms around Bernadette's neck and kissed her like a sister.

'You're pretty,' Bernadette said to Nicole. 'Lovely pair of *nichons* you've got, *chérie*.'

'Have you a lover, Bernadette?' Nicole asked.

'Yes,' she said, looking curiously with dark-brown eyes at Nicole, 'I have a man of my own. Are you in love?'

'I was, but it was painful and I want to be free of it.'

Lucien was sitting on the side of the low bed, still fully dressed, listening to what they were saying and trying to make sense of it. His male part was hard and jumpy in his trousers, he pressed his hand over it to calm it.

'Painful, oh yes,' Bernadette said. 'I know what you mean – men are pigs.'

The two women were close together, bare breasts touching. Bernadette grinned and put a hand between Nicole's legs. *Ah oui*, Nicole said as Bernadette pressed a finger into her and tickled her secret bud.

'You like that?' Bernadette asked.

'I am an addict of love,' Nicole said, 'as some are addicted to drugs or alcohol. I suffer because of it, but if I am ever cured of my addiction I shall fade and die.'

With a hand on Nicole's hip and the other between her thighs, Bernadette pushed her back to sit on the edge of the bed by the side of Lucien – he was staring eager-eyed at the two naked bodies so close together. Bernadette knelt in front of Nicole and pushed her knees apart. She touched the soft lips she had exposed.

'You're wet,' she said. 'Do you prefer women, then?'

Nicole shook her head.

'I've never been with one before,' she said, 'but I know I despise men.'

Bernadette ducked her head and touched the tip of her tongue to the little pink bud of Nicole's *joujou*. She opened her wider so she could lick it.

'You do not love for love, I know that,' Nicole said in a shaking voice, 'but I respect you, Bernadette, because I believe you understand the agony of a broken heart.'

Bernadette said nothing, she was busy earning her living. Nicole fell back on the bed, her legs wide apart and hanging over the side. For Lucien, open-mouthed in astonishment, this was too much for him to bear a moment longer. He stood up and moved round behind Bernadette, flicking his trousers open to let his stiff length leap out.

'My poor Lucien,' Nicole said softly, seeing him loom over Bernadette. 'You know the pain of unreturned love.'

Lucien was not listening. He was down on his knees behind Bernadette, pressing himself to the wobbly cheeks of her bare bottom. His arms were round her and his hands were between her legs to feel the brown-haired patch there.

'*Ah, ça commence*,' said Bernadette, as if expecting this all along. 'Two at the same time, eh?'

Her tongue sent tremors of pleasure through Nicole and her bottom was exposed to the attentions of Lucien behind her. He brought the purple head of his shaft up between her thighs and pushed strongly into her capacious *joujou*.

Nicole on her back on the bed was sighing and writhing to the touch of Bernadette's wet tongue. Her beautiful breasts rose and fell to her rapid breathing.

'Destroy me,' she moaned, her head rolling rapidly from side to side. 'Destroy me, Bernadette, I beg you.'

Lucien had Bernadette's big fluid breasts in his hands and bounced them up and down while he thrust forcefully into her.

'Nicole,' he moaned. '*Ah chérie*,' – just as if he was thrusting into her instead of a girl picked up on the street.

Bernadette meanwhile was banging her bottom against him to increase the penetration of his jabs.

'*Ah oui, ah oui*,' he gasped, his eyes staring wildly.

Nicole shrieked as the moments of ecstasy arrived for her. Lucien stared intently at her over Bernadette's shoulder. A moment later he shook convulsively and gave a long sigh as he spurted his wasted desire.

More From The Diary – Sept 14 – Friday

When we'd finished with the hotel room Bernadette went back to the Place Pigalle – with her black raincoat belted tightly about her waist – and I noticed that she left the top button undone. The pale cleavage of her breasts was bait to attract the next client. But whoever she took to the hotel after Lucien and me, and whatever she was asked to do, it would be trivial and prosaic.

This ordinary woman with the big bottom and spreading breasts had been caught up in a special enchantment for half an hour – she had been the recipient of a tremendous outpouring of love. It was frustrated love, to be sure – that outward surge of emotion from me and, in his own way, from Lucien. Did she understand that, I ask myself.

We parted from her outside the hotel entrance and Lucien and I went to the nearest bar we could find. It was a gaudy place with a red neon sign outside and a big plate-glass window – it was packed with tourists at that time of the evening. I got drunk on cognac. Lucien got half-drunk, but he was able to get me into a taxi and into my apartment.

I woke up alone, naked in my own bed. He'd undressed me and my clothes lay scattered about on the floor. I remember nothing of that undressing. Perhaps Lucien opened my legs and lay on my belly to calm his frustrated love – but I can't remember that either. I hope he did so – he deserves a little happiness in his life. He is a good friend and sometimes I wish I could love him the way he'd like me to.

When Nicole told Jacques Lecomte about her nocturnal

visit with Lucien to the Place Pigalle, his consternation was obvious.

'Good God,' he said – and he was so agitated that he got up from where he perched on the edge of the desk. 'But this is appalling.'

He took his dark-framed glasses off and waved them about while he strode two or three paces up and down the consulting-room.

Nicole shrugged.

'Love leads us all up strange alleyways,' she said.

'Love,' Jacques said sharply. 'After the things you've told me I can't make out whether you love Remy or not.'

'I adore him.'

'So you say – so you may think. But words are easy,' he countered. 'I think you're deceiving yourself. You go with other men so readily that your feelings toward Remy can hardly be a deep attachment – don't you agree? As for your little game with the woman you found – what can I say about that? It seems to me that you and Remy have gone through a phase of passion together, now it is finished and you will move apart.'

'You don't understand me at all,' Nicole told him, crossing her legs gracefully.

She was in one of the armchairs, not on the brown leather couch where patients lay to confess all their innermost secrets to Jacques and open their hearts to him. Or perhaps to open their legs for him – which to Nicole's way of thinking would do them far more good than all the self-indulgent talk and self-analysis in the world.

'You ignore my artistic sensibilities,' she complained. 'You ignore my intellectual need for close human contact.'

Jacques was disturbed – she'd never seen him in that state before and she began to wonder just how strongly he felt for her. Evidently it was more than a psychotherapist ought to feel for a patient. That's if she was his patient – they'd never really settled that between them.

'Human contacts,' he said, not sounding in the least convinced. 'The contacts you prize so highly always seem to take place on a bed.'

'That is a very unflattering view, Jacques. The only men I permit to make love to me are the men I adore and respect. Perhaps it is too hard a truth for you to grasp, but the simple fact is that I can share my love between several men at the same time.'

'Ha!' he snorted. 'More self deception.'

'I've read that in South America and India there are tribes where it is usual for a woman to marry all the brothers of a family and share her love between them – surely you've read of this custom in your learned journals, Jacques?'

'That's not the same thing,' he said at once. 'We are not primitive people and cannot conduct our lives as they do.'

'Love is a very primitive emotion,' she said, smiling at his growing perplexity. 'If a young woman in a jungle can love three or four men at the same time and be loved by them in turn, I see no reason why I can't do the same.'

Jacques stopped pacing and sat down on the edge of his own couch. He folded his glasses and slid them neatly into his top pocket.

'I wonder if you really like men at all,' he said. 'Or do you see them as prizes to be captured – is that it?'

Nicole shrugged again.

'Are you my prize, Jacques?' she asked.

'No,' he said, an intent expression on his face and his voice shaking with confused emotion. 'You are my prize.'

'I adore you when you want to psychoanalyse me, Jacques,' she sighed.

She lay back in the chair as he slid off the brown couch and took her by the shoulders to kiss her hotly. She was wearing the dark-blue Chanel jacket and skirt that day, to appear formal. In view of what she was there to tell him, she thought it might be as well to look responsible.

The jacket was unbuttoned and open. She had an ivory silk blouse on – Jacques' hand found its way inside to knead her breasts. This was no playful caress, his touch was determined, one might even say decisive – he was taking her for his pleasure. She guessed that he was trying to prove something to himself. In another moment her bra hung unhooked and loose and her breasts were uncovered – Jacques' fingers skimmed over her buds to make them firm.

'So I am *your* prize, am I?' she murmured. 'Tell me what have you done to win me, Jacques.'

He didn't answer the question. He was on his knees on the carpet by her chair and his hand was up her skirt, groping so insistently that she was sure he would ruin her black lace knickers – she'd bought them that morning to match those Bernadette had worn under her shiny raincoat.

The bulge in Jacques' trousers was very noticeable – Nicole couldn't help smiling to see its twitching movement. There must have been something in her little story of the adventure shared with Lucien up in Montmartre which had either enraged or aroused Jacques – or both – she found that thought delicious.

Jacques ripped his trousers open – out sprang his stiff part, huge and hard and hot.

'Nicole—' he said.

He didn't finish what he intended to say – what he wanted to say – he stared at her with eyes clouded with indescribable emotions. She guessed that he'd like to say he loved her, but he didn't want to commit himself like that – after all, he was married to her good friend.

Apart from words, he was willing to commit himself by his actions. He pushed Nicole's skirt up her thighs and forced her knees apart – she gasped as he threw himself forward on her, as if he was determined to overwhelm her and crush her under his male domination. His cheeks were flushed red, he put his face between her elegant bare breasts. His stiff part was squeezed and held between his own belly and her black lace knickers.

'Nicole, oh Nicole,' he gasped – and all the time his body was jerking convulsively between her spread thighs.

'*Chéri*,' she murmured, and gripped him tight between her knees.

She was waiting for him to rip her knickers off and penetrate her. But he lay on her as he was and rubbed against her belly, breathing hard. He was going to spurt in three more seconds, she was sure of that. This was strange and it intrigued her that the man whose profession was to help others to recognise and restrain their inconvenient emotions had lost the will to control his own.

He started to moan loudly. Nicole grinned at the idea of Josette Anvers getting up from her typewriter in the next room and putting her head round the door to see what the noise was about. If that happened it would be like the little adventure at the seaside, when a chambermaid came into the room while Alexis was making love to her.

In retrospect, Nicole believed that those next ten seconds with Alexis in his hotel room at St. Raphael were perhaps the most exciting of her life. Alexis had frozen under the eye of the astonished chambermaid, but Nicole's body had carried on by itself, so to speak, the muscles inside her belly working, tugging and squeezing Alexis' throbbing part.

The maid turned her back and fled blushing, but before she was out of the door huge waves of ecstasy crashed through Nicole and made her gasp and cry out.

She was going to tell Jacques all about that and ask him to explain to her why her emotions had welled up so massively in those moments. He'd have a real problem psychoanalysing her emotions then, she thought. But for now, Jacques' face was pressed between her breasts, he was moaning and rubbing against her. He couldn't see the look on her face – which was fortunate for the preservation of his male ego, for her grin had spread broadly.

Well now, dear Jacques, she said in her mind, *so I am your prize – is that what you believe? You love me secretly and dare not admit it. You try to psychoanalyse me away from loving other men. But you must be brave and accept that I am no one's prize, chéri, not yours, not Remy's, not anybody's. I am free and independent and I love whoever I please to love. I let you adore my beautiful body – maybe one day I may decide I love you, if the mood takes me. First there are things you must learn – important things about me and about yourself, things they never taught you when you were a student.*

'My little black lace knickers,' she said, to see how far she could tease him. 'You like them, *chéri*? But you hardly took a moment to look at them and see how well they fit over my bottom and up between my legs. When I put them on I stood and admired myself in the long mirror.'

'Oh yes, yes,' Jacques gasped, his fingers were clenched on the warm flesh of her breasts.

'The girl we picked up in Montmartre – Bernadette – she wore knickers like these,' Nicole said. 'That's why I bought them. They excite you, don't they? You are rubbing against them and taking pleasure from the touch of your flesh on them.'

'Oh,' he moaned, 'oh—'

'Can you feel the warmth and softness of my flesh through them – tell me, Jacques – can you?'

He shook and spurted. She felt the warm wetness soak through to her skin and she laughed. As suddenly as it had happened, it was finished. Jacques gave a long sigh and moved away from her belly. He sank back on his heels, with his sticky length standing out of his open trousers.

'What are you doing to me, Nicole?' he said, his gaze troubled. 'You make me forget I am a professional man and I behave like a student with his first girlfriend. Why do you want to destroy me?'

'Oh Jacques, you've got that completely the wrong way round. I have the highest regard for you – you are the one trying to destroy me. When I explain my problems you tell me I don't really like men at all. What do you think that does to my self-esteem as a woman?'

'I should never have said it,' he admitted mournfully. 'It was said in a moment of exasperation – which in itself is unforgivable. Can you ever forgive me?'

'You crushed my pride,' she told him, trying to sound serious, 'but I admire you too greatly to have any resentment against you.'

She stood up from her chair and slid her little knickers down her legs and off. They lay on the carpet in front of Jacques, made wet by his uncontrollable passion. He stared and said again with a sigh, 'I am like a young student with his first girl—'

Nicole stretched out her hand toward him – he was very comical there on the floor with his limp part dangling out of his open trousers and she wanted him to get up. He took her hand and rained kisses on it.

'Why am I such an idiot about you?' he asked. 'Can you tell me that?'

'I don't see you as an idiot, Jacques. Just the opposite. When you give way to your feelings for me and force me to make love here in your consulting-room, I find it charming and very exciting that you have such passionate emotions about me.'

'Truly?' he said, swallowing her words whole.

'Come and sit with me on the couch,' she said, smiling down at him and tugging at his hand. 'There are things I must tell you – very important things, believe me. In fact I feel that my entire life and happiness are in your hands.'

They sat on the brown leather couch, his arm around her waist in a most unprofessional way. He'd tried to zip up his trousers when he stood up from the floor, but she'd put her hand on his to stop him.

'Leave it, *chéri*,' she said. 'Even small and at rest it is charming. Furthermore, I have no knickers. I am bare under my skirt because of what you did to me a moment ago. In all fairness, you must be as bare as me.'

The little black knickers lay on the floor where she had dropped them. They had an abandoned air about them, as if she'd never pull them up her legs again. And they had a long dark wet stain. Jacques sat staring and seemed unable to look away from the evidence of his passion for Nicole.

She told him about a dream she'd had. She was standing in a large open space – she thought it might be the large picture gallery in the Louvre, but she couldn't be certain about that. She was quite naked in the dream and there were several men lying on the polished wooden floor about her. The men were all naked too – their heads were toward her and their feet away from her – and their shafts all stood up stiff.

'They were like the spokes of a wheel,' she said, 'and I was the hub – do you understand what I am saying?'

'Yes,' Jacques breathed. 'I understand that very well. Tell me – was I one of the men?'

Nicole's hand was inside his open trousers and she was holding his fleshy length. It was no longer quite so small and limp, it was starting to grow hard and long in her warm hand.

'Perhaps,' she said. 'I don't know. It's very strange, but I didn't recognise any of them. There was an attendant in uniform by the door and he was glaring at me in disapproval – perhaps he was you, *chéri*. Do you think he was?'

'Have you had this dream more than once?' he asked, ignoring her pointed question. 'When was the last time?'

In her turn, Nicole ignored his question.

'It was so strange, so unreal and yet so overwhelming,' she told him. 'The half-hour I passed in a hotel room with Lucien and the girl in the black raincoat we picked up in the street. On the surface it seems very simple, but it isn't at all. The more I think about what we did, the more subtle and unreal it seems to me.'

'Why does it seem unreal to you?' he asked.

Nicole was playing with his hard shaft while she talked, sending little ripples of pleasure through him. His arm tightened strongly about her waist and he put his other hand inside her open blouse to stroke her bare breasts.

'I was on my back on the bed, you must understand,' she explained. 'My legs were dangling over the side and Bernadette was kneeling by the bed to kiss me. She pushed my legs apart and opened me – she was licking me and I was on the verge of orgasm almost at once.'

'Have you been with a woman before?' Jacques asked.

Nicole paid no attention to his question.

'I could see Lucien standing behind Bernadette,' she went on. 'He tore his trousers open to let his shaft flip out and knelt behind her. He was pushing it into her from behind.'

'Ah, Nicole-Claire—' Jacques sighed – he was on the verge of spurting from the simple movement of her hand inside his open trousers.

'He was clutching Bernadette's breasts while he stabbed into her,' Nicole said. 'Somehow it was as if he was playing with my breasts, not hers – my nipples stood up as if his fingers were plucking at them.'

'Imagination,' Jacques breathed.

'I could see Lucien's face over her shoulder – he was

staring down at me and saying my name. Between my legs Bernadette's tongue was driving me mad with desire. I stared into Lucien's face over her shoulder and I felt as if he was stabbing into me, not into her.'

'Transference,' Jacques sighed. 'A fantasy.'

His hand was up Nicole's skirt and his eager fingers were dabbling in her warm *joujou*.

'Of course, if you say so,' she murmured. 'But I knew for certain that when he spurted into Bernadette I'd feel it inside me — it would send me into orgasm — commonsense tells me it was a girl's tongue giving me those sensations but I knew it was really Lucien doing it to me.'

'Because you wanted it to be him?'

'No. In my mind Lucien is associated with Remy, and because I hate and despise Remy bitterly it rubs off onto Lucien, poor dear. No, at that moment I hated Lucien and wanted Bernadette to do it to me. I hated the impression that Lucien seemed to be doing it to me — when I had gone to all this trouble to arrange for him to see I despised him by having a paid girl do it to me.'

Jacques paused to consider her complicated statement.

'But the man you hate wasn't there to watch you,' he objected. 'It was another man entirely.'

'Yes,' Nicole agreed. 'Everything was confused in my mind. But there was great pleasure — and more than pleasure. I can't explain it.'

In her hand Jacques' male part was throbbing wildly. She held on to it while she half stood to made a quick turn before she sat down across his thighs facing him. She pushed flathanded against his chest to make him slump back on the couch. She raised herself and guided his stiff length into her very wet *joujou* as she sat down astride him.

'Why am I the only one to be confused?' she asked as she rode up and down, making him slide in her with exquisite sensation. 'How about you, Jacques — do you hate and love at the same time? I know that you love me because you always want to make love to me. And I think you hate me because you want to make love to me — isn't that so?'

'Nicole . . . *je t'adore*,' he moaned. His hands were on her thighs, gripping the smooth flesh above her stocking-tops. '*Je t'adore—*'

'Men are all alike,' she said fiercely. 'Remy, Lucien, you – there is no difference – you are a length of stiff flesh joined to a body. You might as well be Remy.'

'No,' he gasped, 'I am me.'

'You are Remy,' she contradicted him. 'I am using your body to shame you because you humiliated me with another woman.'

'Yes, shame me,' Jacques sighed. 'Shame me, shame me . . .'

He was bucking up into her in time with her fast little down-strokes.

'Get the hatred out of your soul, Nicole,' he said. 'Use me to free yourself from it.'

'I hate you,' she moaned as she thumped down on him and drove him deep into her belly.

'I love you,' he gasped, and he stared up at her with wild eyes as his fingers sank bruisingly deep into the flesh of her thighs.

His back arched off the brown leather as he spurted up into her – and she squealed and writhed in urgent release.

Nicole's Secret Diary – Sept 23 – Sunday

I have met her at last – the woman who destroyed the happiness I had with Remy. I went to the encounter hating her bitterly. Before our hands touched I stared at her face and wished she was dead. We clasped hands warily, like two boxers in the ring, making a gesture of false courtesy before the fighting begins and blood flows.

At the moment our hands touched I fell in love with her, body and soul. I knew what a man must feel like when he meets a beautiful woman he desires, his eyes blazing and his male part stiff in his trousers.

This is absurd, I told myself, she is my enemy and she is a woman. Two final and unanswerable reasons why it is impossible for me to have these tender feelings toward her.

Nicole lay awake in the darkness of her bedroom. Beside her Remy lay asleep, breathing slowly. Their love-making had been lengthy and voluptuous. He was naked under the satin sheet, and so was she, her body caressed by the smoothness of satin and cradled on the softness of down-filled mattresses.

Remy's loving that night had an unusual quality – by turns sensitive and fierce. Her beautiful body responded to his caresses as eagerly as it always did, her orgasms were long and lingering and full. At times he kissed her breasts gently – at others his mouth covered and sucked ferociously at her firm little buds.

His fingers stroked gently between her open thighs – then gripped her soft *joujou* cruelly as if he would torment her. He kissed her feet and murmured her name, then his naked body lay full length on her, pressing down on her belly and breasts to dominate her with his masculine weight. She moaned and sighed and shook while his hands and his man's stiff part explored every part of her and exploited her yielding flesh.

Now he was asleep and she was awake and thinking furiously. Tonight he did all this to her and made her sob with delight, but last night he had most probably done exactly the same to this other woman of his, Chantal Lamartine. Worse even than simple betrayal was the thought that perhaps he couldn't tell the difference between them.

Perhaps Nicole and the other woman were alike in Remy's coarse male consideration. A pair of breasts to feel, a pair of thighs to part, a soft opening to ram into, a warm place for his satisfaction. This was an intolerable thought. For that Nicole could find it in her heart to kill him – to drag the swans-down pillow from under his head and clamp it over his face until his breathing stopped.

He had made love to her most pleasingly. She was devoted to him – he had only to smile at her and put his hand on her knee in a taxi or at a café table and she was his to do whatever he pleased with. Nothing had changed since that first day when she met him at the Dome, when she had stared into his eyes and silently pleaded with him to rip her knickers off and bend her backward over the little round table on the pavement.

It had been a dreadful mistake to let him read a page of her journal when they were on holiday in St. Raphael because now he was confident of his power over her. He had read in her own words that she would lie back and open her legs in full sight of passers-by if he wanted to unzip his trousers and slide his stiff part into her.

This couldn't go on, Nicole decided, lying awake and silent in the night. Her hand lay lightly over her neat little patch of brunette curls and her fingertips touched the soft lips Remy had penetrated and ravished so satisfactorily. She was allowing herself to become a victim of love – something drastic must be done.

Something drastic had been done – and it had failed. In expectation of making Remy jealous she had encouraged Lucien to make love to her. To be truthful she had almost compelled him to. But her expectations had been disappointed, her little scheme had failed miserably. Remy was still infatuated by Chantal. Even after a month of sharing a bed every night with Nicole at the seaside, he had gone back to Chantal within a week of their return to Paris.

There must be a way of getting back at him, some way of bringing him to his senses, a way to reduce his insufferable male pride, some way of humbling him. And in the middle of the night, in the silent and scented darkness of her bedroom Nicole realised how it could be achieved.

She had reached a decision of great consequence. She would steal this Chantal away from Remy. Suppose that it was possible to beguile Chantal into bed with her – Remy would be shattered when he heard about it. He would be forced to accept that the two women he had taken as his lovers preferred each other in bed to him.

Her mind was made up. After a late breakfast the next day, after Remy was gone, she phoned Lucien to ask him to introduce her to Mademoiselle Lamartine. He dithered and hesitated and argued against it, even though he had no idea what Nicole was planning. He could guess that it was nothing to Remy's advantage. But he was too devoted to Nicole to resist her persuasion for long.

'But what shall I tell her?' he asked plaintively.

'Nothing,' said Nicole. 'You will take her to a café or a bar to talk about design and furniture and I shall be there by chance – and you can introduce us.'

'Where – Left Bank?'

She thought for a moment.

'No, at Fouquet's. Let me know what time.'

'Any day?'

'No Lucien, not any day – today.'

At five-thirty she made her way along the Champs Elysées through the Sunday strollers, from the Metro station toward the red awning of Fouquet's. She looked casual, but she had spent hours getting ready for this moment – washing her hair, painting her nails, making up her face and choosing what to wear for this critical encounter.

The result was dramatic and yet relaxed – she wore a

black rollneck sweater in fine wool to outline her perfect breasts and emphasise her elegant long neck. A chic grey and black check skirt flattered the slimness of her thighs. And a short tan suede jacket to complete the impression of elegant informality.

Lucien's table was back near the door, not next to the pavement – he evidently felt nervous of being seen with the two women together. He was glancing about, trying to seem natural and unworried – but not really succeeding. Nicole glanced in his direction as she strolled past, pretended to notice him – and gave him a casual little wave.

Lucien stood up and smiled and beckoned her to join him. There were coffee cups and glasses on the table – and beside him sat the woman who had ruined Nicole's happiness. She wore an expensive looking apricot dress in crêpe-de-Chine, with long close fitting sleeves – and a strand of green jade beads. An elegant jacket of the same colour hung over the back of her chair.

Nicole approached the table without hurry as she appraised her rival – from her chestnut-brown hair to the full round breasts under her dress. She was older than Nicole, though only a few years and she certainly wasn't thirty yet.

'What a pleasant surprise to meet you here,' Lucien burbled on. 'Let me introduce you—'

He recited their names, they touched hands for a moment and said they were enchanted – as everyone does without thinking when introduced. But in this instance it was the truth – Nicole had fallen under an enchantment. Lucien ordered a drink for her. The three of them chatted of nothing for a quarter of an hour. No one mentioned Remy Toussaint.

Now she had met Chantal, the first step in Nicole's plan to even up her dealings with treacherous Remy, she had no idea how to proceed. Chantal was so very obviously an agreeable person. And Lucien kept on interrupting, as if he was afraid that Nicole was about to say something dreadful and insulting to Chantal.

To cut him out of the conversation Nicole told Chantal that she liked her dress very much – the colour was exquisite and the green jade was marvellous with it. Chantal smiled with pleasure and told her where she had bought it. Lucien sat and twiddled his thumbs.

'It suits you so well,' Nicole said.

'It would suit you well too,' Chantal said. 'Your colouring is right for it. I think we are near enough the same size.'

'Except in one respect,' Nicole agreed, eyeing the other woman's breasts. Her own were somewhat smaller and more pear-shaped.

Chantal grinned.

'You simply must try it on,' she said.

In no time at all the matter was settled. The two women wished Lucien *au revoir* and left him to find a waiter and pay the bill while they went off together to look for a taxi. Chantal lived in an apartment at Passy, only a street or two away from Jacques and Annette Lecomte. Events were moving so fast now that Nicole could hardly believe it. She had thought to face an enemy – instead an instant compatibility had shown itself – it was beyond comprehension.

'We'll have a drink in a moment,' Chantal said while she put her key in the door, 'but try the dress on first – I'm curious to see if it will suit you.'

The bedroom was very pretty, white and pink and fragrant. A spray of long white flowers stood in a tall crystal vase on a dressing-table. Chantal slipped her elegant jacket off and threw it on the bed. She stood facing Nicole while she took off the apricot dress, raising it gracefully over her head.

Nicole had taken her jacket off and was sitting on the side of the bed, admiring the ivory embroidered spread. She looked at Chantal, her full round breasts supported by a lacy white bra. Her belly was slightly plumper than Nicole's – or so Nicole told herself.

She was wearing a narrow white garter-belt to keep her stockings up – it lay across her belly, just below the deep button. The cheeks of her bottom in small white knickers were slightly fuller than Nicole's – so Nicole decided, to her own advantage. But in truth Chantal's body was elegant and desirable.

Chantal handed her the dress she had just taken off, it felt slightly warm from her body and the fragrance of her expensive perfume lingered on it. Nicole was tempted to bury her face in it, but she kept a tight rein on herself. Things were moving too fast, her plan was sliding out of control.

'There – try it on,' Chantal said.

'But I am not you, Chantal,' she said. 'I am me – and I can never be anyone else.'

'Wearing the dress will not change you – you will change the dress,' Chantal said with a smile.

Nicole shrugged and stood up to pull her thin sweater over her head and drop her skirt. It was no secret to her now that Chantal wanted to see her body – she pretended to be looking at the fastening on the apricot dress while she stood still for Chantal's eager inspection. For this occasion Nicole was wearing jet-black underwear that covered very little of her belly and breasts – she had a beautiful body and was proud to let Chantal stare at her with enthusiastic eyes.

It was no longer a question of luring Chantal into bed. It was now a matter of not appearing too eager – the situation had changed so much that it was almost comedy – this was the thought in her mind while she slipped the warm dress over her head. Chantal fussed round her busily, smoothing the thin crêpe-de-Chine down her body and over her hips with gentle hands.

There was a long mirror standing by the window to catch the light – the two women were side by side in front of it to see the effect of the exchange. Nicole was deciding whether she really liked the apricot dress she was wearing – and Chantal in her white bra and knickers and stockings was trying to decide if the dress really suited Nicole. Each was secretly admiring the elegant lines of the other's body. And when Nicole realised this she found herself disconcerted by the strong emotions she was experiencing.

This was not what she had planned. She had lost control of the situation – it had taken on a momentum and a logic of its own. As she stared at the reflection of Chantal's full breasts in the mirror, at her smooth belly and her long thighs – Nicole knew that she needed to be alone for a while to consider what was happening to her.

She stepped back from the mirror and pulled the apricot

dress over her head. Chantal looked at her with a question in her eyes, but she said nothing. While Nicole was putting on her own sweater and skirt she said she was ready for the drink Chantal had promised – she'd wait in the sitting-room while Chantal dressed.

The disappointment was clear to see in Chantal's eyes, but she nodded and Nicole left her standing in her knickers by the long mirror. The sitting-room was expensively and ornately furnished – with crystal mirrors and bright watercolours in silver-chrome frames. There was a black velvet chaise-longue – Nicole had never seen one like it before. It suggested sensuality and luxury – with perhaps a delicate hint of perversity.

That being so, Nicole sat herself on it, ignoring the half-dozen modern-looking chairs placed about the room. There was the latest copy of Vogue magazine lying on a glass table – she picked it up and flicked through the pages – her mind was in a turmoil and she didn't know what to do for best now.

Last night – in the small dark hours, with Remy asleep beside her, everything had seemed simple and straightforward. She would make the acquaintance of Chantal Lamartine, dazzle her with charm and elegance, overwhelm her by strength of purpose and character, talk her out of her clothes, caress her body and ravage her sexually. Then walk away with a shrug and a smile and tell Remy what she had done to his girlfriend.

But now she had made the acquaintance of Chantal, nothing was simple. Everything was *dessus-dessous* – upside down and inside out! She felt as if she had been struck by lightning at the moment their eyes met across a café table and their hands touched. Nicole had fallen in love. And to judge by Chantal's eagerness to undress, she had heard the same roar of thunder and had been struck by the same bolt of lightning.

'But this is absurd,' Nicole said aloud, letting the glossy magazine slide to the floor.

Another two seconds and she would have been off the black velvet chaise-longue and out of the door, running away in consternation from an impossibly obsessive situation – but then Chantal came into the room. She had put the beautiful apricot dress on again. She smiled faintly when she saw where

Nicole had chosen to sit – and came across the room to sit down beside her.

'What shall I get you to drink?' she asked.

'A glass of chilled white wine,' Nicole suggested.

'A glass of champagne will be better,' Chantal said. 'There is something I want to ask you – if you'll tell me – was it really an accident, running into Lucien at Fouquet's?'

Nicole didn't answer the question directly. 'Before we met I made Lucien describe you to me,' she said at last. 'He told me you were beautiful, which is true, of course, you are very beautiful. One takes that for granted, almost. But being a man he left out all the important things about you.'

Chantal understood what she meant. She lowered her eyelids for an instant and sighed softly as she took Nicole's hand and held it to her. Nicole's palm lay lightly over a full soft breast. She knew at once that Chantal was naked under her dress. Before putting it on again she had taken her bra and knickers and stockings off – the gentle warmth of her flesh came through the thin crêpe-de-Chine.

'I want you to kiss me,' Chantal said.

Nicole gave the breast she was touching a gentle squeeze – she thought it would be pleasant to kiss Chantal there. But for the moment she contented herself by kissing her on the mouth. Chantal slipped her arm round Nicole's waist and kissed her in return – she kissed her with passion. In another moment or two they each had their arms tightly round the other and were pressing their bodies together, breasts against breasts, thigh against thigh.

'Nicole *chérie*,' Chantal murmured.

They overbalanced slowly and gracefully sideways, much like ballet dancers held in each other's arms, and lay along the black velvet chaise-longue, mouth to mouth and belly to belly, showering kisses on each other's face and cheeks and eyes and mouth.

'You are too beautiful,' Nicole sighed. '*Je t'adore, ma* Chantal.'

'And you are beautiful,' Chantal said. 'We are both beautiful – we are beautiful for each other, we adore each other.'

'None of this makes sense,' Nicole said. 'But does it really matter?'

'I want to touch you,' Chantal said. 'Let me touch you.'

They sat up, Chantal helped Nicole out of her white sweater and her skirt – she knelt on the floor in her apricot dress to roll Nicole's stockings down her long elegant legs. She kissed inside Nicole's thigh, her tongue flickered over the smooth flesh.

Nicole's bra and knickers lay discarded on the carpet while she helped Chantal pull her dress over her head, so they were both naked. They lay on the chaise-longue again, warm belly to warm belly and bare breasts to bare breasts, mouth pressed to mouth in an endless kiss.

'This moment was destined,' Chantal moaned softly. 'That's why it makes sense.'

Her hand was between Nicole's thighs, caressing her *joujou* very tenderly. Nicole's hand was between Chantal's thighs, fingertips stroking along the soft lips. As desire grew, fingers pressed between moist lips, touching secret little buds, teasing and tantalising. Mouth to mouth, wet tongues touching, fingers busy between legs, sending fast little spasms of pleasure through the two intertwined bodies.

'*Je t'adore*,' Chantal sighed languorously.

'*Je t'adore, chérie*,' Nicole sighed back.

Their orgasms began at the same moment, their fingers dabbled in slippery warmth, their backs arched and their bellies jammed together – while their long sobs of ecstasy mingled.

When they were calm again they lay in each other's arms on the black chaise-longue as if they had been lovers for years.

'There is so much unspoken between us,' said Nicole. 'I hardly know how to begin, *chérie*. I suspect that you know what I came here to tell you.'

'I know Remy is deceiving both of us – you with me and me with you – that's what you came to tell me, isn't it?'

'How did you find out?'

'When Lucien phoned to ask me out today I was surprised – I don't know him all that well. At first I thought he wanted to try his luck with me – whenever I've met him with Remy he's looked at me with big eyes that make no secret of his desire to get my clothes off and do things to me. That one expects, of course.'

'Of course,' Nicole agreed. 'We expect men to try to get us into bed because we are so marvellously sexy.'

'But,' Chantal went on, 'there was such a strange air about the invitation to meet him for a drink that I started thinking – I made him tell me why he wanted to meet me. He's easy enough to wheedle, as you must know yourself.'

'Knowing what you knew – that I was the woman with whom you were sharing Remy – you still wanted to meet me?' Nicole said, 'you wanted to see what I'm like – as I needed to see what you were like.'

'That's right,' Chantal agreed.

'What did you think when Lucien informed you that Remy was faithless?'

'I burst into tears. Then after I'd bathed my eyes in cold water I made him tell me everything. And you – what did you do when you found out about Remy's double-dealing?'

'I don't cry easily,' Nicole said, 'I became angry.'

'Then we are different – I was too hurt to be angry.'

'Well then, between us we seem to have run the gamut of the emotions possible to women who have been ill-used by a man,' Nicole said.

'Did you only want to see what I was like,' Chantal asked, snuggling up closer. 'Or did you intend from the start to make love to me?'

Nicole smiled and explained.

'First I tried to hurt Remy by making love to Lucien – on Remy's own desk,' she said, making Chantal laugh. 'When that failed I was seething with anger. So – although I am not attracted to women – I decided I must have you, *chérie*, to get my own back on Remy. Do you understand that?'

'Oh yes, if I were brave enough and ingenious enough I might have tried the same myself. You realise, I suppose, that what you've done to me has freed me from Remy. Now that we've retaliated and are equal with him – who is going to tell him, you or I?'

Nicole shrugged.

'Strangely, it's not important now whether you or I or Lucien tells Remy about us. It doesn't matter if he ever finds out or not.'

'To me it matters,' Chantal said. 'I want him to suffer.'

'We can rely on Lucien to tell him.'

'He means well, but he's an idiot,' Chantal said. 'When you had him, was he any good?'

'Average,' Nicole said, 'to me the important thing was to do it in Remy's office and right on his desk. It was a Saturday morning when I knew Lucien would be there alone.'

'If only I could have seen it,' Chantal said. 'His partner having his girlfriend on his own desk'.

'When I thought about it afterwards, it was comical,' said Nicole. 'Perhaps Lucien found it romantic. What happened was that I took my knickers off and lay on the desk with my knees up and Lucien lay on top of me and pushed it in – he was finished in less than two minutes.'

'*Oh la la* – how very boring,' Chantal said with a giggle. 'But as it was the principle of the thing that mattered, I suppose you didn't mind too much if it was short and sharp.'

'To tell you the truth, *chérie*, the idea of getting back at Remy by letting his partner ravish me on his desk was so exciting that I reached a climax even before Lucien did.'

'*Oh chérie*,' Chantal sighed. 'How could you?'

Nicole stroked her long bare back, from her flat shoulder-blades down to the round cheeks of her bottom.

'I surprised myself,' she said.

'I think we should go into the bedroom, don't you?' Chantal said as she slid her hand between Nicole's thighs, 'I haven't heard you shriek yet – but I know I can make you.'

From The Diary – Sunday

It was love between us – yet it was more than love – it was an enchantment. I felt delight – so did Chantal – we embraced and kissed without impatience, we were assured in our hearts that the pleasure was there for us all the time.

In her pink-and-white bedroom Chantal took the embroidered cover from the bed and the two naked women held it between them while they folded it and put it aside. Nicole put her arms around Chantal and held her close while they kissed, their bare bellies touching – Chantal put her hands on Nicole's shoulders and pressed her down to sit on the edge of the bed.

'Tell me that Remy made love to you on this bed,' Nicole said with a smile. 'Tell me it is so, *chérie* – it is all the more piquant if you and I do it where he had you – together we shall erase all memory of him.'

'It is our reprisal,' said Chantal, returning her smile. 'You may be sure he has had me on this bed many a time.'

'Our reprisal together,' Nicole agreed, 'and more than that – it will be a true act of love between us, Chantal.'

'Yes it will,' Chantal said. 'It really will.'

She was enchanted by the little patch of brunette curls between Nicole's legs and couldn't take her eyes away – and it seemed she couldn't resist giving an expression to her admiration another moment. She knelt by the bed and laid her hand over those curls – Nicole obligingly moved her knees a little way apart.

'I am not vain but I know I'm beautiful,' Chantal said. 'Men always tell me so – always – and I can see as much for myself in my mirror. I'm glad I'm beautiful because I want to give myself to you completely and I want you to adore me forever.'

Nicole touched her cheek. Chantal stroked the trimmed patch of curls between her legs and told her it was charming. Nicole smiled and opened her legs wider so that Chantal could touch the lips of her *joujou* with gentle fingers.

'And I am glad I'm beautiful for you to have,' Nicole said. 'Am I beautiful between my legs, Chantal?'

'Oh yes, yes, yes,' Chantal sighed. 'You are exquisite.'

She parted the soft lips and saw the moistness inside – the little bud was standing proud and pink. Chantal put her head down and touched the tip of her tongue to it.

'*Ah, je t'aime*,' Nicole murmured.

Chantal opened her wider and licked the little bud. Nicole fell on her back on the bed, her legs open and over the side. She was offering herself without any reservation to the other woman, she was begging her to ravish her body. Chantal flicked her tongue over her bud and her cheek was pressed to the smooth flesh of an inner thigh.

Nicole cupped her own breasts in her hands for a moment – then reached down her belly to her groins and stroked Chantal's face.

'Chantal,' she gasped. 'Oh yes *chérie*—'

The climax of sensation came very quickly – her bottom rose off the bed and her back arched – she collapsed again and her spine was on the bed – then up she lifted once more – and fell back. Her body was caught in a long regular rhythm of rise and fall to the sensations washing through her – like waves of the sea rolling in to shore.

'Chantal – do you love me?' she moaned. 'Say that you love me – say it—'

An hour later, when they were lying at ease in each other's arms, the phone began to ring out in the sitting-room. Chantal ignored it, they kissed again and stroked each other's flanks and breasts. After a long time the phone fell silent.

'We are not at home to anyone,' Chantal said with a giggle.

But fifteen minutes later, when Nicole was lying over Chantal to kiss her breasts, the phone rang again.

'Oh damn the thing – you'd better answer it,' Nicole suggested as she slid off Chantal's soft body. 'Otherwise your persistent caller will keep on disturbing us all evening – and maybe all night too.'

Chantal grimaced and got off the bed sighing – the buds of her breasts were standing firm from the loving attention paid to them by Nicole's tongue. She draped an ice-blue satin dressing gown about her shoulders and went off muttering to answer the unwanted caller. It was at least ten minutes before she came back, her open dressing gown fluttering behind her. Her full round breasts and her thighs were uncovered – and so was the triangle of dark curls between her legs.

'Ah, you are truly beautiful,' Nicole said, watching her cross the room from the door to the bed. 'Why were you so long – I've missed you, *chérie*.'

Chantal climbed on to the bed without taking off the satin dressing gown. She didn't lie down – she sat with her knees up and her back to the headboard.

'You'll never guess who that was,' she said.

'Tell me then.'

'It was Lucien, of all people.'

'Lucien? But what did he want?' Nicole asked, her eyebrows rising.

'He asked how you and I got on together after we left him. He sounded worried – I think he imagined we fought over Remy and scratched each other's eyes out.'

'Lucien is a complete idiot,' Nicole said. 'I suppose he's been trying to ring me at home as well.'

'Yes, he said he had. He asked if you were here with me.'

'Did you tell him?'

'Of course I did,' Chantal said. 'I told him everything – I said we were naked in bed together and we'd been making love all this time and were going to do it again – and again. You should have heard his gasp when I said that.'

'I don't suppose it pleased him or put his mind at rest,' Nicole said. 'But at least he knows the truth now. What did he do – slam the phone down? My guess is he'll go out to the nearest bar and get drunk.'

'Why would he do that?'

'Because he knows he'll never have me again,' Nicole said, sounding surprised that the question was even asked.

'Well, he didn't slam the phone down, *chérie*. He begged me to tell him all about our love-making. He asked what we did to each other – was it with our fingers or our tongues? How many times had we done it since we left him at Fouquet's? Which one of us started it all off? He wanted to know everything.'

Nicole wrinkled her forehead and said nothing.

'He asked if we'd kissed in the taxi coming here,' Chantal went on. 'And did we put a hand up each other's skirt – that's what he'd do in a taxi with either of us, I suppose.'

'He was acting like a pervert making an anonymous phone call to a stranger,' said Nicole. 'How odd – but I imagine he was driven to rage and despair by the mortification of being left out.'

'I was shocked by him at first,' Chantal said. 'But then I realised how absurd he was – comical even – though he didn't mean to be.'

Nicole laughed.

'Poor Lucien,' she said. 'Reduced by his disappointment to becoming a phone pervert – an intriguing thought! I wonder if he had his trousers open and his stiff part in his hand while he was asking you questions.'

'Do you think he would do that?'

'He's a man,' Nicole said, as if that settled it.

'You'll never guess what he said to me then.'

'Nothing would surprise me – tell me, *chérie*.'

'*He sounded angry. He said: you can kiss Nicole's breasts and you can caress her joujou and you can make her kick her heels up and cry out – but you can't do what I've done to her – you haven't got what I've got.*'

'Men,' Nicole said with a contemptuous shrug. 'They think the world revolves around their fifteen centimetres of stiff flesh.'

'When he stopped ranting I laughed at him and told him that I didn't need what he had between his legs – I had no use for it – because in one hour I'd given you more pleasure than he ever did, all the times he'd made love to you. That made him splutter down the phone. He wanted to know how.'

'What did you tell him?'

'I told him to use his imagination and hung up.'

'After that, he'll certainly tell Remy about us, after he's calmed down,' Nicole said. 'Well, we've done it, *chérie*, we've punched our dear friend Remy in the eye.'

'Not in the eye,' Chantal said with a giggle. 'I think we've punched him lower down, where it hurts him more.'

While Chantal sat with her back to the headboard and related her curious conversation on the phone, Nicole was lying on her side with her legs stretched out straight. Chantal was looking at her all the time she was telling her what Lucien said to her and what she said to him. The way Nicole was lying gave Chantal a tantalising glimpse of the inside of her long smooth thighs.

More than mere admiration was involved now – Chantal's face was flushed a pretty pink and her gaze was fixed on Nicole's elegant breasts. Their charming little buds stood as firm as if they'd been fondled. Chantal reached down to touch the nearest with a gentle fingertip – and soon her gaze slid down Nicole's smooth belly. Finally she was staring in affection at the little triangle of dark-brown curls.

At this Nicole smiled knowingly and reached up to stroke the inside of Chantal's thigh.

'*Chérie*,' she said. 'I see that talking to Lucien has made you excited – so what am I to believe? Am I to conclude that you want him to roll you over on your back and push his very ordinary part into you?'

'Don't say that,' Chantal breathed as her thighs opened for Nicole's stroking hand. 'Don't even think it, *chérie* – I wouldn't let Lucien touch me with his fingers, far less with his *you-know-what*.'

'But you are excited,' Nicole said while her fingers traced lightly over the lips of Chantal's *joujou*. 'Why then?'

'All the time I was telling Lucien that we were together I was thinking how we made love to each other and I felt myself becoming wet – I had to put my hand down between my legs.'

'I was right – it was like an anonymous phone call,' Nicole said with a grin.

'I knew it was all ridiculous, yet I couldn't help myself,' Chantal said, pink-faced in some small confusion. 'I wanted to end the conversation. I knew I had to break away from Lucien's voice and his words before I went too far and gave myself a sudden climax with my fingertip.'

'And all because you were thinking about me?' Nicole said with a lifted eyebrow. 'Am I to feel flattered?'

'There was also what you said about punching Remy – and what I said,' Chantal added.

'I can see there is passion in the way you are sitting with your knees apart and in the way your body is trembling,' Nicole said. 'But I do not believe this passion was aroused by desire for me – it springs from a lust for revenge on Remy. Confess it now – when you were having me a little while ago, you were really getting your own back on him.'

Chantal didn't answer. With her long blue satin dressing-gown flapping open around her she rolled Nicole over on her back. In another moment later her face was between Nicole's thighs. Her wet tongue flickered over the lips of her *joujou* before probing inside – to settle in earnest on Nicole's pink and secret bud.

'Chantal,' Nicole moaned – and she broke into little gasps and squirmed and twisted on her back until Chantal had to grip her thighs and hold her down on the bed.

This talk of Remy and putting him down had its effect on Nicole as well as Chantal. Both women were aroused – they shook with strong sensation, their thinking was focussed on the need to achieve an urgent release of their emotions – a release which would celebrate their liberation from Remy and their triumph over him.

Pinned on her back as she was, Nicole's legs flew up in the air, sometimes kicking wildly at nothing at all and sometimes clenched tight round Chantal's head. She lifted herself on her arms, she fell back again, she lifted her bottom off the bed – she wriggled and quaked – she moaned in a hot sexual frenzy.

The orgasms ripping through Nicole's beautiful body were too many and too close together for Chantal to keep count of. And she herself was in so powerful a fury of desire that she was unable to stop bringing them on – she used her tongue relentlessly. This went on for what seemed an eternity to both women, but Nicole's frantic struggles stopped eventually and she fell limp.

'No more now . . .' she murmured. 'No more, *chérie*.'

At about ten that evening they compelled themselves to break away from each other while they ate and drank. They sat naked in Chantal's kitchen and ate cold chicken with their fingers, and then Camembert cheese with a bunch of grapes. They told each other their secrets while they were drinking a bottle of chilled white wine.

Chantal revealed that her first lover had been a woman. That was when she was seventeen, she said. The woman who had taught her to love had been witty and charming – and about ten years older than herself. Her name was Mireille – Chantal had slept in Mireille's scented bed many a night, enduring black looks and questions at home from her parents.

When Chantal was twenty she fell in love again – with a man – to her astonishment. His name was Charles and he happened to be her own sister's husband. Chantal couldn't understand what was happening to her heart. As for Charles, he was infatuated by his little sister-in-law and he pursued her ardently.

Chantal didn't resist. She wanted to know what this emotion was that drove men and women so fiercely together – however unsuitable they might be for each other. She let Charles do what he knew how to do well – he took her out in his car one evening and parked in a quiet place. He kissed her and fondled her breasts and put his hand up her skirt.

Before very long he had her knickers off and his trousers undone – she was holding a length of stiff flesh in her hand. This was the first one she'd touched in her life – the size and strength of it amazed her – and frightened her a little. Minutes later she and Charles were in the back of his car – he was sitting and she was straddling his thighs, while he guided her down and his hard shaft up and in.

Chantal was used to the tenderness of Mireille's fingers and tongue between her legs. After that, the long hard penetration by Charles was startling. It gave her sensations which were uncontrollable – and very soon they became staggering in their intensity. Charles had her by the nape of her neck, his mouth glued to hers, while he made fast little thrusting movements into her wide-stretched *joujou*.

Conventional wisdom says that a girl's first time with a man never leads to an orgasm. For Chantal it did – Charles' urgent little thrusts stirred her so powerfully that she reached a climax before he did. She clung to him frantically while her body bucked and squirmed on his fleshy length.

After that first stupefying time in the back of a Peugeot, Chantal was addicted and couldn't get enough. Charles was in seventh heaven – he had a beautiful young girl so eager for him that she couldn't keep her hand out of his trousers. He met her at every opportunity and he pounded away at her until they achieved temporary satisfaction.

But it was never often enough and Chantal hounded him until her sister became suspicious. Suddenly Charles was never there when Chantal tried to get in touch. As for Mireille, she also suspected what was going on and she was angry and hurt. But that affair too was over, now Chantal wanted a man's version of love.

In the years since Charles, she told Nicole, there had been many boyfriends – some better at love-making than others.

'How many – I want you to tell me – ten, twelve, more?'

'More than twenty,' Chantal said, 'but Remy was the last. No man will ever betray me again.'

Nicole sighed.

'If only it were that simple,' she said, 'we let men betray us only because we betray ourselves. Let me tell you about the husband of a dear friend of mine. His name is Jacques and he is in love with me in spite of himself – he hates me because he loves me. He makes me take my knickers off and do things to him in his office – with his secretary listening on the other side of the door.'

Chantal giggled and demanded to be told more.

At eight on Monday morning the alarm clock woke them up from an untroubled sleep. They had slept mouth to mouth and in each other's arms, sweetly fatigued by their long hours of stroking and loving. Chantal groaned and kissed Nicole's cheek before rolling out of bed and making for the bathroom naked. Ten minutes later she came back and began to open cupboards and drawers in search of underwear.

'I refuse to believe this is happening,' Nicole said, staring at her in outrage. 'What are you doing? It's far too early to get up. Are you going somewhere?'

'To my office,' Chantal said. 'I have to work for a living. It's Monday morning and there will be meetings and discussions and phone calls to make. I wish I didn't have to leave you, but I must.'

'How boring,' Nicole said, stretching out luxuriously in the bed. 'Must you really go?'

'We'll be together this evening,' Chantal promised as she stepped into a pair of small black knickers and slid them up her long legs.

'You're hiding just what I want to kiss *Bonjour*,' Nicole said, her eyelids lowered provocatively.

She threw aside the covers. She was lying on her side, her beautiful body naked. Chantal stood and stared at her – all she had put on so far were the little black knickers, her full round breasts swayed as she moved a step closer to the bed.

'You're a beast,' Chantal sighed as she sat on the side of the bed and leaned over to stroke Nicole's bottom. 'You're doing this to torment me.'

Nicole turned on her back and put one knee up to open her legs and display her neat little triangle of curls.

'You don't have to go if you don't want to,' she said. 'You can phone and say you are not well and need to stay in bed.'

Chantal leaned down to kiss Nicole's breasts and run her tongue over the little buds until they stood firm.

'You're right,' she sighed. 'I can't leave you now, I adore you too much.'

She flung herself on top of Nicole, breasts to breasts and belly on belly, legs between her legs, soft flesh rubbing over soft flesh until both women were sobbing with a pleasure beyond words. They writhed and twisted together and entwined like two snakes coupling – Chantal was on top of Nicole, then she underneath her, Nicole was lying on Chantal and grinding her belly against hers.

'*Je t'adore*,' Nicole moaned.

'*Je t'aime*,' Chantal moaned back.

That afternoon they shared a scented bubble-bath, kissing lightly while they washed each other with gentle hands. When they climbed out at last and patted each other dry with fluffy towels, Chantal sank to one knee, her hands on Nicole's hips while she kissed her little patch of dark brown curls.

'You keep it so pretty,' she said.

'I think a straggly little fur coat looks very unpleasing on a woman,' Nicole answered. 'Don't you agree?'

'I've never given it a thought. I've always been *au naturel*, just as you see. Would it look better if I trimmed it?'

'I'll do it for you,' Nicole offered.

In the bedroom they spread a large white towel over one side of the bed for Chantal to put her bottom on. Obeying Nicole's instructions, she lay back on the bed, her legs over the side and her feet on the floor. She lay with her knees well apart while Nicole used the little nail-scissors from the dressing table to trim her curls – the colour was a rich chestnut-brown, very stylish, but Chantal's patch was too large and unshapen.

A minute's work reduced it to a clear-edged little triangle, thinning out what Nicole said was excessive growth. After that came an application of the little razor Chantal used for under her arms. The blade slid over the soft skin of her belly like a kiss – she gave little sighs of delight to feel the touch of the sharp steel edge.

'*Voilà*, now you are chic,' Nicole told her. 'Lie still and I'll smooth some of your moisturising cream in to prevent any soreness.'

Chantal closed her eyes and felt Nicole's hands on her belly, smoothing and kneading.

'Have you made me very beautiful?' she asked.

'I've made you so beautiful that you are irresistible. It's lucky for you there's no man here with us – one look at your *joujou* now I've barbered it and he would fling himself on you and ravish you senseless.'

Her fingers were on Chantal's open thighs and in her bare groins, stroking and pressing. They touched the lips of her *joujou* and caressed up and down the length of them before they opened her gently.

'Not just lucky for me – it's lucky for both of us Remy's not here,' Chantal murmured. 'You are as naked as I am – if he was here he'd have you on your back as well as me.'

'No, he wouldn't,' Nicole said firmly. 'He's a creature of the past – remember that. I'm the one who's about to ravish you senseless.'

A throb of delicious sensation ran through Chantal and made her tremble. She opened her eyes to see Nicole's head between her legs and felt her hot tongue press into her just-bathed and scented *joujou*.

'You are the only one I adore, Nicole,' she said in a husky voice. 'Not Remy and not any man – you, *chérie*, you.'

The smooth tip of Nicole's tongue slithered over Chantal's bud and sent little spasms of pleasure through her. Very soon Chantal felt the urgent approach of her climax. She jerked her belly up and down – her back arched and her heels drummed on the soft bed.

'Nicole,' she cried out, ecstasy flooding through her.

Sept 25 – Tuesday

Time was passing as if in a dream – hours became a day, then two days. We kissed and talked and loved, minute by minute and hour after hour, never knowing or caring whether it was night or day outside. We never left Chantal's apartment, except for an hour in the evening to eat in a restaurant. Then back to her bed, where we lay naked, exhaling and inhaling love and desire.

After a lunch that was only a toasted sandwich and a glass of wine in a café near the Montparnasse Metro station Nicole took Chantal to her own apartment. She felt they needed a change of scene – and for herself she needed a change of clothes. There was a letter waiting for her when they arrived – there were several, in fact – but the one that caught her attention had no stamp on it. That meant the writer must have delivered it by hand.

Nicole took Chantal into the sitting-room and was pleased when she said how elegant it was. After a while they went into the bedroom – Chantal insisted on seeing it – and said it was perfect. She looked at the broad rosewood bed in a meaningful way.

'New bed, new love,' she said.

'Ah, you are as insatiable as I am,' Nicole said with a smile. 'But let me see who this letter is from – it might be important.'

She tore open the pale blue envelope and pulled out the folded pages inside. What a surprise! It was a letter from Jacques Lecomte – which made Nicole wrinkle her forehead in mild bewilderment. He'd never written to her before and she could think of no reason why he should write to her now.

More surprises were to come. Jacques wrote that he had been trying to phone her for days because it was very urgent, but she was never there. He assumed she must be away somewhere with Remy Toussaint.

It's none of Jacques' business where I am, Nicole told herself, *and he's terribly wrong about who I've been with – what a shock for him when I tell him I've spent the past days with a beautiful woman. He'll go very solemn and tell me I've developed a complex with a long name and that I need to be psychoanalysed instantly.*

'Well, is it important?' Chantal asked, seeing the puzzled look on her friend's face.

'I don't think so,' Nicole said. 'At least, it doesn't seem to have any significance for me – but I'll tell you in a minute.'

Jacques' letter went on to say that it was essential that he talked to her, though he didn't explain why it was essential. He begged her to phone him the moment she found his note.

But that was only the beginning of it – there were two hand-written pages. Nicole read the letter through quickly and couldn't make out what it was about – or why Jacques had written it to her.

'Listen to this,' she said to Chantal. 'And tell me what you think.'

She read from halfway down the first page:

What I need to believe is that you are capable of feeling so much for me that you cannot at the same time be interested in another man. But that would be to deceive myself cruelly – I know you too well and I understand your nature – I must accept that it is impossible for you to feel very strongly for any man – for me, for Remy, for Gerard – or for any other.

There is a fearful and painful joy in loving you, Nicole – in loving you and knowing that however receptive you may be at the time, you can never really love anyone whole-heartedly.

Chantal was standing by the window, her round-breasted body was in silhouette against the light. She'd picked up from the bedside table a copy of Nicole's novel, *The Anxious Heart*, and was flicking through the pages.

'Who's the letter from?' she asked. 'It's nonsense.'

'It's from Jacques Lecomte – I told you about him.'

'Your psychoanalyst admirer, you mean?'

Nicole nodded.

'The man with the strange ambition to caress your mind as well as other parts of you?' Chantal went on. 'The solemn idiot you ran away from in his consulting-room with his trousers undone and your knickers wrapped round his length – that man?'

'You make it sound like his entire dismal life-story. But yes, that's him,' Nicole agreed.

Chantal looked at her for further explanation.

'It's weeks since I saw him,' Nicole said. 'I don't understand why he's written this to me now. He's never written to me before.'

'There's no mystery about it – he's telling you that he's in love with you,' said Chantal, turning to face her with a smile on her face.

'Oh that, yes,' Nicole said, shrugging casually. 'Of course he's in love with me – I expect no less. But Jacques is a self-aware man who keeps his own emotions well hidden while he investigates other people's emotions and fears. This sort of confession isn't his style at all.'

'He's been missing you, that's obvious,' Chantal said. 'He's desperate to have you with your legs in the air.'

'There's never been anything serious between us,' Nicole said, still puzzled by the letter. 'We play a game together, that's all.'

'The only game men understand is kicking a ball about,' Chantal said dryly. 'They never understand our sort of games – they think they can change the rules when it suits them.'

'I suppose you're right, *chérie*.'

'Of course I'm right. Your friend Jacques wants you to rush to him and let him take your knickers down so that he can psychoanalyse you.'

'This presents certain problems,' said Nicole, folding up the letter and putting it back in the envelope. 'His wife Annette is a dear friend of mine and the last thing I want to do is upset her.'

'That ought to have crossed your mind the first time her

husband put his hand up your skirt,' Chantal said with a shrug.

There was a lot to be discussed in Jacques' letter – and yet from another point of view there was nothing to be discussed at all. Before the two women could involve themselves any further in the matter, the doorbell rang abruptly.

'*Merde*,' Nicole exclaimed. 'That could be him now – he might be here to make sure I've got his idiotic letter.'

'He sounds very impatient to get in,' Chantal said as the bell rang again continuously – as if whoever was outside was leaning on the push with his thumb. 'Impatient for your door to open and then your legs.'

'Oh God, he'll try to make a big scene about how he loves me and I don't love him,' Nicole said. 'Thank heaven you're here with me – he can't do much of a broken heart routine in front of you.'

'That's true,' Chantal said. 'He'll have to keep the details of his *fearful and painful joy* to himself. Though I must say I'm fascinated to see what he's like, this idiot psychoanalyst of yours.'

'Go into the sitting-room and make yourself comfortable while I let him in,' Nicole suggested. 'Between us we'll soon get rid of him.'

She went to the apartment entrance, paused to take a deep breath and put an impassive look on her face – her intention was to pretend she had no idea of what Jacques' letter meant – he'd have to explain it to her – and with Chantal present and listening that should embarrass him to the point of running away red-faced.

She opened the door. There to her consternation stood not a lovelorn Jacques but an angry-looking Remy Toussaint in a blue suit. Naturally, this moment with Remy had to happen sometime – the confrontation was inevitable – but it was unexpected just then. She stared at him blankly.

'Nicole – what have you done?' he demanded, without a word of greeting. 'I can't believe what I've been told – I want the truth.'

'Do come in, Remy,' she said ironically as he pushed past her – as if he owned the place.

The sitting-room was empty – Chantal was not to be seen. She must have recognised Remy's angry voice at the door and was keeping out of the way. Nicole was on her own to face him in his baffled fury. He stood facing her, he refused to sit down – she tried to defuse the situation by taking an armchair herself. But as soon as she sat she saw it was not a very good idea, because it meant he was looming over her.

'What's the matter, Remy?' she asked, trying to sound unconcerned.

'You and Chantal Lamartine,' he said angrily. 'Is it true?'

'Is what true? You're being very obscure.'

'You know what I'm talking about – there's no point in pretending not to. Were you in bed with Chantal on Sunday when Lucien phoned?'

'Is it true that you were in bed with her last Thursday, Remy?' Nicole countered.

'You're trying to evade the question,' he said. 'Have you and Chantal been to bed together – yes or no?'

'I'm not evading anything – there's no reason why I should, I'm not the one feeling guilty. But fair is fair. You know very well that I've been to bed with Chantal and I know very well that you've been to bed with her too. Does that even things up?'

'Nothing makes sense any more,' he said passionately. 'I thought you loved me – you told me you loved me – I believed that you love me. How can you do this to me?'

'You told me that you loved me, Remy. You also told Chantal that you loved her. Either we were all mistaken or some of us were lying.'

'No, no, no,' he said, his anger evaporating quickly now – in fact he sounded as if he would burst into tears at any moment. 'I've never lied to you – I swear I love you, Nicole.'

'And tomorrow when you see Chantal you'll tell her that you love her. Maybe she'll believe you, but I don't.'

Nicole was not feeling well disposed toward Chantal at that moment. She felt she'd been deserted at a difficult time and left to face Remy by herself.

'How can I persuade you?' Remy said in a heartbroken tone, 'I know I've been stupid – what can I do to make up for my stupidity? I'll do anything – just tell me what will convince you that I'm sincere.'

Nicole stared at him doubtfully, wondering if he intended to get down on his knees and grovel and kiss her feet in abject apology – perhaps even shed a few tears. It would be amusing to watch him abase himself in the hope of regaining her affections. Then she would have the further pleasure of disillusioning him before kicking him out.

Before any of that could happen Chantal made a grand entrance into the sitting-room – barefoot and naked. She'd stripped off in the bedroom for this moment – except for her small white knickers with the lace edging. Remy swung round when he heard the door open and stared in open-mouthed amazement at Chantal. She was enjoying the moment to the utmost as she walked towards him over the parquet and the carpet, with her full round breasts swaying.

'Nicole *chérie*, what's taking you so long out here?' she asked, ignoring Remy as if he wasn't there. 'Come back to bed, I'm lonely and bored without you.'

She had an alluring smile on her face, directed at Nicole. Then her smile vanished dramatically as she pretended to catch sight of Remy for the first time.

'Oh, it's you,' she said, putting her nose in the air. 'What do you want?'

Remy was gesturing with his hands and making gobbling noises. The enormity of the situation seemed to have reduced him to near-idiocy. Chantal strolled casually past him, to where Nicole was sitting in her armchair. She displayed her bottom to Remy as she leaned over to kiss Nicole – he stared blindly and open-mouthed at two shapely cheeks in thin white knickers. Chantal sat down on Nicole's lap and hugged her.

'I've borrowed some of your perfume,' Chantal said. 'Do you think it suits me – it's a little more musky than the one I usually wear.'

She lifted her bare breasts on her palms a little to let Nicole catch the expensive fragrance between them.

'My very favourite perfume,' Nicole said fondly. 'I've worn it for years – I think it suits almost everyone except very thin women. It's very sexy on you.'

'I dabbed a little of it between my legs,' Chantal told her with an affectionate smile.

'In case I kiss you there, I suppose,' Nicole said, stroking a pink-tipped bare breast lightly with her fingertips.

They talked as if they were alone, as if there was no dumbfounded Remy standing almost within touching-distance of them, staring as if his eyes were on stalks. It took a little while before he realised how totally excluded he was from the events and with a snort he turned on his heel and strode out of the room. Three seconds later they heard the door slam hard and they giggled.

Nicole took Chantal in her arms and hugged her close.

'It was a stroke of genius to take your clothes off and walk in like that,' she said. 'Remy knows the truth now – he's seen with his own eyes what Lucien told him. We're rid of Remy and his lies and deception.'

Chantal chuckled and slipped her hand up inside Nicole's black rollneck sweater to undo her bra and cup a breast. There had been no time for Nicole to change her clothes before Remy arrived and she was wearing the same sweater and skirt as when they first met, which was days ago – though for most of the time between she had been naked.

'It destroyed him to see us sitting here like this,' she said happily. 'Me naked on your lap. And it excited him – did you see the bulge in the front of his trousers when he was staring at us? He wanted to drag us both into the bedroom and throw us on our backs with our legs in the air – and he knew that he never would.'

'I didn't notice that,' Nicole said, trembling a little at the touch of Chantal's fingers on the firm tips of her breasts. 'I was too occupied in enjoying the stunned expression on his face, I didn't look at his trousers.'

'We gave him what he deserves – we humiliated him,' Chantal said. 'He was definitely stiff in his underwear – the bulge was unmistakable and that's I had to try hard to stop myself giggling at him.'

'We've finished with Remy and what he has in his underwear,' Nicole said. 'Turn your thoughts and desires to what I have between my legs, *ma chére* – it is much more beautiful and sexy than what he has.'

Their lips touched in a soft kiss while Chantal's hands were gliding over Nicole's perfect breasts under her fine wool sweater. *Oh yes* she sighed to the caress of fingertips on little buds.

'This is a moment to remember forever,' Chantal said. 'The first time we make love in your apartment.'

'Our very first time ever was on your marvellous black velvet chaise-longue,' Nicole said softly. 'The instant I saw it I knew I had to have you on it. The black velvet appealed strongly to my imagination – it suggested luxury and sexuality – and a most delicate perversity that excited me. I could visualise your beautiful naked body lying there, a contrast against the black – it was very thrilling.'

By now Chantal was sitting on the carpet between Nicole's feet and pressing her knees apart.

'In the bedroom,' Nicole whispered. 'Let's lie on my bed for our first time here.'

'In a moment,' Chantal said.

She undid Nicole's check skirt and slid it down her legs – and then her jet-black knickers, to reveal her neat little patch of curls. She leaned forward to trail her wet tongue very slowly down Nicole's belly and flick it over the curls and the soft lips.

'Yes . . . yes . . . yes,' Nicole sighed faintly.

She pulled her sweater over her head and was naked except for her stockings. She brought her knees up, with her heels on the edge of the chair-seat and her thighs splayed wide, a frank posture that exposed her *joujou* completely. She was murmuring to herself while Chantal kissed the smooth flesh of the insides of her thighs above her stocking-tops, up into her groins.

'Remy has never kissed you as sexily as I do,' Chantal said.

She pulled the lips of Nicole's *joujou* open and slid her tongue between them. She ran the tip over her bud and made her moan and shake in delight.

'No one has ever kissed me as sexily as you, Chantal.'

Her *joujou* was an open pink blossom and Chantal knew that she was very near already to orgasm. She gathered her legs under her and rose slowly with her wet and open mouth sliding slowly up Nicole's naked body, from her *joujou* to her breasts.

Another moment and all would be over in gasping spasms and shuddering limbs – but Chantal stopped in time and grinned and offered Nicole her hand. They went into the bedroom together – Nicole stood with legs apart while Chantal knelt to roll her stockings down her legs and take them off.

'Will you be my sex slave, *chérie*?' Nicole murmured.

'Whenever you want me,' Chantal said.

She rose to her feet slowly, steadying herself with both her hands on Nicole's hips, until the two women were eye to eye, nose to nose and breast to breast. She pressed her mouth to Nicole's mouth and pushed her tongue inside, while her long fingers stroked gently down between her thighs.

'Was Remy your sex slave?' Chantal asked when the long kiss finally ended.

Nicole was puzzled and not at all pleased by the way Remy kept creeping into the conversation at a time like this. Evidently Chantal wasn't able to get him out of her mind. If so, that suggested all sorts of needless complications – and it also suggested that the feelings between Chantal and herself were not as they seemed and perhaps never could be.

'I hardly think so,' said Nicole.

She sat on the side of the bed and leaned back on her arms, with her legs stretched out in front of her. Chantal looked in admiration at the slender and naked body spread out for her – at Nicole's pointed breasts, at her smooth belly and her little triangle of brown curls.

Nicole looked back at her, her eyes half-closed. Her glance moved slowly down from Chantal's flushed face to her breasts and then to the neat little patch between her legs. She smiled and said nothing, but she was deep in thought about the future.

Chantal dropped to her knees between Nicole's legs and stroked her *joujou*.

'Just between us – will you miss the feeling of a man's hard thing inside you?' she asked quietly.

Nicole said nothing yet, but she began to move her hips and belly slowly, only a few centimetres, but enough to rub her trim little thicket against Chantal's hand.

'What are you thinking?' Chantal asked. 'Are you asking yourself if you'll miss being penetrated by a long stiff thing – are you asking if my tongue will keep you happy and satisfied forever? Tell me.'

'And you, *chérie*,' Nicole said slowly. 'Will it be enough for you?'

'Always,' Chantal assured her at once, but she said it too sincerely to convince Nicole that it was the truth.

As if to demonstrate her undying devotion, Chantal turned her hand over, palm upward, and drew her middle finger slowly up between the lips of Nicole's *joujou* to open them. Nicole continued to move her hips and rub herself against the fingertip inside her.

'You haven't answered my question,' Chantal said.

'Not yet,' Nicole said.

'I must know – tell me now,' Chantal insisted.

She threw herself on top of Nicole, pressing her down flat on her back on the bed. Her thighs were between Nicole's thighs and her mouth was pressed over Nicole's mouth. Nicole held her tight, her hands clenched hard on the cheeks of Chantal's bottom.

'*Je t'aime*, Nicole,' Chantal sighed.

Nicole gripped her tighter and rolled over and over again until they were full-length on the bed and facing each other. Her hand was between them to caress Chantal's *joujou*. At once Chantal sobbed and pushed her bare belly against her.

'Yes,' Chantal was moaning. 'Don't stop, *cherie*—'

'Oh yes, yes . . .' Nicole murmured.

They clung to each other eagerly. They were lost in love and pleasure and wanted it to last forever – and they both knew it wouldn't.

Nicole's Diary – Sept 26 – Wednesday

Today I learned something very important to me – the truth is that I am only a tourist in the beautiful island of Lesbos, I am not a citizen. But then, it is vacationing tourists in all the world's desirable places who enjoy the natural amenities more than those who were born there and have lived all their lives there and take these delights for granted.

It was after ten in the morning Nicole's doorbell rang. By then Chantal had been gone for hours – she insisted she really must go to her office. She brought Nicole a cup of coffee in bed and pulled her nightdress up and kissed her belly warmly and departed, promising to phone later. Nicole lay comfortably propped on the big soft pillows while she drank her coffee and considered the events of the past few days.

There was much for her to think about and try to make sense of. For a start, the end of her passionate love affair with faithless Remy and then the beginning of a new love affair with beautiful Chantal. These events had developed so quickly that Nicole felt she had no influence over her life – at least for the moment, and this displeased her.

Two hours later she was still in bed, not even thinking of getting up yet, when the doorbell announced an unexpected caller. She slipped into a short and lacy negligee and went barefoot to see who could be at the door.

Perhaps it was Remy, returning to beg her again to forgive him. If it was, then Remy was due for another ritual humiliation, however sincerely he might beg and plead. Nicole thought she would enjoy that, letting him stare with big eyes at her body through her open negligee and her flimsy nightdress – that would make him suffer, not being able to touch her.

As soon as she saw a bulge in his trousers at the sight of her almost unconcealed charms she would laugh in his face and kick him out of the apartment.

Or it could be Jacques at the door. In his mysterious letter he'd said that he must speak to her urgently – Nicole hadn't given herself the bother of phoning him. He might have a lot to say to her, but for the moment she had nothing much to say to him. But she admired Jacques, and if it was him outside, she'd ask him in and offer him coffee.

It would be amusing to tease him by making him sit in the kitchen with her while they drank it. He would be big-eyed with desire as he stared at her beautiful body through her flimsy negligee and nightdress. He'd cross his legs to hide his stiffness and his cheeks would turn pink.

He'd want to get his hand up her nightdress and fondle her breasts – every man she ever met wanted to do that. And for Jacques she'd flirt a little while she secretly laughed at him. When he tried to put his arms about her and kiss her and slip a hand into her negligee she'd tell him that she was in love with Chantal.

That news would disconcert him. Being an expert, or so he believed himself to be, on the reasons why people did what they did – a trained psychoanalyst with a big leather couch for patients to lie on – he'd want to ask Nicole a thousand questions about why she was attracted to another woman.

Poor Jacques wouldn't get an answer to his questions, of course. She had no intention of explaining herself to him. Instead, she'd ask him to explain what he meant by his letter – she was sure that would embarrass him. If he became suitably humble, she might let him kiss her lightly on the mouth before she sent him back to Annette.

Because that's where he belonged, with Annette. Nicole was clear now that she ought never to have permitted her friend's husband to make love to her in the first place. It could only lead to difficulties and broken friendship. Jacques would have to learn how to confine his passions to his own home and bed.

So all that was settled in Nicole's mind while she went to answer the doorbell. When she opened the door, it was neither

Jacques nor Remy standing there with hearts full of hope and remorse and other emotions too complicated to bother with. It was Gerard Constant – someone she hadn't seen for a long time – at least a month.

In fact, she hadn't seen him since the July day she was strolling by the Seine and met him by chance – he was on his way back to his office after lunch. As things turned out, he didn't get as far as his office that afternoon because he went home with Nicole instead.

Not that she had had any intention of letting him make love to her, not after the despicable way he'd treated her by marrying someone else. She'd taken him home with her just to tantalise him and make him suffer by making him realise what he'd lost.

With that in mind she took her clothes off and lay on her bed for his admiration and to make him despair. She made it clear that he could only admire her with his eyes – no hands or touching were allowed.

But as is very often the case, one thing led to another. She still had a lingering affection for Gerard and after a while there seemed no harm in letting him kiss her bare belly – that would really make him suffer the pangs of frustration, or so she told herself.

Naturally, she was deceiving herself with these rationalisations of her own unacknowledged desires. Or perhaps only half-deceived herself. She made no objection when Gerard raised his lips from her warm belly and kissed her between the thighs. He kissed her so nicely that her thighs moved apart on the bed to let him continue. Gerard was more aware of her unacknowledged desires than she was herself.

Certainly he knew what he was doing. He was trying to excite her past caring and then he'd jump on her. But that would be a complete surrender on her part – and it was unthinkable. She reached down to take hold of him by the shoulders and pull him up over her body – as if inviting him to put his belly on hers and penetrate her.

He fell for her ruse, he slid up over her and showered hot kisses on her breasts. And she put a stop to his ambitions to claim his rights over her body – while he was engrossed in kissing her breasts she took hold of his throbbing part. He thought she meant to steer him into her – she had something quite different in mind. Her fingers flicked up and down and he was so aroused that he spurted over her smooth bare belly.

He'd been wearing a white summer suit that July afternoon. Today he was in stylish light grey, with a blue-striped silk tie when she opened the apartment door and found him standing there.

'Oh,' Gerard said uncertainly, looking at Nicole's negligee and bare feet. 'Have I disturbed you – is someone with you?'

'No one is with me,' she said, 'all you have disturbed is my train of thought. Come in, Gerard.'

She held out her hand to him with a smile – in some strange way she couldn't explain to herself she was pleased to see him. He kissed her hand and then her cheek. Before he could put his arms round her for any more intimate embrace she led him to her bedroom. There she took off her negligee and got back into bed.

'I'm not ready to get up yet,' she announced casually, 'I hope you've no objection to talking to me in bed. Bring up a chair and tell me why you are here, Gerard.'

He was at a loss, of course, as she intended him to be. Of course he had no objection to conversing with her in bed. He stood with his mouth open, staring at her, as any man would. Nicole's nightdress was square cut and low across the breasts, and threaded with pale blue ribbon. She lay propped on her pillows, her slender arms and her shoulders bare, the bedclothes lay across her waist.

'A chair,' she repeated. 'Sit down, Gerard.'

He stood there looking at her, his eyes bright with his undeclared but unconcealed desire.

'You ask too much,' he said.

'Be calm,' she said. 'Or I shall insist that you leave.'

'I will try,' he murmured, his trousers bulging, 'but do not be too harsh on me.'

He didn't bring up a chair, he sat on the edge of the bed and she let it pass. After a moment or two he took her in his arms and hugged her.

'It is enough just to see you,' he said huskily.

'But what do you want, Gerard?' she asked – she was trying to maintain her casual approach, though it was an unnecessary question. 'Why are you here?'

'For love, love, love – I want love,' he said, holding her tighter to him. His hands felt hot on her back through the thin nightdress.

'Am I only a plaything then?' she asked. 'You expect me to lie on my back and allow myself to be used by you?'

'I mean love,' he said. 'Sincere and enduring love – I want to be with you all the time. I will crouch at your feet and lick your shoes if you ask me to.'

'You have a poet's soul after all,' Nicole said. 'But only consider, *chéri*, life is not as simple as you might wish it to be – you have a charming young wife at home waiting for you – and I love someone you do not even know.'

'None of that matters,' Gerard said forcefully. 'None of it is even worth a mention.'

His hands were no longer on her back, he'd slipped them up inside her short nightdress and they were gliding over her breasts. She sighed when his fingertips touched her little buds. She had clear memories of the impressive proportions of what was to be encountered inside Gerard's underwear.

The fact was that Gerard was more than handsomely provided – he had a solidly imposing shaft. In the days when they were lovers she'd nicknamed it *Gerard-le-Grand* and she'd delighted in holding it in two clasping hands with fingers interlaced. So much hot hard flesh – even now the memory sent a quiver of pleasure through her belly.

Besides his obvious advantage, dear Gerard was so very easy to tease – Nicole decided there was no reason to deny herself half an hour of amusement.

She sat up in bed and stretched her back like a cat before pulling her nightdress above her breasts. Gerard ducked his head and kissed them. His tongue flicked over the firm pink buds. Nicole drew the nightdress over her head and dropped it on the bed. Gerard threw the bedclothes aside and trailed his tongue down her bare belly.

'I am not your plaything,' she sighed faintly. 'If you want

to stay you must crouch at my feet and beg me not to send you away – that's what you said you'd do.'

He slid to the floor on his knees. Nicole moved to the side of the bed and turned toward him. She put her feet flat on the floor and smiled down at his serious face.

'Well?' she said, her eyebrows arching upward.

'*Je t'adore*, Nicole,' he murmured, and he took her left foot in his hand and kissed it hotly.

This is not a love affair, Nicole said to herself, *it has nothing to do with love or with respect or anything important. The one I love is Chantal, no one else. I want nothing more to do with deceitful men. But for the simple sake of my artistic integrity I ought to remind myself of the sexual sensations of being penetrated by a man – and who better to experiment with than a man as massively well-built as this particular man down on his knees at my bedside?*

Having explained to herself, to her own satisfaction, why she wanted to do what she was about to do, she did it. She slid her knees apart – instantly Gerard leaned over to push his tongue into the open pink interior of her *joujou* and lick at her secret bud.

'I have always been very fond of you, Gerard,' she said, stroking his hair. 'You know that – and you take advantage of my affection for you. You turn up unexpected and unannounced to abuse my body for your selfish pleasure.'

'No, no,' he said. 'It is you who always takes advantage of my helpless adoration for you.'

'Do you adore me, Gerard? It hasn't been very obvious – I thought so once, but you insulted and demeaned me and hurt me by your actions.'

'But you have forgiven me,' he said knowingly. 'Otherwise you wouldn't let me be here with you now.'

He was smiling up at her while he expressed his impudent thoughts. But what he said was true, and Nicole didn't deny it. And even though he was on his knees on the floor, Gerard somehow struggled out of his clothes. His stylish grey jacket, shirt, blue-striped tie, trousers, underwear, black silk socks – all scattered about him carelessly on the bedside carpet.

Nicole was captivated, as she always had been in the past, by his broad chest and the dark curly hair on it and by his lean belly. Most of all she was fascinated by the stiff length of flesh standing up from between his thighs.

He bent to kiss her *joujou* again, then straightened his legs slowly and pushed upward. His mouth moved up over her belly, up to her breasts, then higher still, and he was rearing over her with his body between her spread thighs. Nicole wanted to hold his long stiff male shaft, she wanted to feel its hardness and its strength. She reached for it and pressed it between her breasts.

Gerard gasped and slid with little jabs along the smooth skin of her chest – he was making love to Nicole's breasts in celebration of their perfection. He put his hands on her shoulders to hold her close. Her cheek was against his belly and with both hands she squeezed her breasts about his solid fleshy part.

'Oh Nicole,' he gasped – his body was shaking violently.

His little sliding strokes became fast and furious. Nicole stared down in fascination and saw him spurt up as high as her throat and chin. She sighed and shuddered deliciously as she watched his passion fountain up from between her pink-tipped breasts – and it was in those moments that there came into her mind the certainty that her sexuality required men for its complete fulfilment.

In truth, she realised, she had never been more than a casual visitor to Lesbos. Her love-making with Chantal had been a pleasure trip to an unknown place. Chantal had guessed that at the time and tried to explain it to her. *Will you miss being penetrated by a man?* Chantal had asked her while they were making love. *Will my tongue keep you happy and satisfied forever?*

This sudden understanding of her own nature at the moment of Gerard's ecstasy aroused Nicole even more – she clung tightly to him while he gasped and sprayed his sticky desire over her smooth body.

When he was calm again she told him there was much they had to talk about – and she made him do what she wanted him to do before – bring a chair to the bedside and sit on it. He sat there naked, silently adoring her, his knees apart and his thick shaft dangling slackly between his strong thighs.

Nicole used her discarded nightdress to wipe away the wet smear from her chin and chest – by then it had trickled down between her breasts to her charming little belly button. Gerard watched her with shining eyes.

'I adore you more than I can ever tell you,' he said. 'But I find you impossible to understand.'

'Why should you expect to understand me?' she said at once. 'Do you take me for a simple housewife, Gerard?'

He knew better than to involve himself in that discussion. It would inevitably lead to reproaches about his own wife at home. Better to steer Nicole in a different direction.

'Not long ago you told me that you were in love with someone else,' he said, 'and to be truthful, my impression is that you still are – yet you have made me deliriously happy today.'

'If I tried to explain myself to you, you'd still not understand me,' Nicole said with a curious smile.

She was wondering what Gerard would think – and what he would say – if she told him that her lover was not another man and that she was in love with another woman?

'I meant what I said,' he told her. 'I was utterly sincere – believe me – I'd crawl on my belly to your feet and kiss your shoes, if that would please you.'

Nicole was still sitting on the side of the bed, facing him with a friendly look on her face – although she had put her knees together modestly now, to provoke his emotions.

'I believe you,' she said, stretching one perfect leg out to touch his dangling shaft with her toes. 'You kissed my foot – and that little gesture of devotion persuaded me to let you kiss me somewhere else.'

'Ah,' he said with a charming smile, 'if that's what kissing your pretty feet leads to, I'll go down on my knees and kiss them any time you'll let me.'

Under the rub of Nicole's bare toes with their pink-painted nails, his male part was starting to thicken and lengthen. She watched closely as her toes slid under it and lifted it as it straightened and began to stand upright.

'Any time at all?' she said, 'well then, demonstrate the sincerity of your adoration for me by kissing my beautiful backside, Gerard.'

'Oh yes, gladly,' he breathed.

He slid off the chair down on to his knees again. Nicole got off the bed and turned her long slender back to him – then she knelt herself. Her arms lay on the bed and she leaned forward to present the elegant cheeks of her bottom to him. He held her hips and rained kisses on those two smooth bare cheeks.

She trembled and sighed as his fingers stroked up the deep groove between the cheeks. She glanced over her shoulder with a little smile when she felt his wet tongue trailing over her warm flesh.

'There is no need for you to understand me,' she said, 'none at all – it's enough for you to adore me.'

He shuffled in close on his knees to press his upright shaft and his belly against her bottom. His hands were underneath her, holding a bare pointed breast in each palm.

'You're right,' he murmured. 'Understanding is meaningless.'

'It's good when you adore me,' Nicole said, and she rubbed her soft bottom against him.

'Then you must let me adore you all the time,' he said.

He responded to the wriggle of her bottom against him by kneading her breasts and running his fingertips over their firm little buds.

'Not all the time,' she said softly. 'You must remember that you are not the only one who adores me, *chéri*.'

Gerard sighed to hear this unwelcome reference to his unknown rival – but he was in no condition to object to it or even to argue about who adored her the most. Her round bare bottom was thrust at him in invitation, her thighs were parted and the pouting lips of her *joujou* were ready for him between the neat little brown curls.

His massive male part stood eagerly – he guided it to the waiting lips and a strong push took him in until his belly was tight against her. He gripped her waist while he slid in and out. Nicole met his long thrilling strokes by jerking back against him. Unseen by him her eyes were half-closed and she was sighing hard – she was so excited already that she was nearly at her ecstatic destination.

'I want you all the time, Nicole,' Gerard panted. 'All

day and all night – I can't stop thinking of you and wanting you—'

'Oh Gerard,' she sighed fondly, 'I can feel how much you want me.'

Indeed she could – his great hard shaft was sliding in her slippery *joujou*. It stretched her wide, it probed, it filled her, it sent shivers of delight through her panting body.

'*Je t'aime*, Nicole,' he gasped, ramming into her warm wetness with frantic strokes.

He spurted powerfully into her and her body bucked to the long spasms that shook her. There was no doubt in her mind now that these mighty sensations were what she truly wanted. She didn't love Chantal – making love with her was a pretty game – this was the reality.

She didn't love Gerard either – she didn't have to love him. To achieve the pleasure she needed constantly she only had to let Gerard love her – and express his love through his monster of a male part.

Secret Diary – Sept 28 – Friday

Annette phoned this morning and asked me to meet her. She made it sound urgent. If I could have guessed what she had to tell me, I might not have gone – the unexpected is sometimes very inconvenient. We do not always want to know our dear friends' secrets. On the other hand, there was a certain wry amusement in what Annette had to say – and proof that when we believe we understand someone, we are mistaken.

The Café de la Paix on the Place de l'Opera was busy at eleven in the morning. Nicole walked along the pavement on both sides of the café looking for Annette at the tables. She couldn't see her anywhere and went inside – and there she was, at a window table with a cup of black coffee and a small glass of cognac.

They kissed each other on both cheeks. Nicole looked at Annette's face closely, wondering what was in her mind. She showed signs of agitation, her cheeks were slightly flushed under her make-up.

'Jacques is having an affair,' Annette announced.

'What?' Nicole exclaimed.

Suddenly she was afraid that Annette knew about her and her husband. That would be a catastrophe. She had told herself a dozen times that she never should have let her friend's husband make love to her in the first place – but the past was the past and it couldn't be changed. It was true that she had promised herself not to let Jacques touch her again – she decided that a couple of days ago, when Gerard was with her. But the past might still return to haunt her.

'It's true,' Annette said. 'He's having an affair – what do you think of that?'

'But with who?' Nicole asked, trying not to panic.

Even as she asked the question she realised that Annette's suspicions lay elsewhere – if Annette believed it was her, she wouldn't sit calmly here in a café talking to her about it.

'I should have guessed before now,' Annette said, shaking her head.

'Surely not his receptionist?' Nicole said breathlessly, 'that would be too commonplace.'

From the first time Nicole had seen Mademoiselle Anvers at her desk outside Jacques' room she had been sure he played with her when no one else was about. There was the time Nicole went to talk to Jacques when Annette had gone to their country house with the baby – and had found Josette Anvers in an ivory blouse with a bow at the neck instead of her usual black business-like dress.

Her hair was fluffed up in soft waves that day, not pulled back over her ears. Josette had made herself attractive for the boss, while his wife was away. Her skirt had been so tight it showed the shape of her thighs and the cheeks of her bottom – and a very round one it was.

There was no doubt in Nicole's mind that Jacques' secretary-receptionist sat on his lap when they were alone – and he put his hand in her blouse to feel her pert little breasts. And took off her knickers and had her on her back on his desktop. Or more likely on his big brown couch for patients.

'Josette Anvers? No, not her,' Annette said. 'Even Jacques is not so big a fool as to be involved with someone so close.'

'Then who?' Nicole asked, trying not to let her mixed emotions show in her face. She didn't love Jacques, of course, but she respected him and she admired him. And it so happened that she regarded him as more or less her property.

'One of his patients,' Annette said, looking displeased. 'You won't know her – Madame Fabre.'

'Fabre – but I think I've met her. Always very elegantly dressed. In her forties – is that the woman you mean?'

Annette nodded.

'Jacques has been going to her apartment regularly,' she said. 'He pretends he is continuing her analysis when she is too upset to visit him.'

'Well, that doesn't necessarily mean he's having an affair with her,' Nicole said warily. 'She could be genuinely upset and he goes there to help her.'

'She's divorced – we can guess how he helps her,' Annette said. 'I know what's going on. He's been acting very strangely lately. Though I've had my suspicions for quite a long time.'

Privately Nicole had to agree that Jacques was behaving strangely – the letter he'd written to her had been very odd. But she wasn't going to mention that to Annette.

'What are you going to do?' she asked. 'Will you confront him with what you know? Will you threaten to leave him?'

'I've already done what I intend to do,' Annette said with a little smile of ill will. 'I've started an affair of my own.'

'You? I don't believe it – who's the man?'

'Your ex-boyfriend, Remy Toussaint. He came to see me two days ago, absolutely distraught because you'd kicked him out. He wanted me to talk to you and persuade you to forgive him for what he's done.'

'Never,' Nicole said instantly. 'He's a toad.'

'Yes, but an attractive one,' Annette said with a little smile, 'and everything seemed to happen as conveniently as if it had been planned – it almost makes you believe in Fate. I was miserable about Jacques and Remy was miserable about you. We talked and we drank a glass or two of cognac together. I consoled him and he consoled me—'

'And all of a sudden this consolation was taking place in bed, yes?'

'On the sofa in my sitting-room the first time,' Annette said primly.

'The *first* time?' Nicole's eyebrows arched upwards.

'When we got our breath back he took me in a taxi to his apartment and our mutual condolence continued on his bed.'

'I'm lost for words,' Nicole said.

'I thought you would be.'

'But be careful, *chérie*,' Nicole warned her. 'Do not trust dear Remy. He is faithless by nature and not to be relied on.'

'I know that. He told me why you'd shown him the door.

I am using him to alleviate my misery, that's all there is to it,' Annette said with a superior smile. 'He's very good at consolation, isn't he? He ravaged me ruthlessly and it was marvellous.'

'To give him his due, he's good at that. But did he tell you anything about the other woman involved – Chantal Lamartine?'

Nicole was wondering how much Remy had divulged about his two lovers falling into bed together.

'Is that her name? He told me he'd been fool enough to be interested in someone else besides you, but he didn't go into any detail. Do you know her?'

'I've met her,' Nicole said lightly. 'But tell me more – how long did you stay in bed with him – it was hours and hours, I suppose?'

'Do mean the first time I was in his apartment? Or do you mean yesterday?'

Nicole laughed out loud and settled down to enjoy a long and intimate gossip with her friend. After a while she felt secure enough to tell Annette that she had fallen in love with Remy's other girlfriend, Chantal.

Annette stared at her in half-disbelief and said she thought that most unlikely. They were still talking at twelve-thirty – they ordered something to eat and stayed for another hour. Then Annette looked at her little wrist-watch and said she was meeting Remy soon after two and off she went.

With Annette safely out of the way for the whole afternoon in Remy's bed, Nicole decided to see Jacques. They had to meet sooner or later – his letter had made that clear. Now seemed as good a time as any.

She took the Metro to Passy – it was a fine September day for a little stroll. When she dressed that morning to meet Annette she hadn't expected to see Jacques and so her clothes were casual. But elegant, of course – she was wearing a plain white silk shirt with a sleek grey blazer and a black skirt.

At a few minutes after two o'clock she addressed herself to Josette Anvers – who told her that Jacques had appointments all afternoon and couldn't possibly see her. Nicole smiled sweetly and insisted that Josette informed him she was here and simply had to see him. And as she fully expected, Jacques instructed his receptionist to show her in and see to it that he wasn't disturbed until further notice.

Jacques was halfway across the room between desk and door when Nicole went in. He was wearing the usual professional dark-grey suit, with his spectacles tucked into the breast pocket. He shook hands formally with Nicole until Mademoiselle Anvers had left the room, then put his arms round her and kissed her properly.

'I didn't expect to see you today,' he said, leading her to the big leather couch. 'I'm so happy you're here.'

They sat side by side and he was holding both her hands. It was a familiar gesture of his and Nicole wondered it he did it to all the women he talked to.

'Your letter, Jacques,' she said.

'My letter,' he said solemnly.

'Tell me what it means,' she said. 'Why did you write it?'

'Because I am concerned for you. You were in a strange state of mind when I last saw you. That was two weeks ago, I haven't heard a word from you since then.'

'After my little adventure with Lucien and the street girl we picked up in Montmartre, do you mean? But there was nothing strange about my feelings when I saw you the last time – I was devastated because Remy had deceived me again, that's all – a very ordinary human reaction.'

'I've been trying to get you on the phone but you're never there. Are you reconciled, you and Remy – have you been away somewhere with him all this time?'

'Certainly not,' Nicole said. 'We have parted forever.'

'Then you've been with Lucien,' Jacques said, and he sounded pained.

'Dear Jacques, your thinking is very conventional. For someone who is trained to probe the deepest secrets of the human heart you often seem to lack imagination. I have spent the last few days with Chantal.'

He looked astounded at that.

'The same Chantal that Remy was seeing?' he asked.

'The same. She is beautiful and charming and we've been in bed most of the time since I saw you last.'

'I'm not sure I believe you,' Jacques said. 'Why would you want to do that, even if you were able to persuade her?'

'You're the psychoanalyst – if you can't explain it to yourself, then I refuse to help you,' Nicole said. 'Why did you write to me – what does the letter mean?'

'Tell me what you think it means,' he countered.

'*Mon Dieu* – never a straight answer from you, you always ask another question,' said Nicole. 'The letter baffled me, I must tell you. It seemed to mean that you loved me and wanted me to love you. That's not what you said the last time we met.'

'Yes, it is,' he said. 'We were making love here on the couch and I told you I loved you.'

'Oh *then* – but men always claim they love you at times like that,' she said. 'It wouldn't have mattered who you were lying on – women are all alike to you when you're three seconds away from your satisfaction.'

'No, I meant it,' he said. 'Believe me, Nicole.'

'I had bruises on my thighs for days because you gripped me so tight,' she accused him.

Jacques moaned softly, thinking about her bare thighs.

'You know how much I adore you,' he murmured.

He had released her hands and his palm was under her skirt and sliding up her thigh above her stocking-top.

'You've told me more than once that I don't love you,' she told him cheerfully. 'In fact, you informed me not long ago that I don't love anyone at all and never will. Now here you are with a massive bulge in your trousers and your hand up my skirt – give me one good reason why I should let you do this to me.'

'Nicole, *je t'aime*,' he sighed, his hand warm on her bare thigh.

'Just one reason,' she repeated, keeping her legs together.

'Perhaps you don't love me now,' he said, 'perhaps you never will, but I can try to help you. In the past you made being in love too dramatic. With Remy, for instance, and that caused you unhappiness. Let me show you how to love without being tragic.'

'You fascinate me,' Nicole said, feeling his hand slipping

slowly up her thigh. 'You always have fascinated me. I think it's because you understand enough to direct other people's lives. But I do not want anyone to direct my life, Jacques.'

'I desire you in ways deeper and truer than you know,' he said hotly. 'I will help you direct your own life.'

He always had this effect on her – she was sighing and trembling a little. She parted her legs and his hand under her skirt found its way into her tiny knickers and touched her neat little triangle of nut-brown curls and the long pink lips.

'In your letter you admitted that you were deceiving yourself about me,' Nicole murmured, opening her legs wider for him. 'None of this means anything, Jacques, you said it yourself.'

'You misunderstand my meaning,' he said anxiously while he kneaded her *joujou* with his fingers until she was shaking and gasping.

In another moment he had her on her back on the leather couch and her skirt off. His jacket was on the carpet and his trousers were open – his long stiff shaft stood out very boldly. He was bending over her, pulling her silk shirt up to her breasts so that he could kiss her bare belly.

'Perhaps I misunderstood your words,' she sighed, 'but I can hardly misunderstand *this*,' and she grasped his outstanding and twitching part.

Jacques slipped her knickers down her legs and pressed long eager kisses on her *joujou*. He slipped his hands under the small of her back and lifted her hips while he penetrated her, filling her with his length of hard flesh. She arched her back and parted her legs wide to let him penetrate her all the way. His hands were under her shirt and on her breasts, squeezing them and rolling them.

'This I never misunderstand,' Nicole murmured.

Jacques' stiff flesh inside her moved in a driving rhythm. He was so impatient that he was almost savage – she was sure she'd go into orgasm long before he reached his moment of release. The thought pleased her.

He will give me his strength, she exulted in her mind, *he will make me as strong intellectually as he is*.

Her back arched off the couch as ecstasy shook her. She clung fiercely to Jacques and made little moaning sounds. She wanted his hard beating rhythm never to stop – she wanted to feel the ecstasy again and again.

When it was over and they were sitting side by side again on the couch, he with his trousers fastened and she without her skirt or her knickers, she accused him of being a hypocrite – of claiming he loved her while he was having an affair with Germaine Fabre.

'You are the same as Remy,' she told him. 'Faithless.'

That shocked Jacques. He thought of himself as a serious-minded and very honest person.

'Annette has been filling your mind with mistaken ideas,' he said. 'Do not listen to her.'

'Do you deny that you've made love to Madame Fabre?'

'It's all a misunderstanding,' he said. 'It wasn't like that at all, believe me.'

'Then what was it like, Jacques?'

He explained that Madame Fabre had been in analysis with him for almost a year now. It was progressing well, he said. Then one evening a month or two ago her maid had phoned urgently to say Madame was suffering a severe anxiety attack. Naturally, he hurried round to her apartment to see what could be done.

'What was she anxious about?' Nicole asked, crossing her long elegant legs.

Jacques said anxiety attacks were rarely about anxieties as such, they were symptomatic of deep psychological disturbances and unresolved neuroses. Nicole nodded as if she knew what he was talking about, though to her it was complete gibberish.

'What did you find when you got there?' she asked.

'Madame Fabre was curled up on her bed naked,' he said. 'She was lost in her inner dread – so far into her own fears that she was hardly aware of her circumstances.'

'Naked on her bed, was she? That's very convenient,' Nicole commented dryly. 'She's a tall thin woman – does she have an interesting body?'

'I ought not to be telling you any of this,' Jacques said suddenly. 'It is a breach of professional confidentiality – I shall say no more.'

Nicole uncrossed her legs and moved closer to him on the couch. She put his hand between her thighs and clasped it with them, so his palm covered her little triangle of dark-brown curls – she gave him a knowing smile.

'Do not pretend to me that there is anything professional between you and Germaine Fabre,' she said. 'You might as well admit that you are her lover – though you insist that you love me. I want to know what happened.'

Jacques was uneasy, but he told her that he had taken both Germaine's hands in his own and held them while he talked to her sympathetically – he was trying to get her to come out of her psychological condition and respond normally to the world. After a short while she became calm enough to sit up and put her arms round him and cling tightly.

'Letting you admire all her assets, of course,' Nicole said. 'When she's dressed her breasts look small and her hips narrow. Did you find that attractive naked?'

Jacques didn't bother to answer the question. He explained how he'd soothed Germaine by stroking her back – she responded so well that he stroked her sides. She sobbed and told him she owed him her life.

The touch of Jacques' hands was having a very calming effect on her. He continued with the treatment, he stroked under her little breasts. One thing, as usual, led to another. Soon he was stroking her breasts fully and her belly. She released her grip on him to lie down again, so that he could do this.

'Well, well, well,' Nicole said, squeezing his hand between her warm thighs. 'You cured her anxiety very professionally, I can see.'

'I admit that the treatment was unorthodox, but it was very effective in calming the patient,' Jacques said – he sounded slightly pompous about it.

Nicole's hand was inside his trousers – she had opened them again and was holding his half-hard shaft.

'I suppose the treatment also had an effect on *this*,' she said, giving it a squeeze and a tug to make it grow bigger and harder.

'I did not make love to her,' he protested, hurt that anyone should question his motives. 'That wasn't what happened.'

'Really? Then what did happen?'

Somewhat shamefaced he explained he had stroked Germaine's naked body all over – his sole purpose to calm her and bring her out of her anxiety attack. And so very well did he succeed that after a while she jumped up and threw herself at him, she knocked him over on his back on the bed and dived on top.

'She ripped your trousers open and dragged *this out*,' said Nicole, grinning as she visualised the comic scene – Jacques flat on his back and a naked woman sitting on him, determined to have him.

He nodded, unwilling to talk of those extraordinary moments in Madame Fabre's bedroom.

'She straddled you, did she, dear Jacques? She sat over you with her legs wide open? She slid this useful thing of yours up into her – is that what took place?'

Reluctantly he agreed that it was as Nicole said. There was nothing reluctant about the *useful thing* she was holding as he confessed all, it was long and stiff and it throbbed gently in her hand.

'Have you explained to Annette that all you did was to treat Madame Fabre for a severe nervous attack?' she asked with a malicious little smile.

'She wouldn't understand,' he said. 'I've explained to her that there is no question of an affair between us – I expect Annette to trust me and believe me.'

'Of course,' Nicole murmured, her hand moving lightly up and down on Jacques' prized possession. 'She may be annoyed with you now and upset, but it won't last forever.'

At that very moment, Nicole guessed, dear Annette was naked and on her back with her legs in the air – and Remy was on top of her, consoling her boldly, as she'd called it. It was very strange sometimes, the way things worked out in life.

'Lie down, Jacques,' Nicole said firmly.

'What do you mean – you must go now, I have patients waiting for me,' he said, sounding worried.

'They must wait a little longer,' she told him. 'I was here first – and I am feeling very anxious indeed.'

He hardly resisted at all when she pushed him down flat on his back on the big leather couch. She lay on him quickly, she was naked from the waist down, except for her stockings. She reached between her body and his to grip his stiff part and steer it into herself.

'Oh no, no,' Jacques sighed. 'Mademoiselle Anvers may come in at any moment to announce the afternoon's first patient—'

He felt thick and strong inside her. She started to jerk her loins a few centimetres backward and forward, to feel his hard flesh sliding in her.

'Dear Mademoiselle Anvers,' she said. 'If she looks round the door and sees what we're doing here on the couch, she'll understand perfectly. She's been on her back with her knickers off plenty of times on this couch.'

'No, no,' Jacques protested, red of face. 'You mustn't say that . . . I deny it . . . oh Nicole *chérie*—'

He too was jerking now, little stabs up into her while she smiled down at him and held his head between her hands. She kissed his forehead and smoothed the bare patch at the front where his dark hair was receding. For a clever man he was so easy to control – she pressed down with all the weight of her body and rode him harder.

'I believe my anxiety is going away, Jacques,' she sighed. 'In two more moments I shall be happy again—'

'I knew you weren't telling the truth about making love with a woman,' he moaned. 'For you that is impossible – you made it up to try to shock me.'

'Did I, Jacques?' she gasped.

'A fantasy, it was a fantasy, nothing more,' he moaned – and in another second he bucked up hard into her slippery warmth.

Extract From Nicole's Diary – Sunday and Monday

Love is a complicated and many-coloured picture – but it is often possible to recognise certain designs that are repeated again and again. These are the natural patterns of a person's life, and they are never quite the same for each of us. But I have at last seen the outlines of my own nature.

Sunday was the last day of September – Nicole and Chantal were together all day. They had been to the theatre the evening before and they woke in each other's arms in the morning, at about nine o'clock.

They were at Chantal's apartment in Passy, naked together in her big soft bed. The bed was white and pink, as was the whole bedroom, the fragrance of a discreet perfume was everywhere. Chantal propped herself up on an elbow and leaned over Nicole to kiss her mouth.

Nicole took Chantal by her hips and pulled her down on top of herself, belly on belly. Chantal's belly was a little plumper than Nicole's, warm and soft and sexy as it pressed down on her.

'You want me again?' Chantal said with a loving smile. 'But your eyes are hardly open.'

Nicole ran her palms up and down Chantal's long bare sides, feeling the smoothness of her skin. She smiled back without answering the question, Chantal kissed her again, a long and luxurious kiss. Nicole put her arms about her and her hands on the cheeks of her bottom to stroke them.

The skin was like satin under her fingers – Chantal sighed and rubbed her belly over Nicole's belly. The cheeks of her bottom under Nicole's hands were round and full, but elegant. And very exciting to feel.

'Open your legs,' Nicole whispered urgently. 'I am going to love you.'

'With me on top?' Chantal asked lazily.

Her legs lay outside Nicole's. She moved them apart on the bed and Nicole's hand slid between their bellies, palm upward, to clasp her friend's patch of chestnut-brown curls. And to clasp the pouting lips between her thighs. She thought it felt like satin between Chantal's legs, the soft chestnut curls and the smooth lips under her fingers.

Nicole parted those lips and touched with a fingertip to the little bud inside – it was already standing proud. Chantal sighed and pressed her open mouth to Nicole's mouth in a long and burning kiss.

'I want you to know that I love you truly,' Nicole said.

'And I love you,' Chantal murmured.

'Whatever happens to either of us,' Nicole said. 'You must remember that I always love you.'

'I believe you, *chérie*.'

Chantal's naked body lying on her was hot and trembling to the caress of Nicole's fingers. Each time Chantal came close to an orgasm Nicole pulled her fingers away tantalisingly and slid her tongue into Chantal's mouth. After a deliciously long time of this, the moment arrived when Chantal couldn't be halted again – she moaned and shook from head to foot while she bit the flesh of Nicole's shoulder in a frenzy of delight.

At midday they bathed and dressed and Nicole took Chantal to Annette and Jacques for lunch. There were two other couples there, the men were colleagues of Jacques, and their well-dressed wives looked curiously at the newcomers.

Annette was fascinated to meet Chantal – she still found it almost impossible to believe Nicole had abandoned Remy for a woman – especially now that she herself had experienced his love-making.

As for Jacques, he found it even more impossible to believe. He stared long and hard at Chantal when they were introduced. Needless to say, Chantal looked very beautiful and desirable. It was not difficult for Nicole to guess what was going through his mind – he'd like to watch her and Chantal make love to each other – and then have both of them himself.

For a psychoanalyst his desires were remarkably ordinary and easy to predict.

After lunch, when he reasonably could, Jacques got Nicole on her own for a few moments. He was pressing her back against the wall of the short passage between dining-room and sitting-room, between two small Provencal landscape paintings. His wife and guests were only a few metres away, round the corner.

'This is absurd,' he said – he spoke softly but he sounded irritable. 'I simply refuse to believe you are in love with that woman, pretty as she is. You cannot be. It is not in your nature. You have brought her here to annoy me.'

'Chantal is more than just pretty,' said Nicole. 'She is ravishingly beautiful. How is Madame Fabre, by the way? Has she had more fearful anxiety attacks recently and sent for you to calm her – using your controversial treatment of handling her breasts?'

Jacques blushed a faint pink.

'You are evading the issue,' he said, his voice was low as laughter and chatter came from the sitting-room – where the door stood half-open.

'And you are evading my question,' Nicole retorted.

Perhaps it was the mention of Germaine Fabre's breasts and what he did to them that jogged Jacques into cautious action. His hands slid upward from Nicole's hips to her breasts – he stroked them very lightly through her apricot yellow frock – she had borrowed it for the day from Chantal. And the strand of green jade beads that went with it.

'Beautiful or not, you cannot love Chantal,' he said. 'It's utterly impossible. You may deny it out of personal pride or from a desire to be contrary, but I understand your nature and I know that you're not capable of falling in love with another woman.'

'How little you know about me,' Nicole said.

He was holding her against the wall with his belly pressed to hers. He wanted her to move her feet apart and open her legs so he could slip a hand up under her dress and feel her *joujou*. He wanted to pull down her little knickers and push his stiff shaft into her – though even in his half-frenzied state of mind he must have realised that was out of the question.

Nicole found his over-eagerness and his frustration amusing. Let him suffer, she said to herself, *he thinks he has the right to touch me and caress me whenever it suits him. But he's wrong and he must find out the truth – he can only touch me when I choose to let him.*

She forced her hand down between their bodies and gripped his thick shaft through his trousers. It wasn't dangling at all, it was standing upright with its head raised proudly.

'In spite of all your years of training, *this* does your thinking for you,' she said, and she smiled at Jacques as she felt it throb and jerk under the cloth.

'Nicole – I adore you,' he murmured. 'Tell me that there is nothing between you and Chantal – I must know the truth.'

'Why must you? I am not a patient lying on your big couch, Jacques. What is it to you, who I play with?' she asked to tease him.

Through the apricot silk of her dress and through her thin bra his fingers were gripping her breasts and their sensitive little buds. He was pinching them gently – the sensations were not unpleasant – at another time Nicole would have welcomed them. But not then, and not there – and done as if Jacques had the right to handle her.

'Last night I slept in Chantal's bed,' she said, meaning to discourage him as she stared boldly into his eyes. 'Our arms were around each other and our naked bodies were pressed together all night long.'

'No, it can't be true,' he sighed.

'This morning when we woke up, we kissed and made love to each other three times before we got out of bed,' she told him, giving his upright part a hard squeeze.

'I can't believe it,' he said.

'Since you are so very interested in the truth,' Nicole said, 'I can tell you that in two hours between nine and eleven this morning Chantal ravished me more completely than any man ever has, however long he was with me.'

'Why do you torment me with these impossible fantasies?' Jacques sighed.

'Fantasies?' Nicole asked with a cruel smile. 'Does my actuality become your fantasy, *chéri*? Perhaps it is the other way about – I turn your fantasy into actuality with my body? If you had a choice, which would you prefer it to be?'

'We have made love many times, you and I,' said Jacques, doing his usual trick of not answering a question but asking another question. 'Don't you feel anything for me?'

'But of course I do,' she said. 'I admire and respect you but that's a different matter. After all, you were never making love to me, were you? Be truthful – you were merely psychoanalysing my soul when you did all those fascinating things to me.'

'It was more than that,' he insisted weakly.

'Really?' she said with a shrug.

'I can help you, if you admit this so-called love affair with Chantal is only in your imagination,' he offered.

The arrogant assumption annoyed Nicole and she determined to put him in his place.

'When Chantal and I leave here in another half-hour we are going to my apartment,' she said. 'We'll undress each other and get into bed. She will kiss my breasts and between my legs. You'd like to do that to me, wouldn't you?'

'Nicole – I want you to come back into the dining-room with me for a moment,' he said urgently.

'You are impossible, Jacques,' she said, smiling thinly. 'You want me to go in there with you and bend over the table while you pull my dress up over my bottom and slip my knickers down my legs . . .'

'Oh yes, yes,' he sighed. 'Yes, I do.'

'With Annette and your guests waiting in the sitting-room?' Nicole said. 'How could you? You are a monster, Jacques, a monster.'

'*Je t'adore*, Nicole,' he babbled, his stiff part jumping furiously inside his trousers.

'I can imagine it,' she said, leading him on. 'Your hands would be all over me, stroking the cheeks of my bare bottom and between my legs – that's what you want to do, isn't it?'

He moaned under his breath.

'You'd be standing between my open legs,' Nicole said,

'and this huge hard thing would be out and pointing at me like a loaded pistol. You'd push it into me and hold me face down on the table among the used wine glasses while you slammed in and out – I know what you want, Jacques.'

'Please, dearest Nicole,' he begged. 'It will only take a minute . . . only a minute . . .'

'How absurd,' she said. 'How very inferior and mediocre it sounds. A minute, indeed! Have you any idea, dear Jacques, how many times two women can make love to each other before they have had enough? Six times, nine times, twelve times – what do you think?'

'Oh my God,' Jacques groaned, his eyes staring wide open.

'Think about it when you are alone,' she said. 'Picture the scene in your imagination – Chantal and I kissing and playing, both of us naked – there's a fantasy you won't be able to get out of your mind.'

'Please, Nicole . . .' he gasped.

She slid sideways along the wall to free herself. Jacques reached out to grab at her wrist and keep her with him, but she was too quick. She left him staring after her, with a big inconvenient bulge in his trousers, as she went to join the others in the sitting-room.

Monday was the first day of October – and soon after eight that morning Chantal left Nicole's apartment to go to her office. Nicole stayed in bed and went back to sleep for an hour – it had been a long night of kisses and caresses.

If poor Jacques could have been there to watch us, Nicole thought with a smile – if he'd seen how our beautiful naked bodies twisted around each other in hot desire – if he'd heard our repeated sighs and sobs of ecstasy – if he could have seen how often she and Chantal had clung together in fierce orgasm – he would surely have died of envy and chagrin.

Now that she was alone in her bed again, Nicole fell asleep with her hand between her thighs, touching her little brown fleece. Her longest finger lay along the lips of her *joujou,* where moistness still lingered from Chantal's *good morning* kiss.

Two hours later Nicole stirred and sat up in bed. She was naked when she threw the sheet aside and stretched herself – arms above her head and her back arched, her perfect breasts thrust forward. She put on her frilly negligé and went into the kitchen to make coffee. When it was ready she took a large breakfast-cup with her to sip in the bath.

She lay soaking in hot and scented water while she thought about the events of the weekend past. She was pleased with herself. After Remy's betrayal there had been a time of distress and misery, but by strength of character she had overcome that. And truth to tell, the ups and downs of the summer had provided an immense amount of fascinating material for her secret diary . . .

By midday Nicole was dressed and ready – though dressed casually in an orange silk shirt, cut man-style and tucked into a jet black skirt. The black patent-leather belt round her waist matched her shoes – they were also shiny black and they had ridiculously high heels. The effect was distinctly Montmartre, which she thought appropriate to the occasion.

When the doorbell rang she knew who it was – it was Gerard Constant, because that was how she had arranged it. Naturally, she hadn't told him that this was an experiment she'd planned. If he knew he was being used as a laboratory animal it might upset him – and perhaps even impair his ability to respond satisfactorily. It was better if he knew nothing of what was in Nicole's mind.

But an experiment was what was planned. Nicole's interest in herself and her thoughts and emotions was endless – that was why she kept so detailed a diary to record them. Since falling in love with Chantal, she had become curious about her own reactions to traditional male love-making compared with this newly discovered female love-making.

She was going to compare Gerard with Chantal. She intended to contrast her response to each of them and so investigate the breadth of her own sexuality. All through the weekend she had revelled in love-making with beautiful Chantal – now it was time to see what Gerard could do for her.

There had been showers that morning. Gerard was wearing a gangster-style raincoat and a brown hat pulled down over one eyebrow – and he had a bottle of vintage champagne in each hand. He came into the apartment and leaned forward to kiss Nicole, unable to embrace her while he held the two bottles. She felt the dampness of rain on his coat through her thin silk blouse – she had no bra under it – and she eased away from Gerard while he took his coat off and hung it up.

He had a dark blue jacket on and grey trousers – Nicole guessed he'd been in his office all morning and had left saying he was going to lunch with a client and didn't expect to be back. Because she was certain that he wouldn't be. By the time she was ready to conclude her experiment he would be good for nothing but several hours sleep.

He followed her into the kitchen and gave her one bottle of champagne to put into the refrigerator to cool – the other he popped open, warmish though it was, and poured two glasses.

They drank to each other happily, they touched lips again, they smiled knowingly at each other. Gerard was perched on the edge of the kitchen table, Nicole was sitting on a chair to the side of him.

'Shall we take the bottle into the bedroom?' he asked.

He was staring at her breasts – he had at last noticed that she was not wearing a bra – her buds were very prominent under her silk shirt. The tip of his tongue showed between his lips, as if to tell her how eager he was to undo her shirt and lick her pretty buds.

'The bedroom? Oh, yes, we'll go there eventually,' she said, looking at him with a very thoughtful expression on her face. 'But there's no need to be traditional.'

She reached over to grip his inner thigh, high up.

'Do you really see me as a traditionalist, then?' he asked, raising an eyebrow.

Without bothering to answer his question she unzipped his dark grey trousers and eased his big male part out. Even limp, it was big – in her hand it quickly grew bigger. Although Gerard might be slender of body and indecisive of will and artistic by nature, when size mattered he was exceptional – he was impressive and he was superior.

His pride had risen to full stretch, a strong thick shaft in Nicole's hand, almost twenty centimetres of hard pink flesh pointing up at the ceiling.

'There is a traditional use for what you are playing with,' he told her in a husky voice.

'I didn't mean that you are a traditionalist,' she said, stroking his solid length with affectionate interest. 'I'm the traditionalist, though I try not to be. Sometimes the old ways are very hard to diverge from – even when new prospects can be fascinating . . . and rewarding.'

He had no idea what she was talking about and didn't trouble to ask because he didn't really care. He had something more enchanting on his mind than a discussion of tradition. By general tradition – to be pedantic about it – women lay on their backs and parted their legs and men lay on top of them. Perhaps Nicole was suggesting that they should diverge from that and he ought to lie on his back and she climb on top of him. If that's what she wanted, he was very agreeable.

Truth to tell, as long as he could get his throbbing length into her he didn't care who was on top, or if either of them was on top of the other. If Nicole wanted them both to dangle by their ankles from the electric light fitting and make love upside down, that was perfectly all right by him – he was so panting-eager that she could have it any way she wanted . . .

But that wasn't what Nicole had in mind at all. Her secret experiment was concerned with contrasting sensations – to compare love-making by slippery wet tongue with love-making by hard-flesh shaft.

She took her glass from the table and filled her mouth with champagne – she didn't swallow it, she leaned over Gerard and slid the head of his stiff shaft into her mouth, between her tight-pressed lips – until the top third was engulfed. Gerard gasped to feel how the tiny champagne bubbles tingled on the sensitive bare head.

'You'll make *Gerard-le-Grand* drunk like that,' he said. 'He's not used to champagne – he won't know what he's doing.'

Nicole held his twitching length in her mouthful of wine for a long minute, then freed it slowly. Only a drop or two of champagne escaped from between her lips and ran down her chin. Gerard stared entranced as she put her head back and swallowed her mouthful of champagne.

'Don't worry about *Gerard-le Grand*,' she said with a smile. 'If he gets a little drunk, I'll show him what to do.'

'I trust you completely, *ma chérie*,' Gerard said, looking down at his long wet shaft as it jerked rhythmically all by itself. 'But look at him – he's reeling already – I think you've intoxicated him.'

'The poor darling,' Nicole said. 'He needs my assistance.'

In another moment Gerard found himself half on his back on the table, on his elbows for support. His trousers were round his knees and Nicole was standing up and unbuckling her shiny black leather belt. She dropped her skirt and Gerard sighed a long and heartfelt *Oh* as he saw she was wearing no knickers – only a white lace suspender-belt holding up her stockings.

Oh he sighed again as he looked at her smooth belly and her neatly trimmed little patch of dark-brown curls. She moved in close to straddle his thighs – she put a stockinged knee up on the kitchen table, then the other knee – and she was over his loins, her legs splayed and her hand between them to part the lips of her pretty *joujou*.

Oh he said for the third time as Nicole spiked herself on his upright shaft with a slow downward press of her loins. She was so moist that he slid all the way up into her. She pulled his shirt up out of the way to stroke his belly – he put both his hands up inside her silk orange shirt to hold her breasts and squeeze them, while she rode him in an easy rhythm.

Chantal's clever tongue or Gerard's strong shaft – which of them gives me more pleasure? Nicole was asking herself as she slid up and down. It was impossible to choose – the pleasure was intense from both. And as she arched her back and wailed in ecstasy, fierce shudders shaking her lithe and naked body, she decided she wanted both – and she would have both – she would have Chantal and Gerard as her lovers – for as long as they delighted her.